SECOND CHANCES AT THE LITTLE LOVE CAFÉ

LUCY MITCHELL

BLOODHOUND
— B O O K S —

www.bloodhoundbooks.com

Print ISBN: 978-1-917214-17-9

To Catherine, who has read far too many rough drafts and different versions of this book over the years.

CHAPTER ONE

'Alice, I think I might be falling in love with Denise.' Ronald Jenkins, owner of The Starfish Tea Shop in Blue Cove Bay and my new boss, has called to give me what he feels is an important update.

Ronald is different to the other bosses I've had over the years. He never calls to ask whether business is booming in his tea shop. I don't know why but he sees me as an agony aunt rather than an employee.

At seventy-six, eligible bachelor, Ronald boasts of possessing his own teeth, a full head of hair, the energy levels of a twenty-five-year-old, two seaside rental properties, a five-bedroomed detached house, a hot tub and a successful (his word not mine!) tea shop. He often tells me he can't remember the last evening he spent at home alone and he believes he's singlehandedly responsible for an alleged boom in senior dating sites.

My response is a little sharp. 'Rubbish. You've only been on two dates with Denise.' Cradling my phone between my ear and shoulder, I bring out a customer's cup of tea and a custard tart. 'You're getting carried away.'

'But Denise makes me feel like a teenager again,' explains

Ronald as I reach my customer, Betty, and her yellow plastic table. She's fresh from the hair salon and is sporting an impressive head full of tight silver curls. Betty is my first and last customer of the afternoon.

It has been another quiet day here in The Starfish Tea Shop. Ronald should be more concerned about his lack of business than his strong feelings for Denise. What I desperately want to say – and it is becoming a struggle not to blurt it out – is that nothing good comes from falling in love. That four-letter word should come with a health warning.

Ronald has begun to describe his lunch date with Denise. Half-listening and adding a random 'nice', I'm also scanning the almost empty tea shop for Lucas, my six-year-old son who earlier made a rather bold claim. 'Mummy, I am now a good boy.'

After saying that, he disappeared. He hasn't got out of the tea shop because there's a jangly bell on the door so I'm sensing he's ditched the 'good boy status' and is being naughty under one of the tables.

I can't listen to Ronald talk anymore about the seductive way Denise used her spoon to eat her pudding. 'Is there anything else, Ronald?' It's not a good career move to cut off your boss mid-flow, but if he carries on, I'm going to say something I'll regret. This job has been a life saver and I can't afford to lose it. Also, the thought of sitting down with Betty at her table and having a natter is appealing after the day I've had.

Where the hell is Lucas? My eyes conduct a search of the other yellow circular tables and wooden chairs for a small boy. Nothing. Standing on my tiptoes, I survey the back of the tea shop behind the blue shell encrusted counter where the old coffee machine and toaster preside. Nothing.

'Denise wants to see me again tomorrow, Alice.'

For goodness' sake, can't Ronald sense that I need him to get off the phone?

'Do you have any dating advice for my third date with her? Do you think it is time for me to suggest taking a dip in my hot tub?'

Out of the corner of my eye I catch sight of Lucas's curly head from behind the counter and hear the scrape of the plastic crate. With a mischievous grin my son stands on the crate and appears, holding aloft my black purse with one hand and picking his nose with the other. My son is intrigued by my purse and all that is up his nose. Forgetting about Ronald, I glare at my son. 'Don't be a naughty boy.'

Ronald erupts into a coughing fit before croaking, 'Yes, thank you, Alice, for that.'

'Oh God, Ronald,' I gasp. 'I'm sorry, that wasn't meant...' I stop myself from revealing that I've brought Lucas to work with me. Dad would have covered Lucas's school training day, but his shifts were swapped at the supermarket. In view of the lack of customers, I brought Lucas to work with me. This is something I won't be doing again in a hurry as it's been hell. You'd think with only three customers over the course of the entire day, I'd be able to cope with running a tea shop and entertaining my bored six-year-old son. Lucas has stuck his grubby fingers into every teacake while I wasn't looking. He's fiddled with sugar cubes, climbed over the little tables, and keeps taking my purse out of my handbag. As he's so naughty, I have not been able to have a little cry by myself in the toilets.

To my relief, Ronald hangs up before I have time to figure out what to say next. Betty chuckles at Lucas still standing on the crate behind the counter. 'Lucas, your mummy has been telling me about how you're such a *good boy*. I think *good boys* put purses back.' Arching her silvery eyebrows at Lucas, Betty peers over the top of her gold-rimmed glasses.

Scratching his mass of springy black curls, Lucas grins. For a second or two, Betty and I are lulled into thinking he's going to be a *good boy* and put my purse back in my handbag behind the counter. As I turn towards Betty, Lucas tips the contents of my purse all over the counter. Coins, plastic cards, and receipts are sent flying. To my horror most of it falls off the counter and skitters across the floor.

'LUCAS.' My booming voice makes eighty-six-year-old Betty clutch her chest. She leans back in her chair, banging her head against the wall and blinks rapidly. Gasping, I race around to Betty and rub her hand. Oh God, all the colour has drained from her face. 'Please be okay, Betty.'

To my relief, Betty coughs and gives me a weak smile. 'My goodness, Alice, the foundations of Ronald's shop moved when you shouted.'

With a nervous laugh, I push the cup of tea and custard tart nearer to her. 'Eat some sugar quick, Betty.' She nods, picks up her fork and attacks the custard tart. The words, *'Ronald's custard tarts are a bit chewy,'* are jostling around on the tip of my tongue. Betty normally has a teacake, which have their own taste issues, but today she announced she wanted to shake things up with her order. I did try to persuade her to stick to a teacake, but she was adamant she wanted to try a custard tart.

To avoid watching her bite into the custard tart, I crouch down on the floor to retrieve my bank cards, a ten-pound note, a few receipts and an old photo which has somehow managed to survive countless purse changes. Lucas comes to stand next to me. I glance up at his bright blue eyes, widening with excitement at the chaos he's caused. He's still got my empty purse which I try to grab but he runs off with it around the perimeter of the tea shop.

'He loves your purse,' Betty observes as I groan at Lucas. Some children like toys, cars, or books. Lucas, on the other hand, is obsessed with purses, wallets, phones, and expensive watches. It used to be embarrassing when I met up with the posh mums from his old nursery. All his little friends would play nicely with educational wooden toys while Lucas would be sat in the corner emptying someone's purse or wallet. Frankie, my best mate, jokes his godson is destined for the pickpocket trade.

'How are you doing, Alice?' Betty has known my family for years. She used to manage the hair salon in Blue Cove Bay. Dad's mum, my nana, always swore Betty's perms were legendary.

Rising to my feet, I slide into the chair opposite Betty. My brain is searching for a suitable answer which won't involve the tear tap inside my eyes being turned on. Everyone knows Lucas and I are back in Blue Cove Bay living with Dad. Talking about why I've come home is still difficult. Dad has assured me only a handful people know what happened.

Betty gives me a warm smile before leaning across and squeezing my hand. I let out a heavy sigh. That gesture of hers tells me my secret is now common knowledge here in Blue Cove Bay. If Blue Cove Bay's town gossip Betty squeezes your hand, she knows your business and you can be sure everyone in the town also knows.

CHAPTER TWO

Three months ago, my life imploded. The day before my wedding, I caught my fiancé, Scott, in our bed with a woman he'd met on his stag do in Majorca.

'Can we at least talk, Alice?' Those were the first words out of his mouth as he stood in the doorway to our bedroom, with a sheet wrapped around himself, a strange woman huddled in our duvet on our bed and an array of discarded clothes over the carpet.

He reached out to touch my arm, making me flinch. His delusional words will forever echo inside my head. 'We've paid for a wedding, and I still love you. She doesn't mean anything to me.'

The woman baulked at what he said. 'That's not what you told me on your stag do when we were on the beach.' He turned to glare at her.

Blinking back tears, I'd turned on my heel and raced into our toilet to be sick.

Betty brings me back into the present with a tap on the arm. 'It will get easier, I promise. Bet your father is chuffed to have you and Lucas living with him.'

'Dad's treating me like I'm an invalid.'

To my surprise, Betty shoves the entire custard tart in her mouth and leans closer. Flicking my eyes to the table I decide to just talk and silently pray that Betty's dentures can handle Ronald's rubbery custard tart. 'This is a bit embarrassing, but Dad's standard response to all my illnesses and problems in life is *still* – after thirty-six years – to put me under a blanket on the sofa and overfeed me his homebaked chocolate brownies until I feel better.'

Three months ago, Lucas and I had arrived back in Blue Cove Bay. Whereas Lucas was over the moon to be living with Grandpa by the seaside, I was tear-stained and devastated at Scott's actions, the end of our whirlwind relationship and our cancelled wedding. Dad initially ordered me to lie on his old threadbare sofa, with two pillows stuffed behind my head, his travel blanket draped over my legs and a constant supply of chocolate brownies within easy reach.

'Lying on Dad's sofa, day in, day out, eating brownies and staring up at four walls got too much for me and my sugar levels, so I begged Ronald to give me this job.'

Betty is still trying to chew down on her custard tart. Her twinkly blue eyes have darkened, and her face has become shadowy. Why the hell didn't I remove the custard tarts from the counter?

Lucas comes to the table. He stares at Betty with a puzzled look on his face. She now has an audience. I swat away his finger which is trying to get inside one of his nostrils.

Betty is still chewing. The sound of Betty's dentures finally cutting through the custard tart fills me with relief. It takes her a good minute to mash the tart down and then swallow without choking. Finger mopping her mouth, Betty smiles. 'Well, that was an experience. That tart was like a piece of tough steak.' She rubs her chest and drains her cup of tea. 'I can think of worse ways to recover from what you've been through. Thankfully, you have Brian baking cakes for you and not Ronald. Your father bakes the best chocolate brownies. I remember the days when we would all queue for his little bakery to open.'

A faint smile pushes its way onto my face at the mention of Dad's old bakery.

Betty takes out her hankie and cleans her glasses. 'When your mum passed away, we all wondered how he'd cope raising a young daughter on his own. We should have known Brian would do an excellent job.' Her twinkling blue eyes flood me with warmth. 'He's always been an overprotective father.'

Betty puts on her glasses and casts me a puzzled look. 'Now, everyone wants to know why you've chosen to work for Ronald in this...' Betty surveys her surroundings with a look of disapproval. She stares at the old starfish on the wall which has come loose from its hook and is dangling precariously over Ronald's first attempt at a coastal painting. No one can believe he's stuck a £50 price tag on it. To say Lucas could do better is an understatement. Betty turns her nose up at the chipped paint on the walls, the shells missing from the sides of the counter and the malnourished teacakes in the glass jar. '...awful place of Ronald's?'

The reason why I am working in Ronald's teashop is not only due to me climbing the walls with boredom on Dad's sofa but also because things are a bit tight financially at home. It's up to me to put things right. As Scott didn't have much money to put towards the wedding, I stupidly agreed to use my savings. Dad also used his own money to pay for the reception.

My stomach clenches as I remember the chat I had with Dad a few weeks ago. The one which started with him announcing he was increasing his hours at the supermarket. When I'd asked why he was doing extra hours, he went pale.

'I...' Dad stopped and cleared his throat. 'I took out a loan to pay for your reception.' He carefully rolled up the sleeves of his blue shirt as my heart came to a shuddering halt. 'The hotel's cancellation policy meant I lost a lot of my money.'

Dad explained he thought I had my heart set on a big wedding. My body began to tremble. 'Oh God, Dad, please don't tell me you took out a loan?' Air became trapped in my throat. 'You told me you had saved some money,' I croaked, before erupting into a coughing fit.

Scott was the one who wanted a big wedding even though he couldn't afford it. I would have happily got married in a registry office and gone to the pub afterwards. That night I didn't sleep due to crying about how my wedding disaster had also put my father into debt.

Shame and embarrassment loiter inside my stomach. Scott owned the house in Surrey, so Lucas and I didn't have much choice but to relocate across the country and move in with Dad. It's going to take me years before I can pay Dad back for the money he lost on my wedding reception.

'Awful place,' says Betty. 'Why aren't you working with your friend, Frankie Jones?' Craning her neck, she looks out of the window and peers down at the beach below, frowning. 'I still don't know why Frankie painted old Mick's beach café such a dreadful pink colour.'

The Starfish Tea shop sits above the cliffs in Blue Cove Bay. Tourists who want a cup of tea with a picturesque view have an intense thigh-burning walk up far too many sandy steps. Luckily, Betty's son runs a local taxi firm and spends most of his time ferrying her about for free. I've hinted to Ronald that the location of his tea shop might be one of the reasons why business is quiet, but he dismissed it, saying people will do anything for a good cup of tea and a beautiful sweeping view of the little coastal town and golden strip of beach below. If you look out of the window of The Starfish Tea Shop, you can't miss the cerise exterior of Frankie's business below. The Little Love Café, Frankie's café, sits on the edge of the golden beach and overlooks the picturesque shimmering blue sea.

Eighteen months ago, Frankie, experienced what he referred to as a *thirty-something life crisis*. One gloomy Thursday, he reassessed his life, while eating a blueberry muffin at his desk at a swanky London PR firm.

He was supposed to have been thinking about how he could repair the image of a well-known film actor. A series of compromising photos had appeared in the tabloid press, showing the actor in the arms of his mistress, days before his opera singer wife, who had beaten cancer twice, was due to give birth.

Frankie claims that after finishing the muffin and telling his boss there was no hope for the actor, he realised his own life felt stale and he wanted to feel alive again.

So, he walked out of his swanky job, ended his volatile two-year relationship with a YouTube make-up vlogger, put his Soho flat on the market, left London and moved back home to... Blue Cove Bay, a small seaside town tucked into the Devon coastline. I am still in shock about his life-changing decision.

At a service station he called me to explain his idea – 'I'm going to buy Mick's old café and I'm going to turn it into a romantic-themed place called *The Little Love Café*. It will be perfect for loved-up couples to record live on social media their first dates, mid-week date nights, make-up dates post arguments, engagements and baby news announcements,' he gushed without taking a breath.

I couldn't believe what I was hearing. Even though I'm not a fan of romance right now, I still can't quite believe what Frankie has created. It's a beautiful place where loved-up couples drink delicious skinny lattes, soya flat whites and iced frappuccinos, take selfies of themselves in front of a stunning pink flower wall, and nibble on a range of love-inspired cakes, biscuits, and snacks.

Betty taps me on the hand. 'So, why aren't you working for Frankie?'

'The thought of working somewhere with wall-to-wall romance feels like a nightmare after everything...' My voice becomes croaky as Scott's face flashes up inside my head.

Betty reaches over with both hands and squeezes mine. 'Oh, I know, Alice. You're not going to want to watch live marriage proposals...' She stops mid-flow, sensing she might have hit a raw nerve. She peers through her glasses and spots the photo on the table near my arm. I try to stop her, but she grabs it.

It was taken years ago on the day my GCSE exams ended. In the photo, a group of us from school are sat, tanned bare legs and sand-coated feet dangling, on our favourite rock on the beach, against a backdrop of rugged cliffs and a cloudless azure blue sky. Betty's finger slides across to the blond-haired lad who I'm leant against. 'Ah, I remember the Coombes boy.'

'You mean Noah?' Pausing, I lean over and stare at sixteen-year-old Noah.

Betty holds the photo closer and screws up her eyes to get a better look. 'You and the Coombes boy were childhood sweethearts.'

I nod. 'Noah was my first love.' I decide to miss out the bit about how we had a pretend wedding on my sixteenth birthday on the beach as Betty doesn't need to know that and my father is still unaware. Lord knows what he would say if he knew.

Noah wrote me tiny love letters on little scraps of paper and inserted them into my pencil case when I wasn't looking, he wrote me poems in our English class, and he held my hand under the desks in maths lessons. He was the boyfriend who was perfect in every way... until he broke my sixteen-year-old heart.

'I was surprised at seeing you and the Coombes boy together. Your father never had a good word to say about the Coombes family.'

Fidgeting on my chair, I scratch my itchy neck. 'I should have listened to Dad. He was right about that family.'

Betty leans closer to me, her nose twitching inquisitively. 'A few weeks after this photo was taken Noah told me his dad was emigrating to Ireland. He swore to me that he would write me letters, emails, call me and save up enough money to visit me.' I pause and take a deep breath. 'He said we'd one day meet again down by our rock in Blue Cove Bay.'

Our rock is a small one that sticks out from the slate grey cliffs that hem Blue Coves Bay's beach. It has a peculiar angular shape and if you squint it looks like the side profile of an ogre's head with a nose, forehead, and jaw. You can climb up the side and sit on the top of it to watch the world go by or listen to beachgoers below comparing their suntans. I first discovered the rock after Mum died. If you sit on the rock and look up, you can see the edge of the coastal path. Sitting on the rock used to make me feel closer to her. When Noah came into my life, the rock became our meeting place. As teenagers we would run and escape up there. For a long time, it was our happy place.

Betty laces her fingers together. 'The Coombes boy didn't come back to meet you by your rock. I wonder why that was.'

Shaking my head, I let out a sigh. 'He never wrote back or called, Betty. I know it sounds silly, but I've always wondered why he did that. Noah and I had something special back then and we both cried the day he left. I honestly believed him when he said we would one day meet again by our rock.'

'You both were very young.' Betty takes another glance at the photo. 'A handsome boy like that would have been very popular with those Irish girls.' She stops and stares at my face. 'I've said the wrong thing again – haven't I?'

Years of Noah Coombes agitation rises inside me. 'Betty, I know Noah and I were only sixteen and he probably did hook up with a new girl the minute he stepped off the ferry but...' My neck and shoulders stiffen. 'I can't forget about what he did. If I am honest, I'm still mad at him for leaving me hanging on. I know it sounds silly, but I carried on writing to him and he *never* replied.'

Betty fishes out a ball of tissue from the sleeve of her lilac cardigan. 'I think you're still mixed up about what happened with your wedding. Heartbreak can dredge up all sorts of painful memories.'

I let out a heavy sigh. 'I'm not getting my heart broken again. Frankie thinks I'm being negative when I talk like this but falling in love with scumbags and getting hurt is taking its toll on me. No one is going to get a chance to hurt me again.'

Lucas goes off to wander around the tea shop. Betty leans over to whisper, 'I see Pete Towns was in that photo. His mother was never happy with the haircuts I gave her. I don't like to speak bad about the dead, but she was a miserable woman who had coarse black hair. It was like cutting wire. I hear Pete's bought a house on the outskirts of town.'

'Yes, he has.' Guilt at declining Pete's invite to his housewarming party creeps over me.

Betty frowns. 'Wasn't Pete close to the Coombes boy?'

It takes a lot to push the words off my tongue. 'They were best friends.'

Betty flashes me a mischievous smile. 'Good job Noah didn't return – eh?' She glances over at Lucas who is busy sticking his tongue against the front window. 'Lucas looks more like Pete every day.'

A familiar uncomfortable feeling passes through me.

CHAPTER THREE

I t's Sunday and my only day off from Ronald's tea shop. The old grandfather clock in the hall downstairs is chiming to announce it's seven in the morning, which I don't want to know as I'd rather be still asleep. I'm awake with my head shoved under the pillow, although not to block out the noisy clock. It's so that I can rid my nose of foul-smelling dog wind.

Lucas and I are living in my old bedroom. Lucas has my old bed and I'm sleeping on Dad's camp bed, an uncomfortable metal contraption, which is low to the ground. It also doesn't quite fit in the room so we can't fully close the door. This means Bean, Dad's beagle, likes to come in during the night, curl up beside the camp bed and break wind whenever he pleases.

My phone bleeps. It's Frankie. 'Alice,' Frankie croaks, his voice thick with emotion. 'Please come to The Little Love Café.'

'What?' I gasp, sitting up on my camp bed. Luckily Lucas hasn't stirred.

My heart is pounding. Something is wrong. I don't think I've heard Frankie this upset in a long time. 'Now?'

'Yes.' His voice wavers.

Creeping downstairs, I rummage in Dad's desk for a pad of

paper; I need to write him a note and let him know where I've gone. The only thing I can find is the cream letter writing paper I was using when I returned from Surrey. In a tear-fuelled frenzy, I decided to write all fifty-six of my wedding guests a handwritten apology note for the wedding cancellation. My first and only handwritten letter is still attached to the pad.

Dear Ray, Irene, and family,

Thank you for taking the trouble to organise travel down to Surrey and to book a hotel and for buying us a wedding gift. It was appreciated and I'm sorry for any inconvenience caused with our wedding cancellation the day before.

Unfortunately, I found Scott – the two-timing b*s***d in bed with another woman the night before our wedding. I hope he rots in hell.

Hope Stuart is enjoying his first year in university and Emily is working hard on her A-levels.

Kind regards

Alice

Dad had to step in and order me not to send that to Ray and Irene.

After finding a new page, I scribble Dad a quick note to say that I've taken Bean for a walk before Lucas gets up.

Once I've brushed my teeth and swapped my blue penguin pyjamas for my grey jogging bottoms, which were lying on top of the ironing pile, I grab my coat, the dog lead and call Bean.

Stepping out into the chilling morning rain is a shock for both Bean and me. It's the last days of March and there's no sign of spring. A mischievous sea wind lifts my long hair and whips it against my cheeks. Digging my hands deeper into the warm pockets of my coat, I ignore Bean's unhappy stares. He'd rather be asleep next to my camp bed. We hurry along the street and onto the sweeping promenade. We pass the guest houses, the ice-cream shop, and the tourist gift shop. At the far end, on the edge of the beach is The Little Love Café.

Bean and I are greeted at the door by a tearful Frankie.

'Oh my God, what's wrong?' I go to hug him. He shakes his head before dragging me and Bean into the empty café.

At once, I am surrounded by clusters of baby pink tables and chairs. Lining one wall are three pink leather booths and at the far end is a little snug area which can be booked by customers should they want a bit of privacy. The aroma is a mixture of fresh coffee beans, vanilla, and chocolate.

From the pics Frankie posts on his Instagram feed, this place is always full of soppy-looking couples kissing over lattes. I'm glad it's empty right now. Since arriving back in Blue Cove I have done my best to avoid it when it's open. In my current heartbroken state, I couldn't handle seeing wall-to-wall romance.

'Coffee, Alice?' Frankie goes to stand behind the baby pink counter. I nod and he turns to the gleaming stainless-steel coffee machine. He carries my pink cup over to a booth in the corner. A silver iPad and a plate with a half-eaten croissant are waiting for us.

While I settle Bean down under the table, Frankie stuffs his giant six-foot-four frame into the small space opposite me and places his face in his hands. I lean over and give his wrist a gentle squeeze. 'What's going on?'

'It's Mum,' he whispers, scratching his short thatch of peroxide blond hair. 'She's been keeping something from me.'

'What?' Saliva is evaporating from my throat at an astonishing speed. 'Frankie, tell me.'

He takes a deep breath. 'Mum's got breast cancer. She Skyped me in the early hours.' Taking a pink napkin, he wipes his wet cheeks. 'My Wi-Fi was playing up, so I came here.'

'What?' My jaws drop with shock.

'She found a lump months ago,' croaks Frankie. 'Didn't go see a doctor or anything.' Massaging his temples with his fingers, he sighs. 'Don't get me started on how cross I am at her for that.' He stops and takes in more air. 'Her friend persuaded her to get it checked. It's cancer. Stage three, Alice.'

Frankie's loud sobs fill the air. Tears flood my own cheeks. 'Oh, Frankie,' I stammer in between sobs. My chest feels like someone is scooping out yet more of my insides. Rose is one of the sweetest people on this planet. When Mum died it was Rose who picked up Dad and me, cooking us homemade casseroles, raiding our washing baskets and replacing them with bags of sweet-smelling laundry, organising film nights, making my school packed lunches, and playing Scrabble with all of us on Sunday afternoons. She was even my birthing partner when Lucas was born.

Rose has been living in Sydney for the last three years. One Christmas, she surprised us all by announcing she was returning to her home country after years of living in Blue Cove Bay. Even Frankie was shocked at her life-changing decision. She now lives outside Sydney.

I still haven't got used to her not living next door to Dad. Frankie hired a van to rescue me from Scott's house in Surrey on what should have been my wedding day. Once we'd returned to Blue Cove Bay, along with all my belongings, I'd got out of the van, feeling like my world had caved in around me. Instinctively I looked at Frankie's downstairs window for Rose's face. We've always lived next door to Rose and Frankie. Dad has always called Rose and Frankie 'our adopted family'.

Frankie and I both shoot out of our seats at the same time

and hug the life out of each other. This disturbs a sleeping Bean and causes him to bark with disapproval. From the age of thirteen onwards hugging Frankie became problematic. It was at this point in our lives that his body decided to shoot up towards the sky and mine took the unpopular decision that height wasn't for everyone and touching five foot was going to be my limit. So, Frankie and I decided I would hug the hell out of his torso until he lifted me up like a friendly giant in a fairy-tale book. I felt the floor of The Little Love Café fall away as a tear-stained Frankie pulls me up. Closing my blurry eyes, I press my damp face into his blue sweatshirt.

We ugly cry for what feels like an eternity. Over the years there have been a handful of occasions where we've both held each other and wept uncontrollably: the night Frankie's dad left Rose for a woman in Scotland; the day Mum died after she fell and hit her head during one of her hikes on the coastal path, the day I realised Noah Coombes wasn't coming back and I needed to get on with my life and when Frankie arrived to rescue me from Scott's house.

Placing me back down Frankie slides back into the booth. 'I don't know what to think or do. I'm a mess. She starts chemo next week and there's talk of a mastectomy.'

Swallowing back an avocado shaped lump at the back of my throat I try to contain the army of tears which are spilling down my cheeks. 'Come on,' I say, 'we must stay positive. She's going to get through this.'

Frankie sniffs. 'When Mum told me everything a few hours ago, I did think about not telling you. But then I came to my senses.'

I pull away. 'Why would you do that?'

Taking my tissue to blow his nose, Frankie sits back. 'You've been through hell lately.'

'I'm not made of delicate tissue paper,' I exclaim. 'Dad is the same. As you know, he still thinks I should be on his sofa under a travel blanket.'

A tiny smile finds its way onto Frankie's reddened face. 'Bless Brian. He would need to get down to Sofa World if he wanted me to lie on his sofa. I wouldn't want to spend any length of time on that grubby old thing. You have lower sofa standards than me.'

I let out a chuckle and take a sip of my drink. 'Okay, what are you going to do about your mum?'

Frankie shrugs. 'There's nothing I can do. Just be at the end of Skype while she goes through chemo. I want to go to Sydney to be with her, but I don't know what to do with this place.'

'Can't you get someone to manage it for you?'

He rubs his face so hard angry red marks appear. 'It's doing really well.' Fiddling with his watch, he takes a deep breath. 'Mum thinks it will be bad for business if I go and shut it. She's right. I've worked so hard to get it where it is today, and it would be bad for business to close it. There isn't anyone I trust who could look after it for me.'

'What about that bloke who looked after it when you went to Santorini last year?'

'Tommy?' Frankie's green eyes widen with shock. 'The one who helped himself to some of my takings? No way.'

Scratching my neck, I order my brain to come up with some alternative options. I don't have to wait long. 'What about Jake? He could run this place?'

Jake is Frankie's boyfriend. They'd been dating for a year and Jake often helps as he is a trained barista. Frankie shakes his head. 'His father's not well and I don't want to add any more pressure. I've put the word out on all my WhatsApp groups about a café manager, so I'll see whether anyone offers any help. I am not hopeful.' We both drink our coffee. 'Oh, I saw Betty in town yesterday,' explains Frankie, with a mischievous grin.

'How long have you been carrying around Noah's photo?' He arches his left eyebrow at me.

Heat is travelling up my neck. 'I can't believe Betty told you that. For your information, the photo was from the last day of school. There are loads of us sat on our rock on the beach and I happen to be leaning against Noah.'

Frankie chuckles. 'Leave Betty alone. Anyway, I love how you still hold a candle for Noah Coombes, or should I say your *pretend* husband?'

After all these years, Frankie still finds it amusing that, at sixteen, Noah and I had our own makeshift beach wedding. It was the first thing he told Jake about when they began dating. Frankie, who loves a wind-up, missed out the *pretend* bit and convinced his new boyfriend that it had been legitimate. Frankie howled with laughter when Jake asked me seriously over dinner whether it was true that I got married at sixteen.

'I'm not discussing Noah. I've still not forgiven myself for not listening to Dad about him.'

Frankie takes a sip of coffee. 'You've been obsessed with him since he left.'

'Not true. I hardly think about him.' This is a lie. Noah comes into my thoughts at every key moment in my life: when I agreed to go on a date with Pete; when I found out I was pregnant with Lucas; when Lucas was born; when I asked Pete to leave because I didn't love him; when Scott proposed; and when I'd locked myself in the toilet after discovering Scott's affair. It was Noah who I thought about.

Rose once told me, 'You never forget your first love.' She was certainly right about that.

CHAPTER FOUR

'Alice, I have good and bad news.' Ronald's serious tone makes my neck and shoulders become rigid.

It's not been a great day so whatever he's about to tell me is going to be the cherry on top of my *naff workday* cake. The day took a downward trajectory the second I woke up and found myself lying in my crumpled wedding dress on the camp bed with a throbbing purplish bump on my head. Last night, Frankie came over to Dad's with several bottles of wine.

Dad and Lucas went to bed early leaving Frankie and me to talk about Rose, her cancer treatment, and his ideas on what to do with The Little Love Café.

A few hours later, our evening had got messy. Frankie had invited Jake over and they were cuddling in the garden, and I was sat inside, on the sofa, feeling like a third wheel and wearing my wedding dress. I'd put it on in a drunken state after Frankie had suggested we do a few vodka shots. An hour later and he was feeling romantic towards Jake and I was sat alone holding a half-full bottle of wine and sobbing about how I no longer believed in true love.

Frankie and Jake went home in the early hours, and I

staggered upstairs. If you've ever tried to sleep on an old metal camp bed from the 1970s, you will know that these contraptions are not forgiving and can snap shut, at any point, like a Venus fly trap plant. As I was very drunk and emotional when I came to bed, I ended up having a fight with the camp bed. I admitted defeat after it sprang up and thumped me on the forehead. In the end I lay down on it and went to sleep... still in my wedding dress.

To my dismay, at breakfast, I was greeted by chaos. A Batman pyjama-clad Lucas was stood on a chair shouting for his cereal, Bean had left a puddle of dog wee in the hallway and a torrent of water was coming through the kitchen ceiling. Dad was running about with a mop and bucket. 'Lucas decided to run Bean an early morning bath,' gasped Dad. 'It's flooded the kitchen. I've just turned the taps off upstairs.'

With a thumping headache I helped Dad clean up the mess and offered to pay for the ceiling to be repaired. He refused my offer. I made Lucas his breakfast and told him not to run Bean a bath ever again.

My hangover has been brutal. I have spent much of the day on the doorstep of the tea shop getting some much-needed fresh air, feeling nauseous and telling the three customers who had come into the café that I would never drink wine again.

Ronald's arrival had made me so dizzy and I had to sit down.

'Alice, who have you been brawling with?' Ronald peers at my forehead. 'As you know, I don't like to date local women as they do like a punch-up. Seeing you in this state proves my point. Were you fighting over a fella?'

I glare at him. 'No, I had a row with a camp bed.'

Ronald shakes his head with disapproval. 'Anyway, I have come here with good news – Denise has asked me to join her in

Marbella for an extra-long holiday. Alice, things have got serious between us.'

My heart thuds. 'You've only been dating her for a few weeks.'

He chuckles. 'Alice, you know I don't mess about when dating a beautiful woman.'

I roll my eyes. 'What does this mean for The Starfish Tea Shop?'

He clears his throat. 'Ah, the bad news. Business has not been that great. I know you have been working hard but I am afraid I am closing down.'

'Oh.' My fingers are gripping the shell-encrusted counter so hard I have white knuckles.

'I know this news will be a big loss for the town,' he says, staring into space with a dreamy expression on his face. 'Also, I think it will break some hearts when some of the females here in Blue Cove Bay hear I am no longer available.' He turns to me. 'I'll be closing Friday.'

He must have heard my loud gulp. *What the hell am I going to do now?*

Dad is stood by the mantelpiece. He's been quiet ever since I told him my job at the tea shop is ending on Friday. We've also both been struggling with the news of Rose's cancer, so it's been a tough time. 'Alice, I'll go full-time at the supermarket. You don't need to worry about finding another job.'

Scrambling off the sofa, I rush over to him. 'No, Dad, I'll get another job. You retired from your bakery as the long hours were exhausting you. I don't want you to work full time. I don't care what I have to do.'

He rescues his reading glasses which are hanging

precariously off his head. 'You said yourself there wasn't much in the job centre when you asked on your way home.'

'I'll travel further afield then to find work.'

Turning, he cups my face. 'You've been through enough lately, my sweet girl.' Placing his hands on my shoulders, he ushers me towards the sofa. 'Sit down. You look tired and that bruise on your head should be looked at by a doctor.'

'Dad, I'm fine and I'm not lying on that sofa again. For the millionth time, I'm thirty-six, not eight. I don't need to lie down.' Batting his hands away, I go to stand by the window. There must be something I can do. If there's one thing I hate in life, it's not being able to pay my own way and the thought of my dad being worried about money is painful. He doesn't have much these days after retiring.

Our old living room still looks the same with its huge stone fireplace and walls adorned with photos of Lucas and me.

Tucked away on a shelf opposite me is a single photo of Mum laughing into the camera. It's easy to miss. Even after all these years Dad still finds her photo a painful reminder. In the photo Mum's stood next to her best mate Rose outside a white-washed Greek villa. Rays of golden light are reflecting off Mum's blonde hair and her blue eyes are twinkling like crazy. Rose is trying to tame her mass of wild red curls, which look like they are having a party of their own, while hanging on to Mum's arm. They were on a girlie holiday to Greece which had been Mum's idea after Frankie's father had walked out. She and Rose had a great time and they came home with sunburnt shoulders, lots of photos and tales of drunken dancing in a little beach bar.

Wiping my face, I stare at Mum's lovely kind face and the worst idea *ever* pings into my head. It makes the hairs on the back of my neck stand upright and a sinking feeling take hold of my gut. I'm sure Mum's smile just got a little wider. Dad's living room sways. 'I'll manage The Little Love Café.'

'*You* want to manage The Little Love Café?' Dad is staring at me in horror.

The idea takes shape in my mind. 'I will manage it.' Turning my head, I catch sight of a photo of Frankie, Lucas and me standing on London Bridge, beaming into the camera. We'd been on one of Frankie's fabulous day trips during one of his visits to where we used to live. My best mate needs my help. A memory from last night's drinking session rushes back: Frankie crying on my shoulder because he wanted to be with his mum when she started chemo. My chest aches as my mind replays the sound of Frankie's sobs. 'If I manage it, Frankie can go to Sydney.'

Dad touches my arm. 'Absolutely ridiculous. You can't manage that place, Alice.'

'Why not?'

'Your emotions are in a mess. That place would be torturous. All I hear in the supermarket are tales of Frankie's customers proposing to each other. Some days I wonder what Frankie is putting into their drinks. I can't let you do this.' Pointing me in the direction of the sofa, he steers me towards it. 'Right, sit down. I didn't tell you; I've subscribed to Netflix, and they have all your old favourite films.'

'What films?'

Dad points the TV controller and searches for *romcoms*.

My reply is shrill and instantaneous. 'I am NOT watching bloody romcoms!' Oh my goodness, has Dad lost his mind? Seeing everyone fall in love on screen will have me blubbing over Scott again in no time.

Studying my face, Dad's sea-grey eyes narrow. 'If you want to manage Frankie's café then I think you should watch these films.'

'Dad, those films will make me depressed.'

A frustrated wail shoots out of Dad's mouth. 'Listen to yourself.'

'Dad, I'm not a child anymore.'

He rushes over to me, clasping my hands. 'I've only got you and Lucas, so it's my job to look out for you. All those romantic couples will make you think about all that happened with your wedding, and you'll get upset.'

Dad is right. I can't stomach watching romcoms, so how the hell am I going to manage a romance-themed café?

Mum's face finds me again. I stare at her photo. She'd want me to help Frankie and Rose and she'd also want me to make sure Dad's finances are put right.

'Alice, don't do this. There are other jobs.'

Taking his hands in mine, I shake my head. 'Dad, do you think I can lie here knowing you took out a loan to pay for my wedding reception which never happened and now you're having to work extra hours to make ends meet? I also have a son who needs supporting and a best mate who is desperate to go be with his sick mum. I have work to do.'

I grab my coat.

'Where the hell are you going?' Dad's voice is exasperated.

'To tell Frankie I will manage his café.' My legs feel like they are made of heavy stone once I am out of the door, but I manage to rotate them. If I'm quick, Frankie will still be open.

Taking a deep breath, I tell myself that the café will not be empty like it was the other morning when I consoled Frankie. Pulling open the doors of The Little Love Café I gasp and stand with a heaving chest. It takes only a few seconds for me to realise Dad was right. My eyes are met by couples holding hands across the table, couples giggling and couples whispering sweet nothings to each other.

At one booth, I notice the butcher's son, Vince, with a woman I recognise from school, but I'm struggling to remember her name. Vince used to sit next to me in history. His dinner plate sized hands are tenderly cupping the woman's face and she's wetting her lips in anticipation of a kiss.

Noah used to do that with me. Hot tears build up in my eyes. Before they have a chance to fall down my cheeks, Sandra, who used to work in one of the clothes shops on the high street in town, taps me on the shoulder. 'Alice, here, take a photo of us?'

'Huh?' I glance at her sitting on the lap of a man with a huge grin plastered over his face.

'Alice – meet my new Tinder date. He's called Chris,' she gushes. She turns back to the man and they both erupt into a fit of giggles.

I feel sick. Handing Sandra her phone, I catch sight of Frankie at the baby pink counter, talking to a man with his back to me. My best mate is wearing a bright pink apron with the words *Little Love Café* emblazoned across the front. He's running a hand through his short blond hair whilst deep in conversation. Frankie lifts his head and catches sight of me. His mouth falls ajar with what looks like shock.

Ignoring his expression, I race over. If I delay volunteering to manage this place any longer, I won't do it. 'Frankie,' I gasp, 'I'll manage this place.'

Frankie stares at me. 'Eh? What did you say... *Alice?*'

The man's head flicks towards me, but I keep my attention on Frankie. 'Let me look after this place for you while you go to Australia. I've been thinking about it and...'

Frankie points at the man. 'Funny you should say that as... *Noah*... has offered to manage it as well.'

His words ping around my head as I turn and find myself face to face with Noah Coombes. It's him. Noah Coombes. The boy who once asked me to marry him and organised a makeshift wedding on the beach, with cheap silver rings from the gift shop, a dress, flowers in my long hair, and a suit from the charity shop, all our school friends stood around us holding bottles of cider as gifts. The boy who asked Frankie to marry us and crafted our own vows.

The boy who promised me on the day he left for Ireland that we would one day 'meet again down by our rock in Blue Cove Bay'.

CHAPTER FIVE

I t was a scorching hot day when I first met Noah all those
years ago. I was thirteen and already bored. I was only two
days into the school summer holidays, which didn't bode well.
I'd been sat on the rock down on the beach in Blue Cove Bay for
most of the day. Dad was busy in his bakery and Frankie had
gone to Scotland to see his father.

I didn't know Noah up until this point. He'd always gone to
a different school. There was another reason why Noah and I
had never met; the nasty rift between our two fathers which had
started at a wedding reception a few months after Mum had
died. I can remember Dad swinging a punch at Dave Coombes
by the bar. Women screamed as Dad and Dave wrestled on the
floor. I was led away by Rose and taken back to her house.
When I asked Dad the next morning about his puffy purple eye
and bloodied lip, he said we were never to mention the name of
Dave Coombes ever again.

So, there I was, on that sunny day, sucking on my cola ice
pop, swinging my legs over the side, and watching tourists wade
out into the azure blue sea. Above my head seagulls were
playing a noisy game of chase and below me tiny children were

squealing with delight as they toddled over the sand. I didn't notice the yellow haired boy shimmy up my rock and plonk himself down beside me.

When he tapped me on the shoulder and said, 'Hello, my name is Noah,' all I could think about was my swimsuit. Up until the age of thirteen I'd not given two hoots about my body or my choice in swimwear. On the day I met Noah, I'd squeezed myself into my old pink frilly swimsuit from BHS which Rose had bought me. It was my clothing item of choice back then in the summer holidays. Rose had bought it for me when I was a beanpole. The summer I met Noah puberty had given me some unexpected wobbly bits. Let's just say the costume was a *little* tight. But I didn't care.

The moment I saw Noah everything changed. It was as though someone had flicked an invisible self-conscious switch inside my head. He stared at me with his summer sky blue eyes and then reached up to scratch his mass of golden hair, which reminded me of Rapunzel's hair from the fairy books I used to read as a child. His caramel tanned face and his cheeky boyish grin which swept across his mouth gave me a strange sensation in my tummy. My hands went into a frantic search for my towel. I didn't want him to see me in my costume. To my dismay my Barbie towel had slipped off the edge. It was a nightmare. Tucking my legs up to my chin I inched towards the edge in the hope I could climb down and run away.

A few days later Noah told me he was Dave's son and that his father had forbidden him to go near any of the Hiddleston family. It was then I admitted to being Brian Hiddleston's daughter. Neither of us knew why there was so much hatred between our two families. Seeing each other became a thrill. It was exciting and my heart used to break into a wild gallop whenever I saw Noah coming across the beach towards my rock.

We both knew one day our friendship would lead to trouble, but we didn't care.

Those familiar summer blue eyes are now studying my face. His once golden hair is now heavily flecked with brown, and his smooth caramel tanned skin is host to a few crinkles. 'Alice?' He gasps. 'I can't believe you're here.'

History is repeating itself. All I can think about is my outfit, my old grey jogging bottoms, my faded Levi's T-shirt, and my tatty Converse. Lifting my hand, I touch my hair. I can't remember the last time I brushed it or washed it for that matter. God knows what's he's thinking about my dishevelled state.

'Yes, it's me,' I say, flicking my eyes to the floor. This is embarrassing. Here I am talking to Noah Coombes: the person I have been thinking about for twenty years.

'How are you?' His eyes are studying the bruise on my head.

'Good,' I lie, wiping my clammy hands on the top of my jogging bottoms. 'I'm back living with Dad.' I stop myself. Noah Coombes will not be interested in my life story.

Frankie clears his throat and we both turn back to him. 'This is awkward as you both have offered to run this place.'

My shoulders are stiffening at the sight of Frankie nervously glancing between Noah and me. Surely, I should get first refusal? I am his best friend, and he knows how much stress and heartache Noah has caused me. He cannot give the job to Noah Coombes. I need this job. 'Frankie,' I say, casting him a sugary sweet smile. 'Can I have a word... in private?'

Noah gestures towards the leather booth opposite me. 'I'll be sat over there.'

Once he's out of earshot, I lean over the bar. 'What is he doing here?' I hiss.

Frankie studies my forehead. 'What the hell have you done to your head?'

'I had a fight with a camp bed.' Gingerly I feel the lump with my fingers.

'Noah's looking for work. He has moved back.'

'Please tell me you're not considering him over me?' I am now giving Frankie one of my death stares. 'He's been back here for five minutes. Don't I deserve some best-mate loyalty after what he did to me when I was sixteen?'

'Alice, you and Noah split *twenty* years ago,' whispers Frankie, glancing at Noah and then returning to me. 'You were kids back then. No one knows what they are doing at sixteen.'

Grabbing the sleeve of Frankie's T-shirt I pull him closer. 'This job is perfect for me. You can go to Sydney, and I can help pay Dad back.'

Frankie frowns. 'Pay your dad back for what?'

I exhale a long stream of air. 'He took out that loan to pay for my wedding. Look, I think you need to give me the job.'

My heart is thudding. Out of the corner of my eye I can see Noah staring at me. 'Frankie,' I beg. 'Give me the job.'

Frankie scratches his thatch of blond hair. 'Alice, you have a broken heart for starters. You're also emotional and capable of causing all sorts of havoc.' He picks up a cloth and wipes down the counter. 'Anyway, you're still managing Ronald's tea shop.'

Grabbing a pink napkin, I dab at the layer of sweat on my forehead. 'He's closing the Starfish on Friday. Going abroad with his latest love interest.'

Frankie reaches out and places his hand on my shoulder. 'Sorry, Alice.'

'I can manage this place. My emotional state will not interfere with anything.'

Frankie's perfectly trimmed brown eyebrows climb up his forehead. 'This is a romance-themed café,' he explains. 'Do you have any idea how hard it will be for you? Remember the youth club discos when we were teenagers and everywhere you'd look there would be couples snogging – well this place is like that. It's not the sort of place for someone with a broken heart. Also, you keep telling me you would go crazy if you worked here.'

My cheeks are heating up. 'So, you're going to give the job I want... and need... to *him* then?'

'Go sit down and let me think,' mutters Frankie, massaging his temples and avoiding my angry scowl.

With a huff I turn on my heel to face Noah. He smiles and points to the empty seat opposite. 'Sit down.'

We sit in silence for what feels like an eternity. In my head I have a multitude of questions I want to ask him, but my brain is reminding me of how he broke my heart. Noah is fiddling with a red heart-shaped menu, so I've glued my eyes to the varnished wooden floorboards.

Behind our booth a woman is telling her boyfriend in a loud voice that she can't wait for their wedding in three weeks. The word 'wedding' makes me shrivel up inside. She sounds like I did when Scott took me for a romantic Italian meal before his stag do. I made the same high-pitched squeal. Tears prick my eyes and I blink them away. Scott's face flashes into my mind. My mind cruelly transports me back to the scene when I walked into our bedroom.

Inside me a battle is waging. Half of me wants to get out of my seat, lean over her booth and warn her against getting married. The other half is restraining me. Frankie won't give me the job if I start talking customers out of their plans to wed.

Frankie appears at our booth. 'I've made my decision.'

A triumphant grin slides across Noah's face. It makes my blood boil. He thinks Frankie's going to give him the job. If Frankie gives Noah the job of managing this place, we will fall out.

Frankie places a hand on my wrist and one on Noah's arm. 'I've decided to make...'

My heart comes to a juddering halt as Frankie pauses and hangs his head.

'Both of you managers.'

'What?' Noah and I flick our heads towards Frankie.

Frankie's emerald green eyes are dancing with excitement. 'You both can manage this place and I will go to Sydney to look after Mum.'

'Why are you making both of us do this?' I say, glaring at Frankie. 'Why couldn't you just let me manage it?'

Noah's blue eyes have widened with surprise. He's staring at me.

Sliding himself next to me in the pink leather booth Frankie forces me to move up. 'Alice, it will be fun for you, getting to know Noah again.'

My mouth has fallen ajar at Frankie's suggestion. Anger is coursing through my veins and my cheeks are burning. Has Frankie got amnesia? Has he forgotten about how long it took me to get over Noah Coombes? Does he not remember how for six months after Noah left, I played the good (pretend) wife and wrote to my (pretend) husband in Ireland even when he wasn't replying to me? Doesn't Frankie remember how I started dating Pete to make Noah jealous in Ireland and then stayed in a relationship for far too long with the guy? I know we're all adults now but surely Frankie will take my side.

I hope Noah doesn't remember me writing to him about Pete. Deep breaths, Alice.

Noah Coombes is the last person on this planet I want to get to know. 'But I don't want to get know to Noah *again*.'

Noah raises his hand. 'Frankie, let Alice run the café. I'll find some other work.'

I turn to Frankie, fold my arms, and wait for him to put things right.

'No, Alice will be managing this place with you, Noah.'

I let out a wail of frustration. Tugging on Frankie's T-shirt sleeve I shake my head. 'No, no, no, no.'

'Yes, yes, yes, yes, Alice.' Frankie's reply infuriates me.

Noah gets to his feet. 'Look it's been nice to catch up with you both. I'll see you around.'

Frankie reaches out and grabs Noah. 'Please, mate. Do this for me.'

Noah hangs his head and sits back down.

'Right then.' Frankie rests his elbows on the table. 'You will both look after this place and that's final.'

Opening my mouth, I try to say something, but Frankie looks up at the ceiling and places his hand in a prayer pose. 'Thank you, God, for supplying me with two willing volunteers to look after my café, and I'm sorry for pretending to be a man of the cloth on the beach when I married them both all those years ago.'

I look away and ignore Noah's attempts to catch my eye.

CHAPTER SIX

Dad, Lucas, Frankie, and I are sat around the kitchen table eating a late tea. After I'd stormed out the café following Frankie's decision to make both Noah and me temporary managers, Frankie insisted on inviting himself for tea. He called Dad and asked whether there would be enough homemade chicken pie, mash potato and peas for him.

It's a bit of a squeeze. There's no room for elbows on the table. Dad didn't have enough posh chairs, so Frankie is sat on garden furniture. I haven't spoken to him since he arrived. He's grinning from the far end of the table, doing his best to force a smile out of me.

I haven't told Dad yet about Noah. The prospect of telling him that I will be working alongside Noah Coombes is already making my stomach hurt. Dad is going to be so cross, and he's got enough on his plate right now, what with the bathroom ceiling and having his daughter and grandson live with him.

When I got home, I was so cross with Frankie I went and played Batman figure wrestling with Lucas. I took out my frustrations on several small plastic figures which made Lucas erupt into uncontrollable laugher.

'Is there something going on?' Dad asks, glancing at my stony expression and then at Frankie. 'Why does Alice have a face like thunder?'

Frankie chuckles and digs his fork deep into his crusty pie pastry. 'She's a little cross with me, Brian.'

'Oh?' Dad puts down his fork and dabs at the crumbs around his mouth. 'Do you want to tell me about it?'

After taking a sip from the glass of orange squash, which Lucas had made him when he arrived, Frankie stares at me. 'Brian, this afternoon I had two applicants for the role of café manager.'

Dad lets out a groan and massages his forehead. 'Please tell me you didn't give Alice the job. Your café is the last place she needs to work in right now.'

The second frustrated wail of the day shoots out of my mouth. 'For goodness' sake, I am thirty-six years old. If I want to apply for a job in a romance-themed café then I will.'

Dad looks at me, rubbing his grey stubble-coated chin. 'So, did Frankie give you the job?'

Before I can say yes, Frankie interrupts me. 'Yes, I did, Brian, but there was a catch.' Frankie gives me a mischievous wink. 'I also gave the other applicant the job too. There are now going to be two managers.'

Glaring at Frankie I take a sip from my own glass of orange squash. Lucas was trying to show Dad that he was being a good boy now that the bath incident has been forgotten. The sickly strong taste makes me screw up my face. 'Ugh, Lucas, how much water did you put in here?'

Lucas giggles. 'I didn't put any water in yours, Mummy.'

I can't help but giggle at Frankie who is now doing impressions of me tasting the drink. 'Watch it, Frankie Jones.'

Frankie starts to clap. 'She's talking to me again.' He ruffles Lucas's hair and together they give each other a high five.

Dad has taken off his glasses and is cleaning them with his apron. 'So, what was the catch?'

'I also gave the job to an old friend,' explains Frankie, giving me a wink. 'Someone who deserves a second chance.'

Dad puts down his glasses and stares at Frankie. 'You gave the job to Pete?'

Frankie wipes his mouth with a napkin. 'Pete's busy with the magazine and managing his band.' He grins at Dad. 'Noah Coombes, remember him – Brian?'

Dad's face turns an odd pale colour. His sea-grey eyes have darkened, and his brow has become deeply furrowed. 'Frankie, I will never forget that name.'

'Look at all the trouble you've caused.' With my fork I point at Dad, who looks like someone has hypnotised him. He's sat staring into space. Frankie gently nudges his arm. 'Earth to Brian.'

Shaking my head with despair I nudge a piece of pastry with my knife.

Something snaps Dad out of his mini trance. He turns to me. 'Don't do this, please. That family is trouble. His father upset me terribly all those years ago and what he did was truly unforgivable. The apple didn't fall far from the tree with Noah. He won't have changed.'

I reach out to Dad. 'What happened between you and Dave?'

Dad bats my hand away. 'It's not something I want to discuss. Now, please, Alice, take my advice. Stay away from Noah.' Something flickers across his eyes, and I am reminded of the day he caught Noah and me kissing on top of our rock. It was the summer Noah and I turned fourteen. In the May of that year Noah had joined my school and our relationship blossomed. Everyone at school had been sworn to secrecy. Noah and I were Blue Cove Bay's answer to Romeo and Juliet.

Dad was in his bakery when a local woman, who'd never liked Dave Coombes, said she'd seen me down by the beach on a rock with Dave's son. By the time Dad had closed the bakery and marched across the beach Noah and I were on top of our rock, kissing.

I was grounded for weeks and so was Noah. Dad was furious. His sea-grey eyes glowed with a fiery rage. He shouted about how upset he was to see me with someone who I'd been warned about, how irresponsible I was kissing someone like Noah Coombes on top of a rock, how at my age I shouldn't be kissing boys and how he was a single father doing his best to raise his only daughter and keep her out of harm's way.

With fourteen-year-old defiance, I had asked him why he hated Dave Coombes so much. I was sent to my room without any tea. That wasn't the end of Noah and me. We both lied to our fathers and continued to sneak out after school and head for our rock.

When Noah broke my heart, it was Dad who picked up the pieces.

'Brian, that was years ago,' interjects Frankie. 'Alice and Noah were teenagers back then. They're both adults now.'

I stare down at my plate in bewilderment. My life has gone crazy.

It's a good job Dad never found out about the secret wedding. Thank God for teenage secrets! Everyone involved with our wedding was sworn to secrecy. School friends who attended were carefully selected on their discretion. I still can't believe it's remained a secret for so long. If Dad had known all those years ago that Noah and I had organised a wedding, he would have exploded into a fiery rage.

'Brian.' Frankie drapes his arm over Dad's shoulders. 'Noah and Dave are good people. You got them all wrong.'

My heart is pounding away inside my chest and this horrible sinking feeling has taken over my gut.

Lucas jumps down from his chair. 'Can I go play in the back garden with Bean?'

On my nod he races outside with Bean barking at his heels.

Dad pushes his plate away. 'Noah was nothing but trouble.'

Frankie takes a deep breath. 'Good job we never told you that Noah asked Alice to marry him at sixteen and they had a secret pretend wedding on the beach.'

Time grinds to a halt and so does my heart. It's been years since Dad has shouted at the kitchen table. He's normally a calm and placid man. 'HE DID WHAT?'

My father's booming voice brings in Lucas and Bean. I send Lucas back out after telling him Grandpa was telling a joke.

'Frankie,' I gasp, 'stop this.'

Dad is glaring at me. 'What's this about a secret wedding at *sixteen* to Noah Coombes?'

I try to force some words out, but they all seem to be glued to my tongue.

Dabbing his glazed forehead with his hanky, Dad leans back in his chair. 'Alice, you are making a big mistake by working in Frankie's café. As you say, you're an adult, but I want you to know I'm not happy with the thought of you working alongside Noah Coombes.'

'Well, it's too late to back out now.' Sighing, I push my plate away. My hunger has disappeared. 'I have accepted Frankie's job offer. Tomorrow Noah and I start training.'

Dad's chair angrily scrapes over the stone floor tiles as he shoots up out of his chair. 'This is the worst idea I have ever heard. I'm going to take Lucas and Bean for a walk over the beach.'

After the front door slams shut, Frankie places his face in his hands. 'What have I done?'

I'm stood leaning against the work surface feeling light-headed. 'You told him about the secret wedding. I can't believe you did that.'

Frankie groans. 'It came out all wrong. I think I better go to Australia.'

Opening the dishwasher, I load the plates. 'When did Noah get in contact with you?'

'He turned up ten minutes before you stormed into my café demanding I give you the job,' explains Frankie. 'I couldn't believe it when I looked up and saw him. He said he'd heard about the job from one of my friends on WhatsApp.'

I turn to Frankie with narrowing eyes. Is there something my best mate isn't telling me? 'One of *your* contacts knew Noah?'

Frankie shakes his head. 'It's not what you think, Alice. I honestly didn't know anyone from my network knew Noah.'

'Why is he back?'

Frankie shrugs. 'He didn't say. I'm sure once you get to know him again, he'll tell you.'

Grabbing Dad's tea towel, I playfully whip Frankie. 'That's for annoying me earlier and for telling Dad about my secret wedding.'

Hauling himself to his feet Frankie pulls me into a bear hug. 'You know I love you, Alice Hiddleston. I think it's time you made friends with Noah and while you are at it, maybe you can get Brian to make peace with him too?'

'I wish I knew why Dad and Dave fell out.' I stare out of the little kitchen window. In the distance a strip of shimmering marine blue sea calls out to me.

Frankie says, 'Mum refused to tell me, which is unusual for her.'

Opening the kitchen window, I inhale a lungful of salty sea air. A memory of my grief-stricken father from the time he had his disagreement with Dave Coombes rushes into my mind. Dad was sat with his head in his hands at the kitchen table when I'd got home from school.

'Think it was a case of drunken male pride.' Frankie comes to stand by me. 'Dave was a good bloke.'

My mind wanders back to Noah. So much had happened since he'd left twenty years ago. Pete's face appeared in my mind. An uncomfortable feeling takes hold of me. 'I am not sure about working with Noah again.'

Frankie is grinning at me. 'Too late now, Alice.'

CHAPTER SEVEN

'Mummy,' Lucas shouts as he charges into the living room clutching his trainers. He casts me a lovely smile. I ruffle his mop of black hair. His large blue eyes are bright and full of life. Every day he looks more like a mini version of Pete. 'Are we going to Frankie's café?'

Nodding I give his hand a squeeze. 'Yes, but you're going to play football on the beach with Jake. I must do my training.' Jake has offered to look after Lucas for me, which I am grateful for as Dad is working and I'm not sure Lucas could sit still beside me for two minutes of Frankie's training, let alone an hour or so. An ear-to-ear grin spreads across Lucas's face. 'Will Jake buy me an ice cream?'

Crouching down to his level I smile at my happy son. 'Jake will only get you an ice cream if you are a good boy.' Buttoning up his yellow jacket I also help him tie up his trainers. Lucas looks up at Dad. 'Grandpa – are you coming?'

Dad shakes his head. Something which looks like sadness flickers across his eyes. 'I have got a shift at the supermarket today.'

Turning around I make a point of holding my father's gaze.

'Dad, I am going to make this work. I am going to make a success of Frankie's business and pay you back so that you can get rid of that loan.'

Dad squeezes my shoulder. 'Please think again about this new job. Did Ronald pay you yesterday?'

Yesterday Ronald's teashop closed its doors. Ronald turned up with Denise hanging off his arm. They stood in the doorway and Ronald surveyed the empty teashop. 'Where is everyone? Are they hiding out the back?' I sensed he was expecting me to have arranged a surprise farewell party for him. The Starfish Tea Shop finally closed its doors at 4pm. No one had come in all day. I'd even tried to give away his malnourished tea cakes for free outside, but everyone turned their nose up after a peek at them.

Once I have stood up from putting on Lucas's shoes, Dad takes hold of my hands. 'Don't put yourself through that at Frankie's café. I dread to think what it will be like for you working with that Noah Coombes.'

All thoughts about Noah Coombes have slipped from my mind. Last night a drunken Scott deluged my phone with hundreds of texts about why he'd cheated on me. I read a few of them. This was a mistake as I couldn't get the bedroom scene out of my head. I ended up downstairs on the sofa watching Netflix, with his number blocked.

'Dad, I'm a big girl now. I'm sure it will be fine,' I say, taking hold of Lucas's hand.

'Have a good day at the supermarket.'

He surveys my outfit. 'Alice, are you not going to wear something a bit smarter?'

I look down at my old black jeans which are struggling to contain my knees and are ripped in various places. My black T-shirt was grabbed from the ironing pile. It's a bit crumpled but it will do. 'I'll be fine, Dad.' As Lucas and I head out of the door I silently say to myself, *I'm not dressing up for this hellish job nor Noah Coombes.*

~

Frankie, Noah, and I are surrounded by bits of paper containing my handwritten notes and an array of dirty pink coffee cups. We are camped out in one of the pink leather booths. I have positioned myself opposite Frankie, with my back to the customers, so that I don't have to directly look at Noah. Training has lasted two hours. Frankie has also been leaving the booth to serve and make drinks, which each time has left Noah and me in an awkward silence.

Frankie brings out a sheet of typed out notes. 'Pam is the cake supplier. If you need anything extra, then contact Pam. I have left her details.' He beams at us. 'Right then, I have been wanting to attract more locals to The Little Love Café. We have lots of regulars who travel to Blue Cove Bay, which is great, but I feel like some of the people here are missing out. We have a few lonely souls in Blue Cove Bay, and it would make my day to hear that we have helped them find love and that they've come in here for a date.'

'What?' I stare at my best mate in bewilderment. 'Please don't expect me to play matchmaker while you are away.'

Frankie ignores me and reads from his sheet. 'I think we're missing out on the young coming here. There's a lot of lovesick teenagers around. When we were young, *certain* couples would have spent a lot of time in here.' He grins at me and then Noah. 'It would be good if we could somehow appeal to a younger audience. I also think there is opportunity for some of the seniors who live here. Betty tells me Harold and Pearl should be together as they're both widowed. He keeps gazing longingly at her over a cup of tea in the community centre Senior Tea &

Chat session and they were once childhood sweethearts. That's what I call low-hanging romance fruit.'

'Frankie, being a childhood sweetheart means nothing,' I snap, avoiding Noah's gaze. 'Pearl might not want anything to do with Harold.'

Frankie ignores me. 'Now, let's move on to potential new local customers. Phoebe who owns the bookshop on the seafront. Keith, her assistant, tells me she's lonely and is having no luck on the dating apps. She's got two little kids so is looking for someone in a similar position – ideally, we need a single dad.'

'Joy, Esme's sister, is getting friendly with Eric who owns the guesthouse. I saw them flirting over a stand of *'Kiss Me Quick in Blue Cove Bay'* cowboy hats. Get your thinking caps on.' Frankie pauses and swigs his coffee. 'If you could also somehow get Sunny and Lilly together who work in the ice-cream parlour, that would be great. Their constant flirting while I am ordering my usual three scoops of blueberry muffin flavoured ice cream is doing my head in.'

Noah is scratching his head. 'So, you want us to run the café and provide an unofficial dating service.'

Frankie looks at both of us. 'This café is doing well but it could do better. I want you both to see whether you can generate some extra local business, put some events on and get creative with these lonely souls. I think a little project like this will get you both working together.'

I scowl and look away.

'Oh, and I would love it if you could wear The Little Love Café uniform.' Frankie grinned. 'There is a pile of new T-shirts and aprons on the shelf out the back. I think you will both look great in bright pink.' He smirks at both of us.

'Is the uniform mandatory?' I ask. Sensing Frankie is enjoying making Noah and me suffer.

Frankie grins. 'No, but it would mean a lot to me to see you both on the café's social media beaming into the camera and acting like two happy work colleagues.'

'How pink are the T-shirts?' Noah asks.

Frankie laughs. 'You'll look great, Noah. The ladies will love you in pink.'

I scowl and silently vow to make Noah wear the uniform by himself.

'That's enough training for today. Alice and Noah – what do you think?'

'Depends on when you're planning to go to Australia,' I say, forcing myself to sound optimistic. I can't stop thinking about how I have made a big mistake. This is going to be much harder than I first thought. Noah and I have barely spoken. He keeps staring at me, but I avert my eyes to the floor every time I meet his gaze. All I can think about is how many desperate letters I sent him and what an idiot I was clinging onto him. So embarrassing. I also have no idea whether he knows about Pete and Lucas.

'Must be easier for you to just get a flight with your dual passport.' Noah grins at his old friend. 'Always been jealous of you about that.'

Frankie nods. 'Yeah, I can go when I like.'

Every single one of my stomach muscles has gone into spasm at the thought of Frankie not coming home again for months. I'll be left to wither away in this café prison filled with pink hearts, flowers, soppy customers, and Noah Coombes. For goodness' sake, after a couple of months of managing this place I will be tearing my hair out. 'You better come back, Frankie.'

Frankie yawns and stretches out his arms behind his head. 'You might not want me to return anyway.'

Noah opens his mouth, but I beat him to it. 'I *will* want you to come back. I'm already counting down the days until you return.'

Gripping onto the edge of the pink table and making Noah frown at me, I turn to Frankie. 'Have you decided when you're going to Sydney?'

Frankie casts me a familiar mischievous smile. For years I have been on the receiving end of this special facial expression. It basically lets me know that what comes next out of his mouth is not going to please me. Over the years this smile has been the precursor to Frankie playing countless practical jokes on me, Frankie taking the piss out of me for having a pretend wedding and Frankie pointing towards the male stripper he'd organised for me on my hen night.

My heart has started to thud. 'What?'

Frankie scratches his head. 'I was thinking of going soon.'

Nibbling on my nail I take in what he's just said. 'What does *soon* mean?'

He grins at both Noah and me. 'The day after tomorrow?'

Blood is draining away from my face. 'What – that soon?' Noah is looking my way once again. In a few days it will just me and him managing a romance-themed café on our own. What the hell have I volunteered to do?

'You all right with that, Alice?' Noah's voice is soft and contains a hint of an Irish accent.

I release my messy bun, letting my long hair fall onto my shoulders. 'Great,' I say, while inwardly letting out a silent scream.

Frankie taps me on the wrist with his straw. 'I might leave you and Noah so you can discuss how you are going to run this place. A little word of advice, why don't you both spend the first week working together so you can get a feel for the place. Noah – are you handling the social media for me?'

Noah nods. 'Yes, I'm good with a camera and I can make this place look amazing.'

Frankie has hurried behind his counter to text Jake. Noah's

summer sky blue eyes are studying my face. Biting my lip prevents me from asking him why he never sent me a letter back explaining that he wanted to move on with his life, or better still give me a call. It wasn't like he could forget my telephone number as I used to plaster it all over my letters. He also could have got in contact with Pete, his best mate. Those two were close. I will always remember Noah's watery eyes when he hugged Pete and said goodbye. Surely Noah would have said something to Pete about not writing to me? Life wouldn't have been so complicated. Pinching my skin on my wrist I remind myself that was twenty years ago. Noah and I are adults now.

Flicking open my notebook I find a new page and grab my biro.

Noah fidgets in his seat. He loosens his pink shirt. 'Right, Alice... ummm... this is awkward.'

My brain has lost control of my mouth. 'You can say that again.'

'I need to go to the loo.' He shoots up out of his seat. 'Back in a bit.'

Frankie rushes over. 'How's it going?'

I lean over and hiss, 'All I want to do is ask him about why he never wrote back.'

Frankie's perfectly shaped eyebrows shoot up his forehead. 'Don't ask him that. You need to keep quiet about your twenty-year-old grudge. Come on, you've both moved on since then. Let the past go.'

'It is hard not to think about it when I am staring at him.'

Gesturing for me to shift up, Frankie slides into the booth and squashes me against the wall with his giant body. 'Have you told him about Lucas yet?'

I playfully tap him on the arm with a heart-shaped menu. 'No, I haven't told Noah about Pete and Lucas. He doesn't need to know just yet.' Again, I swat Frankie. 'Can we stop raking up the past?'

Noah returns. Frankie gets out of his seat and pats Noah on the shoulder. 'Good to see you again, Noah.'

'You too, buddy.' Noah places his arm around Frankie. 'Like old times, us all being back here. Do you hear from Pete at all? I always wondered what happened to him.'

'MUMMY!' Lucas's voice makes us all look up as my son charges through the café towards the booth and throws himself at me.

Something flickers across Noah's face as he stares at Lucas's mass of black curls and big blue eyes. All I can think about is how he must see a mini version of his old best friend staring back at him.

I hang my head and wish the ground would open and swallow me up whole.

CHAPTER EIGHT

Frankie scoops Lucas up into his arms and grins. 'Did you beat Jake at football?'

Lucas chews on his saliva coated finger and nods. 'He was rubbish.'

Jake comes over, grinning at Lucas. Noah leans over and extends his hand. 'I'm Noah. You must be Jake?'

'Jake, Lucas tells me you were rubbish at football,' announces Frankie, lifting a squealing Lucas to sit on his shoulders.

Jake gestures for me to shift up and sits next to me. 'I was dreadful; Lucas is right.'

Lucas and Frankie do a celebratory dance. Frankie puts Lucas down and my son climbs onto Jake's lap and stares at Noah, who studies his face right back.

My cheeks are heating up. This is getting awkward. 'Time to go, Lucas.' Once I stand up, I grab Lucas's hand and turn to Frankie. 'When do you want Noah and me to start?'

'Monday,' Frankie announces.

I take a deep breath. 'Okay, Monday it is. Noah, are you all right with that?' I turn to Noah. He's been staring at me the whole time.

'Yes. See you Monday, Alice.'

I guide Lucas out of The Little Love Café, stopping briefly so we don't interrupt a glamorous couple having their picture taken by the flower wall. The woman is holding up a baby scan photo and her partner has lovingly wrapped himself around her. Tears prick my eyes. Seeing all this romantic joy is going to be tough.

As Lucas and I hurry out of the café I accidentally bump into a couple who are having a passionate kiss outside the doors. They pull apart with flushed smiling faces and wet lips. The woman apologises. With a head awash with painful memories of Scott kissing me before he went on his stag do, I run with Lucas down the steps and onto the beach.

Once back at Dad's house I create a makeshift sofa bed for Lucas and me. We spend much of the afternoon hiding away from the world. He watches a succession of cartoons while I nibble at my fingernails and think about what a huge mistake I have made.

Dad is quiet over tea. He turns to me and lets his sea-grey eyes study my face. 'I was grouchy at work and had to apologise to Penny on the tills. How was today?'

I want to bury my face in Dad's white shirt and weep. I want to phone Frankie and tell him it has been a big mistake. I want to return to living on Dad's sofa bed eating his brownies and watching daytime TV. The trouble is, I can't do any of these things. Whether I like it or not, I am the new joint manager of The Little Love Café.

My neck is tingling and itchy. I scratch it and try to sort out my head which has becomes deluged with worries about managing Frankie's café.

It is time to put on my big girl pants. Dad's staring at me. I must show him that I can do this. 'Great,' I say, 'I think it is going to be good for me working there.'

'Really?' Dad sounds surprised. He stares at my neck. 'Your rash has come back. Do you want some cream for it?'

I shake my head. 'It's because I'm...'

'Anxious?' Dad interrupts me. 'Enlighten me – why will it be good working at the Little Love Café?'

Swallowing back a tidal wave of emotion I ignore the urge to scratch my neck. I dig my fingers into the side of Dad's old sofa and try to think of something good to say to support my argument. 'Yes, I think it will be good... exposure therapy.'

'You can't lie to me, Alice.' Dad gives me one of his serious stares. 'I know you are too stubborn to admit you've made a mistake. Just know that I am here for you.'

Nausea climbs up my throat as I force out the words. 'I start managing the café on Monday.'

Dad's grey eyebrows rocket up his pink forehead. 'Monday?'

Kneading my knuckles into my chair I stare down at my lap.

'He's leaving you in charge on Monday... as in this Monday?'

'Yes,' I squeak. 'From Monday I will be managing the café with... Noah.' Every time I say or hear his name I get this weird sensation in my tummy.

'I'm not working Monday and Tuesday at the supermarket, which means I can collect Lucas from school for you. I will see what I can do on Wednesday.'

I place my hand on his arm. 'Dad, you don't have to look after Lucas. They are your days off. I will sort something out with Noah.'

Dad's eyes widen. 'Does Pete know Noah's back?'

Shaking my head, I stare down at my plate of half-finished chicken casserole and mash. 'This is a small town, so I suspect he'll find out soon.'

Dad rises from the dinner table and goes to stand by the window. 'I know I shouldn't say this, but I wish you and Pete were still together.'

Agitation at hearing Dad say this makes my neck itch. He reaches up to the shelves near the table and takes hold of his favourite photo. 'Alice, have you been turning this photo around again?'

In the photo Pete and me are on the beach smiling into the camera. I am holding Lucas, who is a few months old and hiding under a giant baby sun hat. We look like a perfect family. 'To this day I still can't believe you and Pete split up.' He gazes at the photo. 'Now that you are back home, I have been hoping this could be a chance.'

'A chance for what?' My voice is sharp and makes Dad jolt.

'You and Pete to make things work. It would make me so happy.'

Closing my eyes, I massage my temples and stop myself from telling Dad for the billionth time that Pete and I have been apart for five years and there is no likelihood of me ever getting back with him.

CHAPTER NINE

It's my first day at managing Frankie's café.

Yesterday I'd said an emotional farewell to Frankie. 'Take care of yourself, lovely girl,' Frankie whispered, his voice thick with emotion.

'Give my love to your mum. I haven't prayed since Sunday School but I'm going to start for her sake,' I croaked, shutting my eyes tight and sending God a quick silent prayer about Rose.

Frankie chuckled. 'You never prayed in Sunday School as we were always too busy messing about.'

'God will understand,' I sniffed, clinging onto my best mate. 'He'll have forgotten about all the mischief we got up to in the vestry.'

Frankie stroked my long red hair, and his finger got stuck in a knot which made us both forget our sadness and giggle.

My day has not started well. I'm outside the café trying desperately to get bird poo off my top with a wet wipe from my handbag.

Dad took Lucas to school, so I decided to go down to the beach and watch the sea rush in and out. I'd hoped it would stop me panicking at the almost impossible task before me. The sea and the weather reflected my mood. An irritable grey sea took out its frustrations on a miserable damp beach much to the amusement of a gang of rowdy seagulls who sounded like they were cackling with laughter.

Last night I'd planned to read through my training notes, but Lucas wanted an extra-long bedtime story and I fell asleep beside him.

Whilst I sat on the beach, I'd taken out my notes from my bag to have a quick scan over. I wanted to come across as knowledgeable and prepared. The seagull poo disaster occurred shortly after I'd placed the notes on my lap and looked up at the sky to silently ask God whether I could outshine Noah at everything today. This would make him question why he was needed at The Little Love Café and possibly leave by lunchtime. God clearly hasn't forgiven me for the mischief Frankie and I got up to at Sunday School when we were kids as I was hit by a missile of seagull poo which made me yell. Frustratingly it had missed my coat and hit my top. I walked along to the café cursing seagulls, Frankie's decision to open a love-themed café and ex-boyfriends who showed up unexpectedly after twenty years of ghosting you.

'Hello.' It's him. He's behind me. I whirl around and he greets me with an awkward glance. I survey his tan coloured leather jacket, a blue checked shirt, and jeans. His outfit suits him. From a young age Noah always wore clothes that looked good on him. He never went through the fashion wilderness which I found myself in between the years of twelve and seventeen, where any combination of colour and patterns were thrown together.

I have opted for an old black long-sleeved top, which now sports an ugly white stain and an old pair of grey jogging bottoms.

To my annoyance his eyes flick to the white stain on my black top. 'You have some white paint on your... T-shirt.'

'It's not paint,' I snap and rummage in my bag for the café keys.

'You can try out Frankie's pink uniform,' says Noah, as my agitation levels rise.

Once the doors are open, I hurry to the baby pink counter and head out the back where Frankie said the pile of Little Love Café pink T-shirts and aprons were kept.

'Have you found them?' Noah asks, standing by the counter.

'Yes thanks, Noah,' I snap. Standing behind a cupboard so Noah can't see me undress, I remove my stained top. I quickly pull on my new T-shirt. As I step out from behind the counter, I look up to see Noah staring at me. His eyes roam my T-shirt and heat travels up to my face.

'Pink suits you, Alice,' he says, as I grab a T-shirt and apron for him. There's no way I am going to be the only one wearing this ridiculous uniform.

He groans. 'Really?'

I take pleasure in nodding and flashing him a fake sugary smile. 'Yes.' He grimaces.

'I don't want to wear this,' he says, holding up the bright pink clothing.

'You don't have a choice,' I snap. 'Put them on.'

When he walks out from behind the cupboard in his new pink attire looking uncomfortable, I turn away and savour this moment. Karma is seeing your ex-boyfriend wear a tight pink shirt with the words, 'LITTLE LOVE CAFÉ,' emblazoned across his chest.

'Let's look at the bookings for today,' I say, ignoring Noah mumble about feeling awkward in his uniform.

Frankie has left us the table bookings log and several sheets of A4 paper of notes. On the top of the first page in big bold letters and underlined are the words: ALICE BELIEVE IN LOVE.

The word makes me flinch.

We check the bookings log. I point to the top of the page for today. 'We have Julie Hanbury and Graham Hitchcock coming at nine.' A groan escapes my lips as I read their requirements. 'Graham's going to propose to Julie and has asked for rose petals to be chucked on the floor and the Snug is to be sprayed with that heavenly floral spray.'

'Sounds romantic.' Noah runs a hand through his golden hair and at once I am reminded of us sat together in class at school. Back then he used to have floppy blond hair. When the teacher wasn't looking, he would turn to me, flick his fringe out of his eyes, and mouth, 'I love you.'

I quickly dismiss the memory. 'What a waste of good petals. Think we can skip that part.'

'Alice, we must give Julie and Graham what they want. This is their special day, and we are here to celebrate them.'

I let out a sigh. 'We don't have to go over the top.'

Noah ignores me and looks at the booking log. 'You look after Julie and Graham in the Snug out the back, and I'll sort out here.'

After everything I have been through, the last thing I want to do is watch someone ask their loved one to marry them. It will bring back the memory I have of Scott bending down on one knee in the Indian restaurant in between courses and asking me to marry him. Worse still, it will take me back to when a certain someone and I had a pretend wedding in front of our special rock.

I can't get the words out fast enough. 'No, I'm not dealing with Julie and Graham. I've had enough of bloody marriage proposals to last me a lifetime...' My voice cuts out and an awkward silence descends on us both. Noah and I both find interesting things to look at on the wooden floor beneath our feet.

Noah speaks first. 'You manage out here, and I'll deal with Julie and Graham.'

'Fine.' Turning away I use Frankie's list as a fan to cool down my warm face.

'I need to sort out the social media, too. Frankie wants me to take some shots of the café.'

This place is hell. I am even struggling with the heart-shaped menus. It's also hard being forced to listen to a man and woman engage in what can only be described as loud kissing. They've been slobbering all over each other for the past half hour. Surely their lips must be getting sore. I can't take this anymore and go to their table near the counter. 'Excuse me?' They both pull apart, breathless. 'Do you think you could do that a little quieter? Many thanks.'

'Graham has popped the question,' announces Noah, coming to the counter with his silver tray. 'She said yes.'

'Lucky her,' I mumble with an air of sarcasm, folding my arms across my chest.

Noah flicks his eyes to his pad. 'They've ordered two...' Noah mumbles something.

'Sorry, Noah, what did you say?'

'Two... *Sexy Hot Chocolates with Whipped*...' Noah mumbles and points to the name of the drink on a heart-shaped menu.

'Oh, right...' I say, feeling my cheeks heat up. Feeling flustered I set to work on the drinks and curse Frankie for his ridiculous drink names.

'They look really happy together; Graham and Julie.'

People used to say that about Scott and me. Tears prick my eyes. We looked happy together. But then Scott went and ruined everything. What sort of man does that the day before his wedding? Did I mean that little to him?

'You don't seem very happy,' Noah observes as I huff and puff behind the counter.

'I'm great, Noah. Here you go,' I say, keeping my eyes firmly fixed on the drinks and trying my hardest not to burst into tears. I should still be in Ronald's Starfish Tea Shop tucked away high up on the cliffs with nobody to talk to but the dodgy starfish hanging on the wall.

CHAPTER TEN

It's the second day of working in Frankie's café alongside Noah. I'm supposed to be making a drink order for the couple on table five, but I am watching Noah take a photo of two women standing against the flower wall.

There's so much I want to say to him. I want to ask him about his life and why he's back in Blue Cove Bay. I want to ask him why he ghosted my letters, but I must keep reminding myself that what happened all those years ago is in the past.

He was sixteen and looked like a Californian surfer dude when he set foot in Ireland. He was probably crushed by a stampede of beautiful Irish girls who couldn't wait to hop into a relationship with him. The last thing Noah wanted was a clingy girlfriend back home in Blue Cove Bay. Irritation nibbles away at me.

'Excuse me,' shouts the woman from table five. 'Where are our drink orders?'

'Sorry,' I say, casting her a fake sugary smile. 'I'm busy,' I say, which is a lie, but, I think she's probably too wrapped up in her tenth wedding anniversary celebration with her husband to notice.

The woman surveys the half empty café and turns back to me. 'You've been stood there for ten minutes staring into space. Please can we have our drinks.'

These customers are infuriating. If they're not slobbering over each other, they're picking arguments with me. With a loud huff I turn to the coffee machine and make their drinks.

'We have Jason Hinich's marriage proposal next,' says Noah, putting his empty tray on the counter. 'He wants us to film it so that it's live on Facebook.'

'You can do that,' I mutter, 'I am busy with... ummm... table five.'

Noah glances over at table five. 'They ordered ages ago, Alice. Have you still not made their order?'

I glare at him and say through gritted teeth, 'I have been *busy*, Noah.'

Noah looks taken aback and runs his hand through his hair. 'I have a doctor's appointment now. I can't film Jason's proposal video.'

'What?' I gasp. My heart is pounding away against my ribcage, and I can feel that itchy red blotchy rash I get when I am nervous spreading over my neck. I resist the urge to scratch. 'I can't do it, Noah.'

He stares at me. 'You stand and press record. It's not hard.'

My brain tries to think up an excuse. 'I'm allergic to... marriage proposals.'

Noah ignores me and checks his phone. 'Sorry, I got to run. Will be back soon.'

'Excuse me,' shouts the woman from table five. 'Where are our drinks?'

Turning back to the coffee machine I curse annoying customers and work colleagues who disappear at the wrong moment for urgent doctor appointments.

Jason has arrived with his girlfriend, Michelle, who

according to the booking log is unaware he's going to propose. He's dressed in a smart cream linen suit and she's wearing a blue silky dress adorned with pink flowers. Her long brown hair has been styled into an elegant braided updo. Jason seats her by the window and comes over to the counter with his phone. 'Hello, will you film this if I go live on Facebook? Frankie assured me someone would assist. We have family in Canada who want to be involved in this special moment of ours. They have got up early for this.'

I nod as he presses live on Facebook and holds the phone up. 'Hi, everyone, this is it. I hope Michelle will say yes. Only one way to find out. I am just going to pass you over to one of the staff at The Little Love Café who will film our proposal. Wish me luck.'

Sucking in a lungful of café air, which is a concoction of coffee beans and Jason's Lynx Africa body spray, I close my eyes for a second. I can do this. The urge to throw down the phone, rush out of the café and run onto the beach is strong. However, that would let Frankie down and I can't do that. My neck and face feel hot. Within a few seconds it will join forces with the blotchy rash, and I will turn the same shade of pink as the walls.

I must do this. This is a live marriage proposal. Just hold the phone at the couple, press record and force out a celebratory smile at the end. This is not hard. I can do this.

With a trembling hand I give Jason a thumbs-up and point the phone camera at him walking over to Michelle. Lowering himself onto one knee in front of Michelle he fishes out a little velvet box from his trouser pocket. A few customers near me gasp at that soft box opening sound.

In a croaky voice Jason speaks to his girlfriend. 'Michelle, I've been in love with you ever since we shared a tray of chips and curry sauce on the beach and looked up at the stars all those months ago...'

'So romantic,' murmurs the annoying woman from table five. She nudges her bored looking husband. 'Why can't we do something like that? Share a takeaway and look up at the stars.'

He yawns and doesn't answer her.

I can see there are people on Facebook Live watching and sending showers of heart emojis. Jason carries on. 'Michelle, you are the person I want to spend the rest of my life with, and I can't imagine sharing a tray of chips and curry sauce with anyone else. I love you. Will you marry me?'

Every muscle and limb of mine has gone rigid. A memory is forcing its way to the front of my mind. It has grabbed my attention. In my head I'm no longer here in Blue Cove Bay, I'm back in Surrey and walking up the stairs to find out what the strange sound is that is coming from the bedroom. I've come home early as Lucas had been unwell at school. My time at work had been spent daydreaming about the big day. Quickly I shut down the memory before I open the bedroom door. The wound from Scott's affair opens inside of my chest. Pain radiates out. I don't want to think about that awful day.

Waves of nausea lap up against the sides of my tummy. I'm blinking faster to hold back the army of tears which are getting ready to charge down my face. Michelle opens her petite pink mouth and before any sound comes out my finger instinctively hits the stop button on the Facebook Live record.

As I gasp to get my breath behind the counter, Michelle shouts, 'YES!' and the two love birds to fall into each other's arms. Everyone, except me, in the café cheers and then Michelle breaks free from Jason, climbs on a chair, and makes a speech. She talks about how she and Jason first met, how they have both overcome personal struggles and how they have a great network of friends and family in the UK and in Canada.

She rambles on about their love for each other and all I want to do is shout about how the concept of love is fantasy and how love comes before heartbreak. I stand and listen to her talk with the phone now by my side. At the end Jason helps her down and pulls her into his arms. 'All our friends and family on Facebook just heard my proposal and your wonderful speech, Michelle, let's go say hi.'

They both look over at me and something flickers across Jason's face. 'Excuse me, aren't you supposed to be filming us?'

'Well... about that...' I mumble, holding up the phone.

The woman on table five turns to Jason. 'I wouldn't have trusted her to film your event. It took her half an hour to make two Magical Mochas.'

CHAPTER ELEVEN

As I needed to take Lucas to school, Noah opened the café this morning. It was a long walk to work, especially after the horrendous day yesterday. Noah returned from his doctor's appointment to find me arguing with Jason, over why I'd stopped filming the Facebook Live video at the bit where Michelle agreed to marry him, and the annoying woman from table five who claimed her Magical Mochas were not only late in arriving, but they were the worst she'd ever tasted. Noah had to apologise to Jason and to everyone in Canada who, according to Jason, were livid that they'd been deprived of witnessing Michelle's answer and her speech.

The day descended into more chaos when I spilt a Passion Milkshake all over a man's lap as he told me how much his girlfriend meant to him, and I got three separate drinks orders wrong. All this was mainly due to working with Noah and having to mentally process the astonishing number of memories of our past together which kept popping up inside my head and distracting me. By the time we closed the café, Noah and I were down to one word replies and no eye contact.

Our first customers today are a male couple who are

celebrating their one-year wedding anniversary. After showing them to their booth I give them both a heart-shaped menu. While they study the menus, I stand in stony silence and wait for them to give me their order. What did I do wrong in a past life to end up working in a love-themed café?

To my horror Noah rushes up to the booth unannounced and stands beside me. 'Hey, guys, how are you today?'

The red headed man raises his hand and grins. 'Not bad, mate.'

I turn to glare at Noah. We agreed that he would be on coffee machine duty while I greet our customers. Noah smiles at the two men. 'What are we celebrating?'

The man with the curly sandy hair points to his husband. 'Been married a year today.'

Noah beams. 'That's fantastic, congratulations.' He nudges me in the ribs. 'Isn't that great, Alice?' My neck and face are heating up fast. Who the hell does Noah think he is?

Once finished taking down their order I return to a whistling Noah at the counter. 'What do you think you are doing?' I hiss.

He gives me a cheeky wink. 'You greeted them like they'd suffered a death in the family, and you were going to sort out a funeral.'

My blood has reached boiling level. I force myself to walk away and sulk in an empty booth. The morning is arduous and challenging. Even though we are equals I have fired Noah many times in my head. He's got an endless supply of energy and has spent the morning bouncing all over the place with a huge smile on his face, and telling everyone love is in the air.

'Alice, why don't you take an early lunch?' he asks as I return to the counter after delivering drinks. 'I'll be fine to manage things here. You look stressed again.'

'I am not stressed *again*, Noah.' With a scowl at him, I grab my handbag and walk out onto the beach which is deserted. A chilly sea breeze and a gang of sinister grey clouds lingering on the horizon are working together to discourage beachgoers today. I decide to walk into town and leave the seafront. Behind the row of shops on the promenade is the town of Blue Cove Bay with a bustling high street filled with a restaurant, an array of clothes shops, an express supermarket, a butcher, a bookshop, two pubs and an empty shopfront. It used to be a wool shop, but the owner has retired.

I grab a sandwich and as I leave the express supermarket I walk into Phoebe from the bookshop a few doors down. Phoebe moved to Blue Cove Bay while I was in Surrey. I've got to know her recently because she has two children, Martha, aged eight, and Flynn, aged six, who is in Lucas's class. We often see each other in the playground or in her bookshop when I am trying to persuade Lucas to choose a book to buy which is not about Batman. My son will only read Batman books which is a little infuriating when I look across at other children in Phoebe's shop proudly marching out clutching books about nature, space, or famous people in history. Phoebe often makes me feel better by saying her son Flynn refuses point blank to read a book and that the children who are buying intelligent looking books are parent pleasers and will shove them under their bed the second they get home.

'Hi, Alice,' she says, with a grimace. 'I'm having a bad day, so excuse me.'

'You and me both,' I say, and she chuckles. She points to the empty shopfront next door to her bookshop. 'I've been praying for a posh florist to open beside me. You know a pretty one which would allow me to sneak away during a stressful author book signing event and gaze longingly at bunches of beautiful flowers.'

'I take it you're not getting a sweet little florist?'

She shakes her head and scowls. 'It's going to be a bloody record shop. Apparently, vinyl is popular again.' After a heavy sigh, she groans. 'I've spent years creating a peaceful reading oasis in my bookshop and now that will be ruined by the sounds of Guns N' Roses blasting through my walls.'

'Sorry, Phoebe,' I say, casting her a sympathetic look.

She smiles. 'What's going on with you?'

I roll my eyes. 'I'm managing The Little Love Café with my ex-boyfriend from years ago.'

Phoebe grimaces. 'Oh, poor you, that sounds hellish. I take it things didn't end amicably between you two?'

'I feel silly for saying this, but he was my first love. We were sixteen when he ghosted me and broke my heart. Twenty years on and I am still struggling to forgive him.'

Phoebe reaches out and gives my arm a rub. 'My first love cheated on me. Nothing hurts quite so much as your first heartbreak. I'll be thinking of you.'

'I will think of you too. When does your new neighbour arrive?'

'Next week he opens, and it's called Vinyl Dreams. I haven't met him yet, but I know I don't like him already.'

I check my phone. 'I better get back to the world of giving my ex-boyfriend death stares over a Cuddle Muffin.'

Phoebe laughs. 'If you ever need to vent, come into my bookshop. We can go sit in the crime section and look for ingenious ideas on getting rid of my new neighbour and your ex-boyfriend.'

We both laugh and walk off in opposite directions. When I return to the café, Noah is hugging an older woman. I am distracted by the past once again. Back when we were teenagers Noah's hugs could solve all sorts of problems from painful period pains, tricky maths problems to uncontrollable sobbing when I missed my mum. One of the sweetest things he used to do was close his eyes when he hugged me. Frankie would always point this out and say Noah would hug me like he never wanted to let me go. The hugs I got from Pete and Scott never came close to the hugs Noah gave.

From what I can hear, this older woman used to know him when he was a child. 'It's wonderful to see you, Noah. You must have been six or seven when we lived next door to you and your father.'

I make myself busy and avoid looking at the two customers who are engaging in a lengthy kiss against the flower wall.

'Excuse me,' says an older man. 'Can you take a photo of us?' His smile stretches from ear to ear. 'It's our two-month anniversary.'

They both giggle like lovesick teenagers. Reluctantly I take his camera phone as they go to stand by the flower wall. I glare at the other couple who hurry away to their seats. After five minutes of waiting for the man to stop whispering sweet nothings to his girlfriend, I clear my throat. My patience is wearing thin. 'Are you ready yet?' I snap.

'Hang on.' She raises a manicured hand. 'I need to apply an extra layer of lipstick.'

'Oh, my dear Sugar Plum.' The man snuggles into the side of the woman, placing his arm over her shoulders.

She giggles and gushes, 'Oh, my big strong, Action Man.'

Rolling my eyes, I let out an impatient sigh. They both stare at me with worried faces. The woman smothers her lips in a bold red colour and pouts at the camera. I take two photos: one is very blurred and the other misses out half of the man's head.

I'm about to hand the man his phone back when Noah comes up behind me. 'I think we can do better than that, Alice.' To my horror he takes the phone away from me. 'Let's take a good shot of you both,' he beams to the man and woman.

I storm off to the counter. He returns a few minutes later.

'Why do you keep doing that to me?' I growl.

'Helping an old friend,' Noah says, in an ultra-happy voice. 'You look like you could do with some help.'

I can't stop the emotion and anger building inside of me. 'You're *not* an old friend, Noah, you're an annoying ex-boyfriend.'

Noah pulls a face at me. 'Oh, ex-boyfriends can't be friends with you.'

Oh God, this man is making my blood lava hot. He is so annoying. 'Noah, let's get one thing straight. We're not going to end up having iced frapps and giggles with each other.'

He smirks. 'I don't like iced frappes so no chance of that.' As he walks away whistling, I turn my back on the café and let out a silent scream.

CHAPTER TWELVE

Noah and I agreed that Thursday would be his day off in the week and I would have Monday as mine. It's my first day without him and so far, it's been bliss... apart from the woman who complained about her Cuddle Muffin being cold and the couple who left me some handwritten feedback on a napkin which read, *to the miserable woman behind the counter – you should smile more!*

I've not missed Noah and his annoying ways at all. I've thought about him and our past a lot, but I think I'm still processing him being back.

The woman on table ten is still sat by herself. She's gazing at the beach out of the café window. Her date has not arrived. 'Is everything okay?' I ask.

She looks at me. 'I don't think he's coming.'

'Oh, I'm sorry,' I say. She casts me a weak smile. I slide into the seat opposite her with my back to the café door. 'Has he not called you or texted?'

She shakes her head. 'No. The last I heard from him was yesterday when he texted me to tell me the date and the time. He's half an hour late. I think he's stood me up.'

'What a dirt bag,' I exclaim, feeling all my pent-up anger over my failed relationships rise inside of me. 'Relationships should come with a health warning. They're not worth it. I've had my heart broken so many times, there's a giant crack in it.' The woman has an odd expression. I ignore her. 'Does your scumbag of a date have a name?'

'I'm sorry,' says a male voice behind me. 'Did you just call me a "scumbag"?'

I shoot out of my chair to find a man glaring at me. He looks at the woman. 'Sarah, I'm sorry I'm late. Let's go somewhere else. Don't think I want to give this place our business.'

Feeling embarrassed, I hide behind the counter.

Pam, the cake supplier, bustles in after lunch and introduces herself. The first thing I notice is her beautiful light silvery hair piled on top of her head. It glistens under the ceiling light. She gestures to it. 'I'm embracing my grey hair. No more hair dye.'

'It's stunning.'

She smiles and touches a flyaway wisp. 'My ex-husband hates it.'

'He has no taste,' I say, which makes her laugh.

Her coffee-coloured eyes are encased in a weary purple shadow, and I can see she's trying to suppress a yawn. 'Can you open the door at the back of the café? Frankie always lets me do that. My van is ready to be unloaded.' She wipes her sweaty forehead and groans as her phone vibrates in her pocket. 'I wish everyone would leave me alone.' She casts me a weary smile. 'Do you ever have days like that?'

I give her a knowing smile. 'All the time.'

She takes out her phone and shakes her head. 'If he is phoning me with another issue I am going to scream.' After rubbing her forehead, she yawns. 'Sorry, I don't mean to yawn. I didn't sleep very well last night.'

I want to reach out to her and say I am having a bad day too, but I keep it to myself. Pam drops off her new batch of cakes and cookies and hurries away.

∼

Later, after closing the café, I walk back home along the beach. The afternoon had been hard. My resentment today at seeing other people happy and in love resulted in three drink spillages, two customer complaints about my poor service and an argument with a newlywed couple after I accidentally dropped their Cuddle Muffins into their laps.

Taking in a deep breath of salty air I gaze out across the rolling marine blue sea. I wonder how Frankie and Rose are doing in Sydney. My heart aches as I think about Rose and Frankie and the gruelling treatment ahead of them.

Under my breath I whisper Frankie a message which I hope the wind will somehow carry to him. 'Even though working with Noah is proving tricky, you don't have to worry about your café.'

My mind nudges me about the customers who have complained about my service and an uncomfortable feeling takes hold of me. *It will be fine*, I assure myself. *The first week was bound to be difficult. Once Noah accepts I don't need or want his help, we will be fine.*

I take out my phone and send Frankie a WhatsApp message.

Thinking of you. Everything is good here.

On the promenade I can hear raised voices coming from the gift shop. The voices belong to the owners, twins, Joy and Esme. Ten years ago, they inherited their family's gift shop.

Joy and Esme used to be in the year above me in school. Joy

spent most of her time at school bossing Esme around. Frankie and I never liked the way Joy treated Esme, so we took Esme under our wing and tried to make her see that she could stand up to Joy. Our guidance didn't work.

Esme, Frankie and I have stayed friends. Esme is one of the sweetest people I know. When Frankie's dad left Rose, Esme would leave little wrapped chocolate gifts on his doorstep. When Noah left for Ireland, she left me tiny bunches of flowers and when Lucas was born, she bought him a Babygro with the words, 'I Love Blue Cove Bay' across it.

'Esme, it's time we both moved on,' says Joy, in her usual authoritative tone. 'This family gift shop has been a weight around our necks for years.'

I stop and stare. Esme loves that little gift shop. She's the one who runs the place as Joy is always out socialising. Inside it's a seaside gift oasis and sells everything from rustic wooden boat and lighthouse decorations, telescope keyrings, sticks of Blue Cove Bay rock, sweet smelling candles, fridge magnets to seaside-themed jewellery and crockery. Recently Esme redecorated the little shop. It has a nautical blue coloured front and a new window display which recreates Blue Cove Bay. To hear Joy say that about the gift shop will devastate Esme. I take a few steps closer as I want to make sure Esme is all right.

'Joy, that's not true,' an emotional Esme cries out. 'Please think about this. I love working here.'

'I've made my decision,' declares Joy, 'we're closing this place and moving away. Esme, you know I'm the one with the business brain.'

My mouth falls open in shock. Why the hell is Joy selling up?

'I don't want to go elsewhere,' Esme cries. Hearing my friend sounding distressed makes me walk toward the door.

'In years to come you'll thank me for rescuing you from this place,' shouts Joy.

'If I have to, I'll run this place myself,' shouts Esme, making me flinch. In all the years of knowing Joy and Esme I have never heard Esme say something as bold as this to her sister.

Joy's peal of laughter rings out across the promenade. '*You* are going to run this place by yourself?'

'Why is that funny, Joy?'

Silence descends upon the gift shop. I reach the doorway and knock. Joy yanks open the door. 'Alice,' she says, before glancing over at Esme.

I crane my neck and wave at Esme. She gives me a thumbs-up and I step away. A few yards down from the gift shop I wait by a bench for a few minutes in case Joy decides to shout at her sister again. There's nothing but the lapping of the sea and the noisy seagulls. Taking out my phone I send Esme a message.

> Hope you are ok – you know where I am if you need to chat x.

Pete is on Dad's doorstep when I get back.

'Hi, Alice,' he says, running a hand through his curly black hair. 'Your dad invited me over for tea.'

Lucas's loud cheer, at the sound of his father's voice, is followed by him thundering down the stairs. He flings himself at Pete. Lucas's goofy happy face makes a lump balloon in my throat. He leads Pete into the living room by the hand and then wrestles with him on the sofa. Even though relations between Pete and me are sometimes strained, I do enjoy seeing Lucas with his father.

Pete holds aloft a giggling Lucas. 'It is time I did more with

Lucas. Now that you're working, Alice, it might be a help for you?'

His announcement makes me a take a step back in surprise. This is unexpected. Ever since Lucas was born Pete's been more of a hands-off father. I wasn't in a relationship with Pete when I got pregnant with Lucas. We'd broken up a few years before Lucas arrived. Lucas was the result of a drunken one-night stand after a karaoke night at a pub in town. In our drunken haste we'd forgotten about contraception.

Initially Pete and I tried to make 'us' work again for the first year of Lucas's life, but Pete enjoyed going out too much and I realised I didn't love him. He took it badly and went to live in London for two years. In that time, he barely saw Lucas. When we lived in Surrey, Pete saw Lucas every few months. Since we've moved back, Pete has changed and has Lucas overnight every fortnight, but he's made it clear that's his limit.

Tonight Pete has swapped his usual dishevelled T-shirt and faded black jeans for a fitted blue shirt, tucked into fitted beige trousers. It also looks like he's tamed his wild black curls which have always had a life of their own. 'I heard you were helping Frankie out at The Little Love Café. How's it going?'

'It's okay,' I say, taking the armchair opposite while Lucas cuddles up to Pete. 'A bit of a steep learning curve.'

'I hear Noah is back.' Pete's face has darkened. 'How is it working with him?'

Loosening my ponytail, I release my hair. 'Odd.'

Pete ruffles Lucas's curls. 'I bet it is after all this time.'

Dad bustles in with a tea towel flung over his shoulder. His face immediately brightens at the sight of Pete. 'Hello, Pete.' Dad rushes over to give Pete a warm hug. 'Good to see you.' Dad has never recovered from Pete and me splitting up. He has always idolised Pete and in his eyes, Pete can do no wrong. Even when Pete went to London, and we didn't see him for two years Dad still didn't have a bad word to say about him.

Pete stands up and grins at Dad. 'I'm going to do more with Lucas. Take him to school and pick him up.'

Dad's face breaks into a huge smile as though someone has just told him he's won the lottery. 'That's the best news I have heard all year.' He drapes his arm across Pete's shoulders and turns to me. 'Isn't this great, Alice?'

Lucas runs to hug Pete and the sight of them all beaming at me tugs on my heartstrings. They all look so happy together and it doesn't take long before guilt eats away at me.

'You've got a nasty hole in your jogging bottoms,' observes Pete as we head to the dinner table for tea.

I shrug and sit down.

Dad smiles at me as he puts a plate of sausage and chips in front of me. 'Isn't this nice. Us all eating together.'

After Pete leaves, Dad takes me aside. 'Pete's a good man, Alice. It would make me the happiest man alive to see you two back together again.'

'Dad, I don't want to get back with Pete.'

He touches my arm. 'Lucas asked me the other day why he has a mummy and a daddy who don't live in the same house.'

Riddled with guilt, I put Lucas to bed and read him an action hero story. At first, he complains that the hero of the book is not Batman, but I am persistent and eventually he lies back and listens. After I stop him from picking his nose, he points to the main character and tells me, 'He's like my daddy.' Stroking his forehead, I smile as his eyes close, and he gives me a sleepy grin. Silently I apologise for all the disruption I have caused him in his little life, and for not loving his daddy.

CHAPTER THIRTEEN

Noah smiles at me as he enters the café the next day. 'Morning, Alice, how was yesterday?'

I give him a weary smile. Lucas woke me at five in the morning to tell me he'd done a wee in the bed and once I was up changing his bedding all hope of returning to my own vanished as he wanted to play with his plastic figures.

We then spent an agonising couple of hours downstairs. Lucas wouldn't stop climbing over Dad's sofa, the washing machine broke while washing Lucas's bedding, Bean did a poo in the kitchen and Dad came downstairs clutching yet more brochures of local houses to rent. They were all on Pete's housing estate. When I asked him whether he was trying to tell me something, he said they were for a friend. It then took him a good five minutes to force out the words, 'I love having you and my grandson living with me.'

'Yesterday was good,' I say, injecting some optimism into my voice. Noah does not need to know it was another disaster. Grabbing my order pad, I head over to two customers who have entered behind him. It's a young man and woman. After I take their order, the woman asks me where the toilets are. Once she's disappeared the man grins at Noah who is loitering at the table opposite. 'You're brave. I couldn't run a café with my girlfriend.'

My response is instant. 'We're not together.'

The man looks surprised.

Noah says, 'We used to go out with each other when we were teenagers but...'

I open my mouth and Noah interrupts me. To my horror he grins at the man and taps me on the shoulder. 'I moved to Ireland thinking we could still be together, but Alice was having none of it. I was dumped by email a day later.'

My heart has stopped beating. Air is trapped in my throat. What the hell did he just say? I never dumped him by email. His email stopped working two days after he'd been in Ireland which I assumed was due to him moving countries, so I sent him weekly letters instead.

The man casts us both an awkward look and I glare at Noah. Anger is coursing through my veins.

Noah and I return to the counter. 'I never dumped you by email, Noah,' I hiss. 'I didn't want us to end.'

Confusion flashes across Noah's face.

I continue. 'You ghosted all my letters. I can't believe the lie you have just told that customer.'

'Alice, you emailed me to say you'd met someone else and that it was best if we split up,' he snapped.

My eyes grow so wide I worry they are soon going to pop out of my face. Has he been living in an alternate universe all these years? 'That is a lie, Noah!' The couple turn around in their seats to stare at us. 'You were the one who ghosted me. I waited for you–'

Something flickers across Noah's face. 'Now you're the one who's lying, Alice.'

I gasp. 'Noah, I don't want to spend any more time listening to your bullshit.' Grabbing an empty tray, I turn my attention to the coffee machine.

He's breathing fast behind me. 'You hurt me all those years ago, Alice. However, I came back and agreed to work alongside you, thinking we could put the past behind us.'

'Please stop lying, Noah,' I snap. 'Also, there are customers staring at us. You're not being professional.'

He laughs, which infuriates me. 'You're the one who needs to think about being professional. Have you seen our social media lately?' He brings out his phone and shows me The Little Love Café Facebook page. On today's post there are a slew of negative comments

> @JanineKingston36: Not great service today. #LittleLoveCafé

> @RuthSayer: I agree @JanineKingston36 – the manager needs to start smiling more!

> @KennyRichards45: Yesterday the waitress took half an hour to make our drinks. She told us she was busy. We were the ONLY customers in there.

I read a few and turned to Noah. 'Isolated incidents. We'll be fine.'

'Alice, we have received these sorts of comments every day since Frankie left. You need to change your ways and stop being so angry. To be honest, I am the one who should be cross seeing how you treated me.'

I have had enough of him, this job, his patronising tone, and his lies. Placing down the milk jug and the espresso cup, I cast him a sugary smile. 'I quit. Have a nice life, Noah.' I collect my handbag, swing it over my shoulder and walk towards the door.

'Alice, you can't leave.'

At the doorway I turn around and look at him over my shoulder. 'Watch me.'

It takes me awhile to calm down after I storm out. I sit on a bench on the promenade for ages and watch two white sailing boats head out of Blue Cove Bay. Everything feels so jumbled with Noah. Why was he lying about what happened? He knows full well he ghosted me after leaving for Ireland. My head feels like someone has secretly turned my kaleidoscope and all the bits of coloured glass at the end are in disarray.

Someone joins me on the bench. It's Esme. She smiles, though her eyes are puffy and pink. Joy and Esme are identical twins, and both were blessed with thick dark hair, olive skin and amazing eyelashes, the ones that don't need mascara. Even though they dress differently Joy is insistent they still both wear their long hair down and draped over their shoulders. I have never understood why Esme lets Joy have control over her hair.

'Hello, Alice,' says Esme, 'thanks for the text the other day.'

I reach over and give her hand a squeeze. 'Are you okay?'

'Joy wants to sell the gift shop.'

'I heard the other evening. I'm sorry, Esme.'

'She has a plan for us,' sighs Esme, casting her gaze out to sea. 'I don't want to leave Blue Cove Bay. This is my home... but Joy...' She stops and wipes her cheek. 'Ignore me. Joy makes good decisions. I should have faith in her.'

She's trembling and looks like she needs a hug. Leaning over I pull her into one. 'Esme, it's okay to not do what Joy wants.'

She nods and changes the subject. 'Are you taking a break from The Little Love Café? I heard you were working there.'

I shake my head. 'I've just quit.'

Esme gasps. 'Oh dear. Are you okay?'

'I am now. It was too much, Esme. I need a different job.'

Flicking back my hair, I dismiss the worries about not having a job and a regular wage to pay Dad back, which are pinging into my brain at an astonishing rate.

'Noah kept going about the customer complaints I have received and then he lied about me in front of some customers.'

Esme gives me a worried glance. 'Customer complaints?'

I nod. 'The first week was never going to be easy and I am struggling with seeing everyone so happy and in love.'

'That must be hard,' she says, 'I'm sure Frankie will understand.'

'Yes, he will,' I say, thinking about how I will explain the complaints to Frankie. I could say that they all overreacted. Frankie will be fine, I reassure myself.

'Everyone is talking about you and Noah in town,' says Esme.

Sitting up I turn to Esme. 'I'm fine. People need to find someone else to gossip about. Noah and I broke up twenty years ago. Let's talk about you.'

She sighs into my shoulder before pulling away. 'All my life I've accepted my place and happily let Joy navigate us both through our years as kids, our teens, our twenties, and thirties. Joy makes good decisions for us both, however she is hard work if I don't agree with her, so it's easier to just do what she proposed.' Esme smooths down her hair. 'It's difficult because right now I love my life where I sell gifts on the seafront and go home to my cats. They don't judge my life. They don't compare me to my twin sister, don't make me feel ashamed... and they don't break my heart.' She pauses and takes a lungful of sea air. 'The other night when she told me about selling up, I found myself disagreeing with her for the first time in my life. Can you believe that, Alice? Joy looked visibly shocked.'

My eyes are widening at what I am hearing. Reaching over I give her hand another squeeze. 'I'm proud of you, Esme.'

She shakes her head and watches a group of dog walkers

venture onto the beach. 'There's something else. Another reason why I don't want to leave Blue Cove Bay.' She pauses. 'I've got close to someone. It's not Steve... or should I say the person who Joy wants me to get back with.'

Neither Frankie nor I liked Steve. He always seemed to be another version of Joy who ordered Esme around and made her look after his teenage daughter from his previous relationship while he spent all his time on the golf course.

I stare at her and wish Frankie was here to witness the change in our old friend. 'Esme, this is brilliant to hear.'

Esme hangs her head and her hair falls over her face like two black curtains. 'I don't want to leave, Alice.'

I take hold of her hand. 'Stay strong, Esme. Joy has controlled you for too long.'

I can hear footsteps behind us. I peer over my shoulder to see a stern looking Joy. 'Esme, it's busy in the gift shop. Can you come back, please?'

Esme shoots up from the bench. 'Thanks for the chat, Alice.'

My brain is desperately trying to think of a piece of advice I can give her. 'Frankie's mum Rose has always told me to follow my heart. Maybe you should do that?'

Esme's face brightens. 'Has that worked for you?'

The urge to tell her at length about how that advice has been the worst piece of advice I have ever had is strong, but I sense Esme needs something to cling onto. I nod and she hurries away.

CHAPTER FOURTEEN

After Esme leaves me, I take out my phone and look at The Little Love Café's Facebook feed and read each negative comment in turn.

An uncomfortable feeling passes over me as I see that they all relate to me. Customers have picked up on my inability to smile, my angry face, my distracted state and the mistakes. Have I been that bad? Blimey, what has Noah triggered inside of me?

When I close my eyes, I can see Frankie's face – his emerald green eyes, his peroxide blond hair and his goofy grin. He will not be happy to hear about what's been going on. Frankie has always prided himself on giving his customers excellent service.

I have gone some way in damaging his café's reputation. Guilt nibbles away at me. Somewhere inside me, a little voice whispers, *Go back to your job and put things right.*

Noah and I could agree to be civil with each other and we could also be strict at ensuring we don't annoy the other. At the end of the day, we are doing Frankie a favour, and this is not a job for life. Frankie has enough on his plate. He doesn't need to hear about this.

I walk back to The Little Love Café and find Noah in the

middle of chaos. There is a queue of dissatisfied customers and he's frantically trying to make drinks. This was not the day to walk out of my job.

After placing my bag behind the counter, I nod at him, before seeing to the queue of customers. With the complaints on Facebook still fresh in my mind I greet everyone with a fake smile and concentrate on getting them their correct drink order.

Half an hour later and we have got things under control. 'You came back?' Noah says, placing two Magical Mochas on a tray.

'Yes. Look, I agree I have not been professional, Noah.'

He looks taken aback. 'You agree with me?'

I nod. 'You were right. Going forward can we put our differences about the past to one side and just get the job done here? We don't have to be friends.'

He raises his hands in defence. 'Fine by me. I just want to do a good job for Frankie.'

'Okay, if you work on the drinks, I will serve the customers. Let's not encroach on the other's role.'

His face softens. 'Yes, I'll do that. I'm sorry if I annoyed you in the week. You didn't need my feedback on your photography skills.'

For the rest of the day, we both concentrate on running The Little Love Café. Noah sticks to our agreement and stays behind the counter. I work the tables and make sure everyone gets the correct drinks and a smile. The wall-to-wall romance still annoys me, but I let it simmer under the surface. Noah and I part ways with a friendly nod which is remarkable given how the morning started.

The following day is easier as Noah and I carry on our

working arrangement. We don't mention the past and we both stick to our allotted areas. I force out smiles when excited couples tell me they are on a date, are celebrating anniversaries or are sharing their baby news by standing in front of the flower wall, holding their scan images while I take photos of them.

When I am alone out the back getting more milk or tripping over the cans of pink paint Frankie has acquired since decorating the place or cleaning the café toilets, I let out a silent scream and tell myself that I don't believe in love anymore.

On my way back into the café after my lunch break, I spot a customer with his head in his hands and an empty chair next to him. 'Noah,' I whisper, 'is the man on table four okay?'

Noah shrugs. 'Why don't you go over and ask him?'

As I get closer the man turns and greets me with a sad face. 'My girlfriend – well, my now ex-girlfriend – brought me here to confess to having an affair with the postman.'

'I'm sorry,' I say, resisting the urge to sit down next to him and tell him all about what happened to me. That would only lead to anger which in turn would impact how I serve customers.

'This place should be renamed Heartbreak Café – right?' He looks at me with watery eyes. In his hand is the bill for two Luscious Lattes.

I tell him, 'Your bill is on the house.'

'That's very nice of you,' he says, rising from his chair. 'I'm going to the pub.'

I try to forget about the man but later an argument breaks out between a couple on table six. 'We are finished, Gareth,' yells the woman. 'I never want to see you or your annoying mother ever again.'

'Fine,' shouts the man, 'I don't want to see you or your interfering sisters again either. Oh, and my mother was right about you – she took one look at your profile on the dating app, and said you looked like trouble... with a capital T.'

Noah casts me an awkward glance as the woman shouts, 'We're finished. Goodbye, Gareth.' She storms out of the café leaving Gareth to stare miserably out of the window.

'Is it me or has the atmosphere changed in the café?' I ask Noah later. We are half an hour away from closing and he's looking at our socials. 'There are a few comments on our Instagram post.' He passes me his phone.

@SnarkySue: 'There was no love in the #LittleLoveCafé for me today. Husband annoyed me so much with his constant moaning I walked out.'

@JeremyLightYear: I got dumped in this place today – should be renamed #HeartbreakCafé

I hand Noah's phone back to him. 'Do you think we should worry?'

Noah shakes his head. 'Probably the weather.' We both glance out of the café window. It's been the first proper warm day in April and a few holidaymakers are still dotted on the beach enjoying the last few rays. As we lock up the café and go our separate ways, I pray things go back to normal soon.

CHAPTER FIFTEEN

A part from a few noisy seagulls arguing over a paper bag, the beach is deserted. I've come to sit down here before work. My head is filled with worries about the café's reputation online and thoughts about Noah. Even though we have a new arrangement it's still hard working alongside him.

I have become distracted by a man swimming in the sea. He's quite far out. When I was younger, I used to be a lifeguard and I saved quite a few holidaymakers on this very beach who got into trouble after going too far out. So I know the water can be unforgiving, even in the summer months, punishing holidaymakers and surfers with chilly currents and boisterous waves.

I look out at the swimmer again. I have a bad feeling about this. Something is wrong. The waves are getting bigger and I can almost feel the sea's excitement.

Once he starts swimming the sea's spiteful waves queue up to crash up against his face. Their persistence pays off as his arms slow. My heart bangs inside my ribcage as a current carries him further away from the shore. Seagulls screech with laughter at the man. Turning his head, he looks back at the beach. Something is wrong.

I get to my feet. My heart beats faster. Flinging myself off my rock I charge across the beach. How long will it take for his bobbing head to disappear under the murky waters? The is sea dragging him out further and he's not putting up much of a fight. I can't watch this. In a flash I strip off my clothes and kick off my plimsoles.

I wade into the water. The icy cold water robs me of breath and my lungs burn in protest. But then my old love of outdoor swimming returns. After my lifeguard days ended, I used to go swimming in the sea all the time. It was a great way to cool off after an argument with Pete. Before I met Scott on a dating app Dad would look after baby Lucas, and I would head down to the beach for a swim. Cold water is invigorating and I would have a buzz about me all day afterwards.

I dive into a wave and power towards the stranger's bobbing head. Instinctively I reach out and grab his arm.

The stranger struggles. 'I don't need your help,' he yells.

A wave crashes over the both of us, making me gasp and swallow a mouthful of salty sea water. Shit. The sea is fighting back. I can feel the water swelling around us. A huge wave is forming. The sea is getting ready to settle things. All it needs to do is unleash one giant wave over us, robbing the human world of not just one but two lives.

'You need to come with me,' I say, through chattering teeth.

'Please,' he splutters, 'I am... okay.' Something flickers across his tanned face as he struggles to keep himself above water. He isn't fine.

Using all my strength I grab him by the shoulders. The man tries to struggle free, but my hold is too strong.

'I don't need your help,' he shouts, before erupting into a coughing fit.

'Come with me, silly bugger,' I yell, lifting him onto his back and heading for the beach. He thrashes his arms and legs.

Anger rises in me. Here I am risking my own life to save him from a cold and miserable death and all he can do is complain. If he carries on trying to shake me off, we will both end up in trouble. My foot lashes out, kicking him in the shin. He yelps and his body sags against me. The sea makes one last attempt for victory, pulling us away from the shore with a strong current. With gritted teeth, I tighten my grasp on the man and swim harder. 'You will not win sea,' I croak.

I shove the man out of the water and we stagger onto the beach. With heaving chests and wet bodies, we bend over to get our breath.

'What did you do that for?' he croaks.

Wiping sand and hair way away from my lips, I snap, 'You were going to become fish food.' His eyes wander over my black bra and pants. Oh God, I have rescued a pervert!

He straightens, stands up, placing his hands on his hips. 'That was my business.'

Irritation at this silly man is making my cheeks prickle. 'The phrase you are looking for is... *Thank you for saving my life.*'

'You kicked me and then dragged me ashore.'

'We were both going to drown out there.'

The man sighs before removing a clump of dark hair from his tanned forehead. 'Look – I am not happy about this. I was doing my own thing out there.'

With eyes widening in horror, I stare at him. 'Well – I wanted to save you and I will do it again if you pull another silly stunt like that.' I am now praying he won't make me enter the icy waters for a second time.

'You should really ask people first if they want to be rescued,' he moans, grabbing his jeans from the pile on the beach. Rolling my eyes, I run to my pile of clothes. He's shoving his wet slippery feet into his trainers by the time I return fully dressed.

'Who are you anyway?' His dark eyes fix upon my pink café T-shirt.

'Look, I don't have time for small talk,' I say, quickly. 'You need to get warm, or you'll freeze out here.' His lips have gone a blueish colour, and his golden tan is fading fast. 'I run the café over there and I'm happy to shout you a free coffee.'

'I have things to do,' he snaps.

My neck and shoulders stiffen, making me spin round. 'Fine – freeze to death on the beach then.'

'Fine.' He shouts back as I march away.

As there is no time to go back to Dad's I stomp to the café. I'm relieved Noah has not yet arrived. My long hair takes forever to towel dry, so I end up piling it into a loose ponytail. My clothes are damp, so I grab a new Love Café T-shirt and apron from the pile Frankie left us. After I plug in the heater and stand by it until I get warm. I should be looking at the booking log for today, but I am freezing.

Noah arrives and spots my damp hair. 'Are you okay?'

'I'm fine,' I say. 'How are you?'

He nods. 'Good, thanks.'

He surveys the damp patches on my jeans. 'Alice, have you been in the sea?'

'It's a long story,' I say. 'We have a café to run.'

At lunch I go home, shower, wash my hair and put on fresh clothes. When I return, The Little Love Café is busier than normal. There is a queue of people waiting to pay and more people waiting for tables to become free. 'What's going on?' I ask Noah, who is frantically trying to make drinks for multiple tables.

'Didn't you read the booking log for today?'

I shake my head. 'No, I didn't.'

'Well, we have a celebrity coming. He knows Frankie from his PR agency days. I think a few of his fans have come to gawp at him.'

'A celebrity?'

Noah nods. 'A film actor. He's popular on social media so we need to impress him and his celebrity girlfriend. Rocco Reid. He's going to propose, I think.'

'I've never heard of him,' I say as the crowd at the door parts, and everyone hushes. I stare in shock as the man from the sea strides into the café.

Clamping my forehead with my hand, my neck starts to feel itchy and hot. Why did Frankie's important customer have to be the man I plucked from the sea earlier?

His brown eyes lock onto mine and with a tanned hand he sweeps his almost black wavy hair away from his handsome face. I can't help but think back to seeing him half naked on the beach. My mind kindly replays soundbites from our strained conversation and I am back to feeling irritated by the sight of him.

Noah comes up beside me and outstretches his hand. 'Welcome to The Little Love Café, Rocco. I'm Noah and this is—'

Rocco interrupts Noah and says, 'The woman who wrestled me out of the sea this morning and kicked me when I didn't listen to her commands.'

Noah casts me a worried look and mouths, 'You kicked Rocco Reid?'

I give him a nervous look. I need to sort out this situation quick. 'Right then,' I say, with a false smile, 'shall I show you to the Snug?'

Rocco turns to look for someone behind him. 'Where did she go?' He asks one of the men stood by him.

'Outside. Instagram shots,' replies the man, with thick rimmed glasses, tapping something into a tablet.

Something flickers across Rocco's face, and he turns to me. 'Do you want to show me to the Snug?'

Once in the Snug, Rocco catches my eye. 'I suppose I better say thanks for this morning.'

'Huh?' I wasn't expecting this.

'You did the right thing.' He sits down and fiddles with the jewelled cufflink on his crisp white shirt. 'I'm sorry if I was a little short with you. Please have a seat.'

I sit as far away from him as possible, crossing my arms tightly across my chest. 'You looked like you were in trouble.'

Rubbing his neck, he bows his head. 'I was in trouble but too proud to say.'

'Where's your girlfriend?'

Rising from the sofa he paces the perimeter of the Snug. 'She's more concerned about her Instagram feed than me.' I detect a disappointed tone.

'Is she famous too?'

Rocco smiles and stares at the flower wall. 'Yes. She's a pop princess. Impressive flower wall.' He returns to his seat. 'Look, I don't even know your name.'

'Alice.'

'It is good to meet you, Alice. Aren't you going to ask me about my next film?'

I cast him a puzzled look. 'I'm sorry but I have never heard of you, but I can ask you if you want?'

His shapely pink mouth falls opens in surprise. 'You hadn't heard of me?'

'Nope.'

He runs a tanned hand through his glossy wavy hair and looks a little lost. 'Blimey, this is new territory for me.'

'How famous are you?'

'Very.' He turns to take one more look at the flower wall behind us.

'What's it like, being famous?'

He goes silent which makes me steal a glance at him. His head is once again bowed and he's staring blankly at something on the floor. 'My girlfriend and I are not really a couple. It's fake. My team have told me my career needs this high-profile engagement as fans will love it. Soon everyone will rush in here and film my big proposal.'

'I am sensing you're not fully embracing this fake relationship?'

He lets out a heavy sigh. 'I just want to be me. Not Rocco Reid. Even that's made up. My real name is Rob Smith. Years ago, I was in love with this girl from my hometown. She was everything to me. I was going to ask her to marry me and then I got a decent part in a film and my life went in another direction. I've never met anyone like her.'

'What's she doing now?'

He shrugs. 'Divorced with a little girl. I often check on her. You see I broke her heart before I left for my big acting career. I ended our relationship, and she was upset.'

This is sounding familiar, and I can feel Noah related irritation bubbling up inside of me. 'Rocco... sorry... Rob, do me a favour and don't go back to your hometown, get a job in a romance-themed café, and start working alongside her. Trust me it doesn't work.'

He's grinning at me. 'Ah, I see. Did that guy out there break your heart? Do you want me to set my minder on him?'

The urge to say *yes please* is strong but I refrain.

Rocco looks at me. 'I am jealous of you two.'

I laugh. 'Jealous?'

'You've been given a second chance. I'd bite someone's hand off for a second chance with Freya. You're very lucky to be in this position.' He looks at me. 'You remind me a lot of Freya: plucky, strong willed and you don't pay much attention to my celebrity status. Those qualities are refreshing. He's a lucky guy out there.'

I shake my head. 'He's annoying.'

Rocco grins and takes out his phone. 'Alice, you have saved me in more ways than one today.'

Before I have a chance to reply we're surrounded by his team and an attractive blonde-haired woman who wants everyone to call her Lil Tia and who won't stop talking about her next album which will be a celebration of her love for Rocco Reid.

CHAPTER SIXTEEN

@NaomiTheTiredMummyBlogger: As you can see from my pic of Rocco Reid striding out of the #LittleLoveCafé by himself, he and Lil Tia have SPLIT up – OMG I am in shock!

@Crazyfakebakeanna: WTF? Rocco Reid has SPLIT from his popstar girlfriend at the #LittleLoveCafé – my heart is broken. He and Lil Tia were everything. Will she scrap her new material and do a break-up album?'

@JennyCranon123 posts: I now agree with @JeremyLightYear – that place should be renamed #HeartBreakCafé

It's the day after my drama with Rocco Reid. I needed a crane to lift me out of bed and Dad and Lucas had laughed at me as I hobbled down to breakfast. Saving Rocco's life in the rough sea has strained every muscle in my entire body.

I walk into work with aching legs and arms. At the café, I

am met by Noah giving me an uncomfortable look. 'Rocco Reid and his girlfriend have split up, Alice.'

'Oh God, really? How do you know that?'

'It's plastered across social media. What exactly did you say to him in the Snug?' His voice has an edge to it.

Staring at him I can feel a red filter sliding over my eyes. 'What do you mean by that? Noah – I don't like your accusatory tone.'

Noah's face tenses. 'You wrestle him out of the sea and then he splits up with his girlfriend after a lengthy chat with you in the Snug.'

'I saved him from drowning, Noah.' In a huff, I storm off to the counter.

Noah follows. 'You kicked him, Alice.'

I spin round to face Noah. 'Rocco Reid was pulling us both under the water. I kicked him to save our lives.'

Noah's eyes are frantically scanning my face. 'What did you say to him?'

'We talked, that was it.'

Noah sighs. 'Well, he's dumped his girlfriend so you must have said something. Did he fancy you?'

The question robs me of breath. I stare at Noah. 'No, Rocco didn't fancy me but if he did – it would be none of your business.'

Something flickers across Noah's face. 'Did *you* fancy him?'

I let out a wail of frustration. 'No, I did not fancy Rocco Reid.'

For a few seconds we face each other. Noah's eyes are focused on my lips, and he's breathing quickly. Something awakens inside of me, sending a rush of excitement around my body. I quickly suppress it and remind myself of everything he has done to hurt me.

Noah breaks our trance and gets his phone from the

counter. 'Social media has gone crazy. Everyone is now calling us Heartbreak Café and Rocco's fans have given it a serious number of likes.'

Frankie's face appears in my mind. There has been no word from him. As Noah shows me the social media, I become wrapped in a heavy cloak of guilt. In the space of a week, we've received a high number of complaints; I've somehow contributed to the break-up of a high-profile celebrity relationship at the café and everyone on social media is talking about heartbreak at The Little Love Café. This is all my fault.

As the morning progresses, the café becomes a graveyard for broken hearts. Everyone who has come here is either doing the dumping or is being dumped. Noah and I groan as two couples argue about their dull relationships and one half of a third couple storms out after his partner commented that his new hairstyle had aged him by ten years.

On my break I walk past the gift shop and give Esme a wave. I'm about to go in and see her when Joy comes into view. With Joy breathing down her neck Esme wouldn't be able to talk.

Instead, I go into town and try to block out the sound of my argument with Noah playing on repeat in my mind. I find myself walking into Phoebe's bookshop. It is an amazing place to go if, like me, you love books. And it's even better if you don't have to go hunting for Batman books with a bored six-year-old tugging on your arm.

Phoebe has split the bookshop into different sections and has used her creativity and artistic skills to bring them to life. Her *Crime Scene* section comes complete with police tape lining the shelves, tiny magnifying glasses attached to the two large bookcases and a table filled with crime and thriller books.

In *Romance Land*, she's erected wooden shelves painted sugary pink. Romance books are scattered over a round table with a pink and white gingham tablecloth complete with little vases of plastic flowers and a fancy tea set.

Her *Fairy Book Kingdom* has a toadstool for the little ones to sit on, plastic flowers, and a magical castle painted onto a giant piece of card behind the shelves. I love the *Young Adult* section which has eye-catching gothic décor, black and silver walls and two high-backed vintage purple velvet chairs.

Phoebe is at the till. She gives me a friendly wave before attending to a customer.

Reading has always been a passion of mine. Whenever I am stressed, I gravitate towards bookshops. My eyes are drawn to the display of bestselling romance author Celia Black's latest novel. The eye-catching cover features two figures sat on a snowy mountain looking up into a starry indigo sky.

Before my wedding and relationship with Scott crumbled, I was an avid reader of romance novels. Celia Black was one of my favourite authors. When I realised I didn't love Pete anymore I found the strength to end that relationship by reading Celia's book, *The Approval List.*

Her new book is titled *Always You.* An uplifting and romantic story about two exes who find themselves thrown together on a charity trek to Base Camp Everest. Over the course of the trek, they overcome many physical and mental struggles, and go on a journey of self-discovery. My eyes are drawn back to the cover. In view of how close the couple are sitting on the mountain; I'm sensing it's a happy ending.

'It's her best romance yet,' says Phoebe, jolting me out of my thoughts. 'The couple hate each other at the start of the trek.'

Noah's face comes into my head.

Phoebe continues. 'She does a great job because when you start reading it you do worry one of the exes is going to push the other off the mountain.'

I smile. 'I'm intrigued how they stop hating each other. Is it soppy though?'

Phoebe shakes her head. 'It makes you think and laugh a lot.'

Keith, her assistant, looks over from stacking books. 'Alice, do you follow Celia Black on social media? Her posts are always soppy and emotional. Personally, I prefer following the crime and thriller authors, they are hilarious. The darker and grizzlier the murders they write, the funnier the authors are on social media. Some of the ones who write about serial killers are such a hoot.'

Keith always makes me chuckle with his observations of the literary world.

'I am going to buy it and treat myself.'

Phoebe pats me on the shoulder. 'I have seen the café's social media about Rocco Reid splitting with his girlfriend. How are you?'

'I'm fine. I saved him from drowning.'

Phoebe and Keith gasp in unison and Keith hurries over.

'I saved him. I saw him in trouble in the sea, so I stripped down to my bra and knickers and swam to save him.'

Keith takes out his hankie and mops his brow. 'You saved Rocco Reid? This sounds like something from one of our romance books.'

I am about to talk more about Rocco Reid when an R.E.M. song comes booming through the wall. Phoebe mutters under her breath. 'Stay here.' She marches outside.

Keith giggles and rushes to the door and opens it. The music stops.

Through the open door, I can hear Phoebe shout, 'One of my customers has just left my bookshop without buying a book because of the noise.' That was a little lie, but I like her style.

A male voice replies, 'Maybe that customer had decided to buy a record instead.'

With an angry screech Phoebe comes storming back. 'That man has been here two days and already he's annoying me.' Once at her till she grins at me. 'We need to get together so you can fill me on saving hunky actors and what underwear you opted for today because whatever you had on, he split up with his beautiful girlfriend hours later.' She gives me a wink.

I laugh. 'Phoebe, it wasn't like that. Anyway, Rocco and I had more of a heart-to-heart talk in the Snug.'

'I need all the details, Alice. Let's get together soon.'

As I pay for the book, I can hear Keith behind me telling a customer about a gothic novel which has come out. 'If you're looking for dark secrets, a castle, random screaming sounds at night, a 200-year-old child ghost, and a lot of ravens that seem to know everything – this is for you.'

Phoebe grins. 'I read that book a few months ago. It kept me awake most nights.'

Keith chuckled. 'Phoebe texted me throughout the night whilst reading it. When I woke up the next morning, I thought someone had died. They were all from Phoebe who was sure ravens were at her window.'

'This sounds exactly the sort of book I like reading,' exclaims the customer which makes me smile. Phoebe and Keith are a good double act at bookselling.

The afternoon at the café is much the same: more tiffs between lovers and one man got a Cuddle Muffin thrown in his face by his angry boyfriend. Later that evening, after putting Lucas to bed, I sit and read Celia Black's book.

The first few chapters make me smile – and laugh in places. The two exes couldn't stand to be in each other's company, let alone climb to Base Camp together. At one point I felt grateful for working in a love-inspired café with Noah, because at least I wasn't hiking up part of a mountain with him whilst battling altitude sickness, extreme temperatures, and painful blisters. Noah and I would not have survived that scenario.

The next day, once I've dropped Lucas at school, I walk to work thinking about the book. What has become interesting is once the warring exes start to work with each other and help others, their fortunes on the mountain change. I have also noted that at the start they no longer believe in love, and it makes everything harder for them as they battle the elements and their strong feelings of love and hatred for each other. This thought makes me feel uncomfortable. I don't believe in love anymore and my life at the café is getting harder. Maybe I need to adopt Celia Black's advice.

At the café, Noah is pacing up and down looking anxious. The tables are all empty. 'It's not working – is it?' He lifts his face towards mine. 'You and me working together. I'm thinking of quitting, Alice.'

The news makes my stomach turn itself into knots which is unexpected. This is what I have been wanting – him to resign and leave. Why am I now feeling uncomfortable? A little voice from deep inside me whispers, *Because it's your fault the café is in this mess.*

'Noah, don't quit. Frankie needs the both of us right now.' I take a seat at a table and gesture for him to sit opposite me. 'I'm the problem. I don't believe in love anymore and it's spilling over into the café.'

Something flickers across his eyes as he stares deep into my soul. My face feels like someone has shoved it underneath a grill and turned up the heat. 'Why don't you believe in love anymore, Alice?'

I take a deep breath. 'Three months ago, I was supposed to marry Scott. Once again in my life I thought he was the one.

The day before we were supposed to get married, I caught him cheating on me.'

'I'm sorry, Alice,' Noah says, quietly. 'What was Scott like?'

Reaching for my tissues inside my jacket pocket I wait for the tears to come. Nothing happens. A few weeks ago, talking about Scott would have left me in floods of tears. 'He was charming, blond and he reminded me of–' My words stop as I realise what I was about to say.

We both flick our eyes to the table. Noah breaks the awkward silence first. 'Pete is Lucas's dad – isn't he?'

His question robs me of breath, but I manage to say, 'Lucas is Pete's son.'

Noah scratches his blond hair. 'Oh... you guys still speaking to each other?'

'Pete's just bought a house on the new housing estate as you come into Blue Cove Bay. Yes, we get on better now than we did when we were together.'

Noah nods. 'So, when did you guys start dating?'

My heart pounds against my chest, and I grip the table. 'Six months after you left, he asked me out. Noah – I'd not heard anything from you.'

Noah nods. 'Pete was always jealous of you and me. He's always been an opportunist. So, you must have been together for years then?'

I shake my head. 'We dated for a few years and then split up as the arguments between us were huge. It was all my fault. I dated him for the wrong reason. Lucas came after a drunken one-night stand six years ago. Pete and I tried once again to make it work but I ended up telling him I didn't love him.'

'I can see why this place must be hard for you, Alice.'

'Really?'

'I know we agreed not to talk about this, but you were the one who ended...'

I can feel the old agitation at him creeping over me. 'Noah, we had an agreement.'

Customers enter the shop behind us. I get the urge to shout at Noah but I must bite my tongue. Turning around, I greet them with a forced smile and welcome them to The Little Love Café.

CHAPTER SEVENTEEN

It's mid-morning. My head is awash with worries about what I have done to Frankie's business. The Rocco Reid drama has not calmed down on social media. It's ablaze with emotional fans saying that his ex-girlfriend is now devastated and has hit the studio with a new record producer.

This morning, two couples had arguments. One resulted in the man walking out leaving the woman he was with in floods of tears. Noah cast me a worried look as I consoled the girlfriend and tried my hardest not to share my own views on love and relationships. Once they'd gone, Noah pointed out that the woman had tagged us into an emotional Facebook post about her horrible break-up argument with her boyfriend, who was now her ex – *the curse of Heartbreak Café strikes again*. It had garnered a lot of likes.

I stand by the counter while Noah makes the coffees for table three. 'I never had to worry about things like the atmosphere or public relations in The Starfish Tea Shop.'

Noah smiles. 'You probably had other things to worry about. I can't believe that place lasted as long as it did.'

'Probably because Ronald was delusional and more

interested in his love life. I need to turn this place around, Noah.' I turn around and survey the café. 'I got us into this mess, so I need to fix it.' I decide to do some cleaning. 'I'm going to do a quick check and clean of the café's toilets as I need to distract myself.'

As I emerge from the final cubicle, I spot a woman washing her hands. Her mass of blonde curly hair is piled on top of her head, two giant golden hoops hang from her ears and her slender arms are covered in an array of colourful and striking tattoos. She turns off the tap and puts her hands under the blowers. Smiling at me in the mirror she squirts on some of Frankie's Little Love Café moisturising cream. 'We need more places like this.'

'Really?'

She nods. 'I spend a lot of time reading all the little heart-warming stories behind the photos on Facebook. When my daughter was born, she had a lot of medical problems with her heart.' The woman holds my attention. 'Sorry, am I keeping you from your work?'

'No, please carry on.'

'We were in and out of hospital. It was a tough time. Things broke down between my boyfriend and I, so we split up. I'd got pregnant on our third date, so we were not really used to being in a couple. There was a lot of stress. Our baby daughter didn't need two bickering parents by her bedside.' She stands and fiddles with a runaway strand of hair. 'When I wasn't at the hospital doing my shift with our daughter I used to log on to X and Facebook. It sounds mad but The Little Love Café gave me hope.'

'Hope – what do you mean?'

'I kept reading the café's social media accounts and hoping things would turn out okay. We decided to give our relationship another go last month and are here to celebrate.

Tomorrow is our little girl's first birthday and she's doing well.'

'That's great to hear.'

She turns to me. 'I've seen the stuff about Heartbreak Café on Instagram.'

My shoulders sink. 'It's all my fault.'

'Oh,' says the woman, looking concerned. 'Why is it all your fault?'

'I lost control of my emotions. You see, I am nursing a broken heart and all my negativity around the concept of love has spilled into this place. I should never have asked my friend, Frankie, if I could manage it.'

The woman reaches out and rubs my arm. 'The Rocco Reid drama wasn't your fault. I never thought that was a real relationship. It was a publicity stunt.'

I cast her a knowing smile.

She continues. 'Some say that this is just a gimmicky romance-themed café but it's much more than that. It gives people hope. Everyone who comes here has a story to tell about love and how it got them through dark times in their lives or reunited two lost souls. Maybe you need to share more customer stories?'

'Do you think so?'

She nods. 'Put more love out into the world and you'll get more back.'

Her words are still on my mind after lunch. Placing down the tray in front of two women sat in the pink booth nearest the flower wall, I can't help but notice their beaming faces. 'Here are your Cute Cappuccinos.'

'Thanks.' The woman with the stylish cropped brown hair nods at me.

'How are you both today?'

The woman gestures to the grinning blonde woman sat

opposite. 'Good, my girlfriend here is treating me to a nice coffee.'

'This is a magical place you have here,' gushes the blonde woman.

'Thanks.'

'I have been a fan of The Little Love Café for ages,' she explains. 'Every morning me and all the nurses in the hospital I work at log on to The Love Café's Facebook to see all the romance stories being shared. Some are so sweet.' She turns to me. 'Lately though, I haven't seen the café sharing as many stories.'

'What do you mean?'

'You've only been sharing photos of coffee cups and the flower wall.'

Maybe I should get involved with the social media too? I've let Noah run that by himself. 'Thanks for the valuable feedback,' I say to the woman with the blonde hair. 'Can I get you both a free Cuddle Muffin as a token of my appreciation?'

As we are closing the café, I remember the two women from earlier and the woman in the toilet. 'Noah, can I have a go at managing the café's social media?'

He nods. 'Be my guest – why?'

'I have been speaking to a few customers today and they think we can do more with social media. I want to give it some thought.'

When Lucas has gone to bed, I sit down with my iPad and look at The Little Love Café's social media. The blonde woman was right. Even though Noah has been posting cute photos of the café, close-ups of drinks and plates filled with mouth-watering muffins, they are lacking something.

I scroll back a few months to when Frankie was managing it, and I can see a difference. Frankie was sharing customer stories and there was more engagement. His posts feel personal and bring out all sorts of funny and heart-warming customer stories about love.

I find myself smiling at the customer who proposed to his girlfriend by making her a mixtape of love songs and in the middle, he recorded himself asking her to marry him.

Then there was the customer whose daughter stuck a message in a balloon about her dad needing a girlfriend as he was lonely. A woman a hundred miles away found it and contacted him.

And the customers who met via a radio phone-in, the customers who met on a ski lift and the customer who married the woman next door after she kept baking him cakes and inserting little messages of love into them. I recall Jason's proposal speech about him and Michelle sharing curry and chips under the stars. I can feel a twang of guilt at ruining their day by stopping their Facebook Live.

I'm about to put down my iPad when an idea for a social media promotion comes to mind. I could title it *Give Love Get Love*. We could encourage people to share their acts of love and tag us. Maybe do it as a seven-day challenge? We could offer a free drink or muffin at the café for the best ones. I am distracted by my bleeping phone. It's Frankie and he's video calling. Panic takes hold of me. With a trembling hand I hold out my phone and press *accept*.

'What the hell is going on, Alice?' His eyebrows have formed a sharp V and his face looks taut and tense. 'I thought to myself, I'll give them a week or two to get to grips with my café before I have a look to see how things are going.' He places his head in his hands. 'My bowels haven't been the same since I saw all those complaints, that Heartbreak Café hashtag and what did you do to Rocco Reid? Mum has had to buy me some stomach settlers.'

'Frankie, listen to me. I'm sorry.'

He lifts his face to the screen. 'I want to fire you both and send Jake in to turn things around.'

'Please don't do that. Noah and I can do this.' I rub my aching chest.

Frankie runs his hand through his hair. 'Jake's father is still unwell so I can't do that, but I need to see a visible change soon, Alice. I can't have all this bad publicity. You are destroying all my hard work. On a separate note, did you end up snogging Rocco Reid or something?'

'No, I did not!' I exclaim. 'For goodness' sake I saved his life in the sea and then we had a heart-to-heart in the Snug about his fake relationship.'

'Oh,' says Frankie, looking surprised. 'I didn't know you'd been in the sea with him. I thought you were busy trying to make Noah jealous.'

I arch my eyebrows at Frankie. 'By throwing myself at a famous actor in the Snug?'

Frankie giggles. 'Trust me I have witnessed some bizarre things in the Snug.'

'How's your mum?'

His face softens. 'She's doing great. I mean she's at the start of a long journey, but her positivity and optimism are so inspiring.'

'Give her our love.'

'Don't let me down, Alice,' he says. 'Control your emotions and sort out the café's social media. I'm not renaming my business – Heartbreak Café.'

As I climb into the camp bed his words are still ringing in my ears.

CHAPTER EIGHTEEN

@The Little Love Café: Today we are kicking off our new 7-day challenge #GIVELOVEGETLOVE We want to bring love back to The Little Love Café. We want to see your acts of love whether that be a bunch of flowers, box of chocolates, cute Post-it note messages in lunchboxes, breakfast in bed or a romantic mixtape. Take a photo and tell us about your act of love. The ones which make us say 'aww...' or smile will get a free coffee. Post your pics using the hashtags #LittleLoveCafé #Letsbringbacklove

I woke up before Lucas and Dad to put my social media promotion live.

By the time I open the café we've had a man tag us into a photo of his wife's breakfast tray containing two poached eggs, toast, and a printout of cinema tickets to see her favourite film later. And a woman has tagged us with a photo of her husband's sandwiches, which she'd cut into heart shapes: 'A little surprise for him during his lunch break.'

Pam is busy unloading her cake delivery; Noah is at the

coffee machine working on some drinks and I am heading back with an order for table two. They're a couple who were pleased to tell me about how they split up ten years ago but had an unexpected reunion a year ago today in Thailand.

As I get back to the counter there's a crash from the back of the café. I rush out to see Pam sprawled across the floor. 'Don't worry,' she says, 'the cakes are fine. It's me. I'm trying to do too much, and I fell over my shoelace.'

I help her up and she brushes down her trousers.

'Have you hurt yourself? Can I get you some water, a cup of tea or coffee?'

She shakes her head. 'I'm fine. You are my customer, and I shouldn't say this, but I would just like time to see my family and not have to spend day and night with my ex-husband. This business we created when we were together has become demanding and I'm working far too many hours.' Her phone is vibrating in her pocket. She takes it out and groans. 'I'm so tired.'

'Pam, you're worrying me,' I say, giving her arm a gentle rub.

She looks at me with pink watery eyes. 'Thank you for worrying about me.'

Once she goes, I return to the counter. 'Pam fell over.'

Noah looks up. 'Is she okay?'

'I think she's stressed. I do hope she's all right.'

He points towards the Snug. 'Will you go check on the couple who are in there? It's Jon and Donna. They're regulars. A bit of background, Donna has been unwell, and Jon is proposing.'

My initial reaction is to shake my head, but I remember Frankie's face from last night. I must turn this place around and that means confronting my phobia of live marriage proposals. I stop shaking my head and nod. 'Okay, will go now.'

Noah looks at me with a shocked expression. 'Are you serious?'

'It's time to face my fears.'

He smiles at me. 'I'm proud of you, Alice.' I feel a fluttering sensation inside my chest as I head out the back to the Snug. I'm bracing myself for a couple gazing longingly into each other's eyes. As I get nearer, I can hear the couple arguing. Inwardly I groan.

'I am afraid we are going to have to leave,' the man – Jon – barks. 'She's changed her mind.'

The woman – this must be Donna – arms crossed tightly over her chest, is scowling out of the window. 'Jon, I need some space.'

'Fine,' snaps Jon, who is wearing a blue shirt and beige jeans. He gets up and storms off through the café.

I take a deep breath and go sit down next to the woman. 'Can I get you a drink, cake maybe?'

She shakes her head and wipes away a lone tear. 'I feel bad now. This sounds like I am being selfish and cruel, but I wanted the fairy-tale wedding, only it looks like my breast cancer has put a stop to that as well.'

Sitting back into the plush sofa I send her a friendly smile. 'You two are Little Love Café regulars – aren't you?'

The woman sits up and fiddles with her short red hair. 'Yes, we used to be regulars. Then I got sick and couldn't come for months. I'm Donna by the way.'

'Alice,' I reply.

'Do you have kids, Alice?'

I nod. 'Yes, Lucas, he's six.'

She rubs her temples. 'We have five kids and sometimes I feel like my head is going to explode. Last night the two boys had a stomach bug, so Jon and I were up half the night. This morning, our eldest daughter informs us over breakfast she wants to go on the contraceptive pill; our other daughter has been caught skipping school; and our little girl fell over the dog and hit her head. Then Jon proposes. I am exhausted and the last thing I want to do is get soppy. We can't afford a big wedding because I haven't worked for months due to my illness, and we stupidly cancelled our insurance policy three months before I got diagnosed. So, things are tight.'

She sighs and picks at a piece of fluff on her top. 'I just wanted to get married somewhere nice and special. I suggested we wait for a bit.' Her face has lost its scowl, and I can see the hint of a smile on her thin lips. 'Sorry for downloading all that. I feel better now.'

'I totally understand,' I say. 'Blimey, you have had your hands full.'

Donna laughs. 'Poor Jon probably hates me now.'

'How long have you and Jon been together?'

Fiddling with a gold heart on her necklace, Donna looks wistfully out of the window. 'When we were kids. He used to pull my pigtails at school. I tried dating others, but Jon's face never left my mind.'

'I'm sure you both need time to cool off.'

Donna sits up straighter. 'The kids have been on at us for years to get married. When I got sick, it was all they spoke about. We've never had much money though for a big wedding, so we are going to go to the registry office and then for a quiet meal in a restaurant on Friday. That's all we can afford. Receptions are expensive. I just wanted something a bit more memorable where I can wear a nice dress and maybe feel a bit special.'

My eyes wander over the mini flower wall behind Donna's head. It is then my next idea pings into my brain. It's mad and both Noah and Frankie will say no, but we are in desperate times. Donna and Jon have a story to tell about love. 'Have your reception here.'

Donna flicks her head towards me. 'We couldn't afford to hire this place. Jon and I don't have much to spend on our day.'

'You will be our first wedding reception and if you let us use your story on social media, I will let you hire it for free.'

Donna puts her hands to her mouth.

'It will just be posh cupcakes and coffee or tea though. Is that okay?'

'Oh my God, Alice, we would love to have our wedding reception here. We could take pictures of us against the flower walls or outside on the beach.'

Jon appears looking sad. Donna jumps up and hugs him. 'Yes, I will marry you next Friday.'

'What?' Jon stares at Donna. 'I came back in here for another row.'

Donna turns to me. 'Alice has offered for us to do the reception here, with no hire fee.'

'Really?' He looks at me and I nod.

'What about a dress?' He turns back to Donna.

It's then I remember the wedding dress which is hanging up at the back of my wardrobe. Remarkably it survived my drunken night on the camp bed. 'What size are you, Donna?'

'Twelve to fourteen – why?'

I take a deep breath. 'I have a wedding dress which might fit you. It's a long, A-line, ivory gold number.'

Donna's eyes water. 'Really?'

Feeling inspired I put my arm around Donna. 'Yes. Let's get you both married.'

After swapping contact details and agreeing timings plus a night for Donna to come to Dad's to try on my dress, they leave holding hands.

Walking through to the café, I feel high as a kite. Noah's

mouth falls open after I tell him about what I have just organised.

'For free?' He looks like someone has given him a fright. 'You do realise this is a business and we are supposed to make money?'

'Noah, they will still pay for drinks and cakes. Look, I have a good feeling about this. If we can get their story on social media and how we have stepped into help them I think it will help turn public opinion. The challenge for us is that it's next Friday.'

His blue eyes widen. 'We are having a wedding reception here next Friday?'

'Yep.'

He looks around the café. 'I don't want to spoil your plan, but we have one stressed-out cake supplier and there are only us two working here. How are we going to make a wedding reception happen?'

CHAPTER NINETEEN

@Sharonandhershoeobsession: My act of love was to buy my new boyfriend a surprise pair of new shoes. He's worn them out today and I think he looks irresistible in them. #GIVELOVEGETLOVE #LittleLoveCafé #RedLeatherLoafers

@MikeFlowers: An act of love is also to say sorry to someone who means a lot to you. @KirstenBall36 – I am sorry I broke up with you. I love you and always will x #GIVELOVEGETLOVE #LittleLoveCafé

'Hello, Alice.' A voice from the doorway makes me look up from the counter. I am busy looking at the responses to my promotion. A familiar young woman, willowy, with black hair approaches. She's wearing a blue denim skirt with a pink T-shirt. 'Remember me?'

'Lilly,' I shout before going over to give her a hug.

She grins. 'I heard you were back, so I had to come and see you.'

Many years ago, I used to babysit Lilly and her brothers.

Lilly hugs me. 'Alice, you had the patience of a saint with me and my five little brothers.'

'You were an angel, Lilly,' I say, draping my arm over her shoulders. 'But your little brothers were a gang of little so-and-sos.'

'Fancy a free drink?' I say, pointing at the coffee machine.

Lilly piles her long hair on top of her head into a messy bun. 'Black coffee, please.'

Once I have made her a coffee, she sits on a stool at the counter.

'What are you doing now? College? Ice-cream parlour?'

She screws up her face. 'I dropped out of college. All that studying wasn't for me. I work in the ice-cream parlour, and I volunteer at the youth club. Remember the old place?'

'The old lifeguard building?'

Lilly nods. 'It's in a bit of a state but all the young people still go there.'

The memory of me kissing Noah at the youth club resurfaces. My face is reddening as I spot him walking into the café after his lunch break. I avert my eyes from him and focus on Lilly.

'Tonight, at the youth club, I have organised a painting party. We're struggling to get the funds to redecorate the place. Paint and all that stuff is costly so everyone who is coming is bringing some spare paint from home. We're going to decorate the youth club area ourselves. The kids are excited.'

I recall Frankie saying something about wanting to attract a younger audience.

Lilly leans in with a mischievous grin. 'I'm also trying to impress Sunny.'

'Ah,' I say with a grin. 'I see.'

She giggles. 'He hasn't made a move yet. I want him to, but I think he's shy. Tonight, over a can of paint, I can work my magic.'

An idea on how to grow Frankie's business unfolds in my mind. 'I have an idea,' I say, thinking on my feet. 'How about I donate some pink paint from The Little Love Café, and I come to help too.'

'You have paint?'

I nod and point out the back. 'Loads of tins. It's pink, but I am sure you won't mind.'

Lilly's face lights up. 'That would be great.'

'I might have to bring my little boy to this painting party though,' I say, remembering Dad's late shift at the supermarket.

'Painting party?' Noah comes over, looking interested. 'Can I come?'

Lilly nods. 'More the merrier.' She glances at both of us. 'I'm so glad you two are back together. Mum heard about it in the supermarket. She said you two were the Romeo and Juliet of Blue Cove Bay at one time.'

'We're not,' I say, feeling my cheeks heat up.

Lilly looks shocked. 'Oh, I'm sorry... I...'

'It's fine,' chuckles Noah. 'You're not the first to ask.'

After Lilly goes back to the ice-cream parlour, I receive a text from Donna confirming numbers for her wedding reception. As I am waiving the hire fee, she has confirmed that they will pay for coffees and cupcakes. She's kept it limited to close family and a few friends so I am sure Pam will be okay. I show Noah my extra cupcake order. 'That's not as big as I thought it would be. Are you going to email Pam?'

'Yes, I will see what she says. Hopefully she's had a chance to de-stress.'

≈

On our way to the lifeguard building Lucas skips along the beach. The low evening sun makes Lucas's shadow stretch across the sand which makes us both laugh. There are still a handful of hardy beachgoers sat on their towels watching the waves rush into the shore and a few have ventured into the sea. Lucas shouts before bending down to pick something up. He squeals with delight, and I let out a groan. He's found someone's black wallet in the sand. I hurry over as an excited look takes hold of his mischievous face.

'Lucas, don't open it.'

He's about to peer inside it when I reach him. Placing my hands on the wallet I bend down in front of him. 'Someone has lost this wallet. They're sad. What shall we do?'

'Sad?' He casts me a thoughtful look and shoves a sand coated finger up his nose.

I bat away his finger and nod. 'Without their wallet they can't buy their boy an ice cream.'

His eyes grow wide, and his little mouth forms an O-shape. 'We must get it to him, Mummy.'

I catch sight of an older man and woman searching their beach towels. Their panic-stricken voices drift over to us. 'I hope someone hasn't stolen it.'

'Lucas, why don't you go ask that couple whether this is their wallet?'

In a second, he grabs it and sprints over to the couple. 'I found it,' he announces with a huge smile. I am filled with pride as I see relief sweep over the couple's faces. The man outstretches his hand and for a few seconds Lucas studies the wallet. 'Give it to the man, Lucas,' I murmur under my breath, praying he doesn't run off with it. He's staring at it and my heart has started to race. I am about to go over when Lucas reluctantly passes the wallet to the man. The couple make a fuss of Lucas and he comes back to me with an ear-to-ear smile. 'I did it, Mummy.'

I plant a kiss on his cheek. 'Lucas, that was brilliant.' He hugs me. 'I'm a good boy now.'

Teenagers are milling around the entrance to the old lifeguard building. They are all clutching tins of paint and plastic bags full of brushes. The air is filled with laughter, excited chatter, and the clicks of mobile phones as several pose for selfies.

I would not normally consider decorating with Lucas. He's not the most patient of little boys. After two minutes of being told to sit still he often decides to do his own thing. Everything he sticks his fingers into goes into his hair – food, fizzy drinks, glitter, half chewed sweets, toothpaste, and the contents of his nose. He also struggles with the phrase 'Don't touch'.

Looking around, I remember waiting for youth club to start. We'd all huddle on the wall. Noah's arms would be around my waist pulling me close and Frankie would be making everyone giggle with his rude jokes. I spot Noah sat on the low wall with the tins of paint from The Little Love Café.

My heart is banging against my ribcage and my mouth is dry as he spots us. 'Hi, Noah. Lucas, do you remember Noah from the other day? He works with me.'

Noah comes over and smiles at Lucas, who shoves his finger up his nose and grins.

'This is a great idea, Alice,' says Noah. 'We can promote The Little Love Café to the younger generation.'

Lilly flings opens the doors. 'Come on, everyone. It is time to get painting.'

Lucas and I have been painting for nine minutes. We haven't painted much as he keeps touching the paint and trying to pick up the roller when I am not looking.

'PUT THAT DOWN, LUCAS.' For goodness' sake – what is it about that phrase my son doesn't understand?

Sweat is pouring off me and my shirt clings to my back. I'm covered in paint and so is Lucas. He's been told off so many times all his stars will be removed from his reward chart when we get home, and he's needed more toilet trips this evening than I have ever experienced.

'Stand there and paint that little bit,' I instruct, at the same time noticing the dark looks coming from the groups of teenagers. Before we all got started Lilly and her army of volunteers drew small square sections in pencil on each of the four walls. Each section was to be painted a different colour. 'Think patchwork quilt,' she instructed as we all got to work. Everyone placed all their tins of paint in the centre of the large room before getting to work.

The youth club room looks the same with the black rafters running across the ceiling and the sloping roof in the far corner. When we used to come here, there was a pool table at the far end, an old threadbare sofa which somehow sat about ten teenagers all squashed together, a pinball machine and a load of plastic chairs at the other end. The grey walls would be adorned with posters of local bands and festivals.

Beside me is a teenage girl with long blonde hair. She's busy painting and at the same time glancing over at the tall boy who is painting opposite Lucas.

Our eyes meet as she goes back to painting after what feels like the millionth glance in the boy's direction. She smiles, leans in and whispers, 'He and I have been messaging each other for ages. I thought tonight we might take things to the next stage.'

'Oh, I see.' Turning my head, I catch the boy sneaking a look in our direction.

The girl giggles as I pretend to focus on painting the square.

She takes another look at the boy who is now putting in his white earbuds. 'He's not going to ask me. I know it.'

'Do you want to be his girlfriend?'

She stares at me in horror. 'No one likes labels anymore. I think he and I should come out of our friendship zones... now and then. Nothing serious or anything. Maybe go on a date once or twice a week.'

Wow, things have certainly changed in the world of teenage love. I remember how good it felt knowing I was Noah's girlfriend. Leaning in I whisper, 'Take matters into your own hands – ask him.' Smiling, I give her a little nudge. We both glance over. The boy is busy painting and engrossed in whatever music is pumping through his earbuds.

The girl takes a deep breath. 'You are right. It's time to sort out my own destiny.' She takes out her phone and taps out a message. I give her a wink.

The boy checks his phone, looks up and grins.

When I turn back to steal a look at what's happening they are both stood holding out their phones and posing for a selfie with each other, heads pressed together, and dreamy smiles plastered over their faces. As the boy returns to his part of the wall, I notice the girl has an ear-to-ear smile. It gives me a surprisingly warm feeling to know that I have helped them. Maybe I should keep my own feelings about love to myself. Just because I don't believe in love, doesn't mean others have to do the same.

I look over to check on Lucas and he's disappeared. Panic sets in. I look around and spot him helping Noah. The sight of them together fills my chest with fluttery birds. As I come to stand near them, Noah's hand brushes against mine. My whole body comes alive. I quickly dismiss the sensations.

Lilly climbs on a box and claps for everyone's attention. 'I want to introduce you all to Alice and Noah who run The Little

Love Café. They've kindly donated us some pink paint. Let's all give them a round of applause.'

A handful of teenagers clap but most take to their phones.

A young girl puts her hand up. 'Hi, Alice and Noah. My mum has text me to say she went to school with you two and she wants to know – are you back together?'

Oh God, my face is now the colour of the paint. Why do people keep asking that?

CHAPTER TWENTY

'How's Lucas this morning?' Noah asks as I unlock the doors and open up the café.

A smile pulls up the corners of my mouth. 'He had to have another bath before he went to school. That child looked like a walking art project by the time we got home.'

Noah laughs. 'His hair made me smile. There was more paint in there than there was on his brush.'

After depositing my bag behind the counter, I set to work on making sure the tables are neat, tidy and all have a good supply of heart-shaped menus. As I wipe one table, I notice Noah is looking at me. This morning I decided to make an effort with my hair by curling it and I added a little eye shadow and mascara.

'I enjoyed last night,' Noah says, from behind the counter. 'You were always doing volunteering stuff like that when we were younger.'

'Me too. I used to enjoy everyone mucking in on a project when we were kids. Although you and Frankie always moaned when I made you do Sunday Beach Litter Cleaning.'

I can hear Noah chuckle. 'No teenager wants to get up early to pick up crisp packets and plastic bottles.'

'Oh, Pam came back and confirmed she will be able to cover the extra cupcakes for the wedding reception.'

He places his hand on my shoulder. 'Good work, Alice.'

The sound of footsteps entering the café make us both look up. It's the girl from last night and with her is the boy with the white earbuds. Her blonde hair is elegantly braided, and the boy's messy brown hair looks like it needs a good brush. Both are wearing T-shirts, denim shorts, trainers, and have rucksacks slung over their shoulders. My eyes are drawn to how close they are standing. They both smile as I walk over to them.

'Hello again. This place is cool,' gushes the girl, fiddling with one of her braids. 'I've never been in here.'

'Why's that?' I ask, keen to know more.

She grins. 'It looks like the kind of place my dad would take my mum when he's trying to get her to agree to him going to watch the footie with his mates.'

Her male friend smirks.

She surveys the café. 'It's the kind of place I'd bring my nana though. I love treating my little nana.'

'Your nana?' I cast her a puzzled look. 'Our friend who owns this place has tasked Noah and me with finding new business opportunities. He thought it would appeal to younger customers like yourselves. So, I'm curious about why you said your nana?'

She nods and looks across at the little pink tables and chairs. 'I'm not sure teenagers like us would come here on dates. It's too bright and sugary pink for us. However, I would bring my nana here.'

The boy surveys the empty café. 'Yeah. I would bring my nana here. She'd love it.'

I cast them both a look of surprise. With a grin, the girl flicks one of her braids. 'Teenagers get a lot of bad press. I can see why, I mean we stay out late, we don't do our homework, our bedrooms are a mess, we are grumpy, we play our music too loud, and we shout at our parents. However, everyone forgets how much we love our grandparents. We love our nanas and grandpas. We love taking them out and treating them. You could run a *Treat Your Grandparent* type promo. I know a few people at college who would love that.'

I turn to Noah. 'What do you think?'

He nods. 'I like the idea a lot and it might help with attracting senior customers.'

The girl giggles and taps the boy on her arm. 'I'll get Georgia to bring her grandpa if you bring your nana.' She turns to me. 'We think Will's great nana and my best mate Georgia's great grandpa fancy each other.'

I smile. 'Well, I love your idea. What's your name?'

She outstretches her hand. 'I'm Ava. He's called Will. I'm also looking for some holiday work. I'm seventeen, I am a hard worker and I have been a waitress before.'

I like Ava. She's bright and could help on a Saturday when we get busy, but she could also help with the wedding reception next week. 'How about a trial on Saturday?'

Her face lights up. 'You won't regret it.'

'You can help sort out our grandparent day promotion and we have a wedding reception in here next Friday? When do the Easter holidays start?'

She grins. 'Next Friday and we have a teacher training day. I'll be happy to help at the reception.'

When they leave, our first customers of the day arrive so Noah and I get to work. At the counter he leans over and says, 'You're like a different person.'

'Really?'

He pauses and holds my gaze. 'It's like the old Alice I once knew is coming back.'

'What was she like?' I whisper, finding myself getting lost in his summer blue sky eyes.

'She had all these big ideas, she loved organising everyone and she believed in herself.'

A ball of warm tingles shoots up my spine.

During my break, I go into the gift shop on the seafront to see how Esme is doing. Luckily Joy isn't working so it's just me and Esme.

She lifts her head from arranging a new collection of Blue Cove Bay mugs and smiles. 'Hi, Alice, how are you after quitting your job?'

I smile and browse her extensive candle collection. 'I went back. Noah and I have agreed to not discuss the past and I am trying my hardest to control my emotions. How are you?'

Esme shrugs. 'Still the same. Joy is still intent on selling this place.'

After smelling a few of her candles, I move on to her range of vanilla and cotton cloud scented diffuser sticks. 'What about you and your secret friend?'

Her face brightens. 'He's great.' She takes out her phone. 'His texts are making me laugh.'

'Are you going to tell me who it is?'

Her dark eyes shine and for the first time in all the years I have known her, she casts me the biggest happy smile. 'It's Keith. He works for Phoebe.'

Seeing Esme happy gives me a rush of excitement. 'Oh wow, Keith is lovely, Esme.'

She nods. 'He makes me laugh, Alice. He takes me for walks on the beach, buys me ice cream, gives me book gifts and he listens to me. And my cats adore him.'

I rush over and hug her. 'Esme, I wish Frankie was here. He would be so happy for you.'

She takes out her phone. 'Every day Keith sends me funny stories about life in the bookshop. This week his stories have been about the guy called Liam who has moved into the shop next door.'

'Ah, the record shop guy.'

'That's him. Well, every day Keith tells me about Phoebe and Liam's arguments.'

I cast her a worried look. 'Arguments? This doesn't sound good.'

Esme grins. 'Keith says he's never seen Phoebe so fired up. She's winning, though, as this Liam guy has turned down his music.'

'Good for Phoebe.'

She looks up and spots Steve walking his dog along the promenade. I follow her gaze to where Steve is getting dragged along by his rebellious Labrador. Steve's struggle to hold on to his dog is pleasurable to watch.

'Why does Joy want you to get back with him?'

'He plays golf with Eric, who runs the guesthouse. Joy and Eric have started dating.'

'Oh, I see.' I recall Frankie saying something about Joy and Eric.

'Eric is selling the guesthouse. He's moving as he's bought a new guesthouse somewhere in North Devon. I think that's where we will be moving to once Joy sells this place.'

I turn to Esme. 'This all feels very convenient for Joy – doesn't it? What about you, Esme, and *your* life?'

She bows her head. 'My life is with Joy.'

'Is it?'

She shakes her head. 'I don't have the strength to fight her, Alice.'

'I didn't think I had the strength to leave Pete but I found it. If Joy wasn't an issue – what would your perfect life look like?'

Esme's large brown eyes widen. For a few moments she doesn't say anything, and I wonder whether I have pushed her too far. To my surprise she gushes. 'Well, I'd stay here in Blue Cove Bay, I'd get into cat fostering as I have always wanted to do that; I'd find a job somewhere. Keith and I would go on day trip dates. And I would cut my hair.'

I smile. 'Cut your hair?'

She nods. 'Joy thinks short hair wouldn't suit me.'

'It's your hair, not Joy's.' It's then I remember Celia Black's book, *The Approval List*. The book I'd read about the young woman who had lost herself after years of people pleasing her friends and family. She'd even created an approval list for any decision she made in life. Things had come to a head when the guy she fell in love didn't perform well on her Approval List. He had tattoos which her mother hated, he had an earring which made her father complain bitterly, he was friends with the people her sister didn't like, and he played football for the team her brother despised. The young woman decides to stop seeking approval and starts living her own life.

'Esme, have you read, *The Approval List* by Celia Black?'

Esme shakes her head. 'No.'

'That book was transformational for me. It helped me so much when I was trying to please Dad and Pete. Let me dig it out for you. I will drop it in.'

'Are you sure?'

'Esme, I'm positive. Just be ready for some life changes.'

CHAPTER TWENTY-ONE

I'm standing at the top of the cliff and looking at the golden strip of sand below. Groups of beachgoers are dotted along the coastline. Above my head is a bright blue sky. It's Sunday and the café is closed. Yesterday was busy as we had student Ava join us and the warm weather had brought out the romantic couples. Ava and I also planned out her *Treat Your Grandparent* promotion. She agreed to help spread the word at college.

Lucas and Dad are baking so I have decided to walk along the coastal path. It's where I feel closest to Mum. Taking out my phone, I smile. On my lock screen is one of my favourite photos of her. The one where she's in hiking gear and boots, rucksack slung over her shoulder, ready for an adventure. She loved walking for miles in the countryside and up along this winding coastal path. I remember every Saturday, Dad and I would wave her off. Even as a child I could feel her excitement on the morning of one of her walks. She'd be laughing as Dad poured her tea into a flask and moaned about how she had packed her rucksack.

Sometimes I look at Mum's face for too long. 'I miss you so

much, Mum,' I croak. 'After all these years without you it still hurts.' Through the blurriness her beaming smile finds me.

The walk I am going on will take me to the little brass plaque Dad and I got made after she died up here on one of her walks. She fell on a piece of ice and hit her head. It caused a fatal stroke.

Dad and I visited regularly in the years after she passed away. Throughout my teenage years it was a place of solace for me. As the little path winds around, I can see a figure stood by Mum's plaque. They're crouched down on their knees and wiping her plaque. My heart thuds. Feeling protective, I walk faster. The figure sees me coming and shoots up to their feet. As I get closer, I gasp; it's Noah.

He gives me an awkward look. 'Didn't expect to see you up here.'

'It was a last-minute decision. What are you doing?'

He nudges a collection of small pebbles with his shoe before casting his gaze out to sea. 'I was on a walk, and I've just come across your mum's plaque.'

'Oh, I see.'

He points to the beach below. 'When we used to sit on our rock, I always used to see you looking up here.'

Smiling, I stand beside him and look down at our old rock. 'You came up here a few times with me – remember?'

His face softens. 'I used to moan a lot about coming up here – didn't I?'

A giggle escapes my lips. 'Yes, you did. I think once I had to practically drag you up those steps.'

'Sorry.' His boyish smile sweeps across his face and my chest feels like it is full of tiny seagulls.

I flick my eyes to Mum's shiny plaque and find myself wishing she'd got a chance to meet Noah. 'You never met Mum – did you?'

He doesn't say anything and returns to staring out to sea.

'She would have liked you,' I say, letting my mind whisk me back in time to when Mum would collect me from primary school in her old leather jacket pretending to be a cool parent.

I get the feeling Noah wants to go. He's shifting his weight from one boot to another and is fiddling with the zip on his red jacket. 'I used to think you were brave dealing with the loss of your mum. I never knew my mother because she left after my first birthday.'

I bend down to run my fingertips over her plaque. 'I think I'll always be dealing with losing her. I like to think she's still with us.'

We walk back along the coastal path towards the steps side by side. Every so often we turn our heads to find the other smiling back.

'Your mum loved hiking, didn't she?'

I nod. 'Mum loved adventure and the outdoors. She looked forward to her Saturdays, when she would head out with her map, her rucksack, and her flask.'

'She sounds like a lot of fun,' he says, quietly.

On the way down the steps, we giggle like school children at the exhausted tourists who are getting their breath midway up, and we try to chase each other down the rest of the steps.

Once we get onto the beach Noah points over to our rock. 'Shall we climb up for old times' sake?'

Before I can blink, he takes my hand, and we hurry across the beach to our old rock. He climbs up with ease. With a sigh I follow him up. I make sure I sit apart from him. Dangling my jean-clad legs over the side, I savour the warm and fuzzy nostalgic feeling of being back sat on our old rock. It's been years.

'I'd forgotten how peaceful it is up here,' sighs Noah,

running his hand through his blond hair. 'It's still one of my favourite places in the world.'

'We used to have a lot of fun.'

He nods. 'We'd race home from school. I'd do my homework and you...'

'Wouldn't do any,' I say, with a giggle. The prospect of spending time with Noah was too much of a distraction for me.

'We'd meet by the seafront and run like mad things over to this rock.'

'With sweets stuffed in our pockets and two sugary drinks shoved inside a picnic blanket.'

The boyish smile is back. 'Listen to music up here and watch the world go by.'

'I never got cold up here considering we stayed out until it got dark.'

'That's because you always stole my coat.'

We both laugh and I notice the sparkle in his eyes.

'I missed this place so much when I left.'

'Where are you staying?'

He flicks back his golden hair. 'I'm renting a tiny cottage in the town. It's just off the high street.'

'Why are you back, Noah?'

His summer blue sky eyes lock onto mine. 'I had a succession of bad relationships in Ireland, and I started to think about why love was so hard for me.'

'Did you come to any conclusions?' I can't drag my eyes away from his.

The atmosphere between us has changed. Our friendly banter has been replaced with intense stares. 'I never forgot about you, Alice.'

We've been staring at each other for what feels like an eternity. A wave of emotion is rising inside of me. On the white crested tip, it carries the words I have been trying to say since he returned. The wave is stronger. After a deep breath the words whoosh out of my mouth. 'What happened to us, Noah?'

He reaches out and touches my hand, sending a surge of electricity through my arm. 'I never wanted us to end.' Leaning back, he breaks our trance and throws a pebble out to sea. 'Did you really write to me?'

I nod. 'Every week. I couldn't post them in the box on our street as I was scared Dad would see me.' I smile. 'Looking back now I don't know why I was worried Dad would see me. Anyway, Pete took my letters and posted them for me.'

Noah is looking at me. 'You asked Pete to post your letters?'

'He was your best mate and I trusted him. He was nice to me when you left.'

Noah looks out to sea. 'When I first came back and I learned about Lucas, I was angry.' He runs a hand through his hair. 'I thought you and Pete had got together because all along you'd...' He stops. 'Oh God, this is silly. Why are we raking up the past?'

A concoction of twenty years of frustration and anger is bubbling inside of me. 'You thought I'd secretly fancied Pete while we were going out with each other – is that what you thought?'

Noah has found another pebble and is turning it over in his hand. 'Did you?'

'No, I did not. I started dating Pete because...'

Noah is now staring at me. 'Why, Alice?'

'To make you jealous.' I hang my head. 'Noah, I was so angry you never contacted me. It was a bad decision. Probably one of my worst.'

He puts a hand on my arm. 'You had Lucas together. He's great.'

'Yes, he is.'

'Did you love Pete?'

I let out a heavy sigh. 'I feel guilty for what happened with

Pete. For years I was waiting for him to lead me back to you but when that didn't happen, I waited to fall in love with him.'

'And?'

I shake my head. 'I never loved Pete.' Noah's intense stare is making me feel light-headed. Our eyes have locked in. We're inching closer. His mouth is hovering over mine. I can feel his warm breath on my chilly lips. In a flash I am whisked back to when we were teenagers, we're on this same rock and Noah is about to kiss me. Just like he used to all those years ago, he presses his soft lips against mine and as we kiss, I plunge my hands deep into his blond hair. His hand brushes against my thigh as our kissing intensifies. A familiar feeling of warmth is emanating from between my legs and making me press myself against him. Parts of me which have been in a deep sleep for years are waking up.

Noah sits up abruptly. 'I need to go.' His tone has changed. It's tinged with a coolness to it. He checks his watch. 'I have got to sort my laundry out.'

I place my hand on his arm. 'Are you all right?'

He nods and sits up straighter. 'Look, I made a mistake kissing you. I'm sorry, Alice.'

'What?'

Pulling himself to his feet he climbs down our rock and strides away.

CHAPTER TWENTY-TWO

S unlight finds a way to overcome my bedroom blinds and pokes itself through the gaps in the wooden slats. As I turn over in my bed, my head screams in pain. Oh God, why did I drink so much wine last night? My dry tongue tries to unstick itself from the roof of my mouth while my stomach considers serving the contents of my gut with an eviction notice. With a groan I rub my sore eyes and think back over the chain of events which led to this fragile state.

It had been a long trek back to Dad's house after Noah had made his sudden and unexpected departure from our rock. I'd climbed down with anger coursing through my veins. I was cross with myself for engaging in that impromptu kiss. Why did he get up and leave like that? What had I done? He was a heartbreaker and hadn't changed after twenty years. Noah Coombes should come with a health warning.

On the way back I'd crossed the promenade and spotted Phoebe with her two children. Flynn was having a tantrum and refusing to go home. His shouts and screams had made me cast weary Phoebe a friendly smile. She waved me over. Her eldest, Martha, was sat on the bench looking angelic. Her little brother clung to the little green beach telescope, yelling, 'NO, MUMMY. I AM STAYING HERE.'

'As you can see, I am having fun,' Phoebe said, with an eye roll at Flynn. 'How's your Sunday?'

I groaned. 'Don't ask. I'm so cross and fed up.'

She grinned. 'Listen, how do you fancy a few drinks tonight at mine? I fancy a good gossip and a moan.'

Dad was home and he could babysit Lucas for me. Plus, I had the day off tomorrow so there would be no need to get up early. 'I would love that.'

'Alice!' I heard someone shout my name. Turning around I saw that it was Esme marching toward us. In her hand she was clutching the book I'd dropped into the shop for her a few days ago. 'I've read it,' she cried, holding it aloft. 'I now want to change my entire life.'

Phoebe smiled at Esme. 'We're going to have a girl's night in tonight – do you want to come, Esme?'

That was how Esme, Phoebe and I found ourselves in Phoebe's living room hours later, drinking far too many glasses of wine.

I remember Esme sat on Phoebe's sofa talking about the book I'd lent her to read. 'That book has triggered what can only be described as a volcanic eruption. I felt shaky and sick as I was reading it. Celia Black held up a mirror as I saw myself in the main character of Lola. All I have done in my life to date is seek the approval and validation of others, mainly my sister and my parents who aren't even alive anymore.'

Phoebe and I had both stared at Esme who was changing before our eyes. 'This will sound a bit random,' said Esme, 'but stay with me. What's the word for one of those things that goes onto the side of a motorbike. It has wheels, a person sitting inside it but it is attached to the bike.'

'Sidecar?' Phoebe suggested.

Esme nodded. 'I don't want to be my sister's sidecar anymore.'

I stared at Esme and at the wine bottle. How much wine had Esme been glugging as that was a bit of a random thing to say.

'In our sister relationship, Joy has been the motorbike and I have been her sidecar for too long,' exclaimed Esme. 'In life I want to be the motorbike. I don't want to be someone's sidecar.'

'This is deep,' I said, which made them both laugh. 'Can someone check how strong the wine is.'

Esme grinned. 'Sorry, ladies, I do love a random analogy when I'm drunk.'

Phoebe nodded. 'No one should have to be a sidecar in life. What are you going to do?'

Esme held up her long dark tresses. 'I'm going to cut my hair first.'

I poured us all another glass of wine. 'Esme, I have never understood the hair issue. Explain it to us.'

Esme took a large gulp of her drink. 'Mum always wanted Joy and me to dress and look the same. She loved us being twins. Joy believes we should carry on Mum's wishes.'

Phoebe stared in horror at Esme. 'I am shocked at Joy. She sounds so controlling.'

Esme nodded. 'She's been like this all my life. When we were kids, our parents reminded us regularly that Joy was the boss because she was the older twin – by fourteen minutes and thirty-six seconds, to be precise. Our mother was always quick to point out Joy hadn't spent the first few years of her life in and out of hospital with an array of infections, like I had; and she hadn't been referred to as the *weaker* twin by the medical profession for the first five years of her life. Joy grew up being conditioned as the twin who was the boss, and I grew up knowing I was the weaker one.' Esme raised her glass. 'Not anymore though, ladies.'

'So, tomorrow you are going to cut your hair, and then...?' Phoebe asked.

'I'm also going to tell Joy I am not leaving Blue Cove Bay.'

Phoebe and I exchanged worried glances. This was a huge step for Esme. We pulled her into a group hug. 'Esme, we're here if you need us,' I said.

'Thanks both,' gushed Esme before draining her glass. 'I need more wine.'

The conversation moved on to Phoebe and Liam, the owner of the record shop. 'Are you still at war with Liam?' Esme asked Phoebe.

'What does he look like?' I asked, trying to imagine Liam. The last music shop in Blue Cove Bay had closed years ago and it had been run by a little chap with long hair and an even longer beard.

Esme began to giggle. 'Have you not seen Liam, Alice?'

I shook my head and noticed Phoebe's cheeks were pinker than normal. Phoebe swept her mane of brown curls from her face and sighed. 'Liam is tall, slim, with brown hair, a designer beard... and the sexiest black shades I have ever seen on a man.'

We all squealed with laugher. She carried on. 'His hair is styled into this elegant male quiff at the front, and he has a famous Australian film star look about him. Let's just say this: it's getting harder to argue with him.' Reaching her glass, she takes a drink of her wine. 'He's got kids and is a widow as his wife died a few years ago.'

'This sounds interesting,' I chuckled.

Phoebe shook her head. 'I don't think someone as handsome as Liam would be interested in me.'

'What?' Esme and I both gasped in unison. Phoebe is

stunning with a mass of brown curls, almond-shaped eyes, and caramel coloured skin.

Phoebe smiled. 'Do you two know Harold Brown and Pearl Williams?'

Esme and I both nodded. 'Harold and Pearl must be in their eighties,' I explained. 'They have lived in Blue Cove Bay for years. At one time Harold owned the car garage on the outskirts of the town and Pearl ran her father's sweet shop. They were once childhood sweethearts but ended up marrying other people. Harold married Edith, who died ten years ago, and Pearl married Bert, who died twenty years ago. They both had children who grew up in Blue Cove Bay and moved away. Harold and Pearl are now next-door neighbours and are always seen walking together.'

'Well, they were in the bookshop yesterday. I'd just come in from arguing with Liam about the position of his shop dustbin.'

'What was wrong with the position of his dustbin?' I chuckled.

Phoebe rolled her eyes. 'It was too close to mine. Anyway, after I threatened to fill his dustbin with rocks if he didn't move it, I went back into my shop. Pearl and Harold were stood by the door giggling like two school children. Keith said they'd been spying on my argument with Liam.'

'That's Blue Cove Bay for you,' I said, 'everyone knows your business.'

Phoebe and Esme both look at me. 'What's happened with you and Noah Coombes?' Phoebe leaned over and winked at me. 'But first fill us in on Rocco Reid.'

'I rescued him from the sea and later he turns up at the café.' I sighed. 'Rocco and I have a chat and the next day he's split from his popstar girlfriend.'

'What did you talk about?' Esme asked.

'He's in a fake relationship and he still thinks of his teenage sweetheart.'

Phoebe gasped. 'Oh, wow. Can you imagine being Rocco Reid's teenage sweetheart and knowing that out of all the women in the world he can choose from, you're the one he still thinks about.'

'How was Noah?' Esme asked. 'After the Rocco split?'

'Rattled,' I say, thinking back to our argument.

'He was jealous,' said Phoebe. 'Did you know you and Noah are the talk of the town. I wish I'd grown up here to witness your relationship all those years ago.'

Esme nodded. 'It was intense. We all cried for Alice when he left.'

Phoebe took a sip of her wine. 'Tell us the current Noah situation.'

I became engulfed in Noah related irritation. 'Well, we started working together and I hated him. My anger at him resulted in a lot of complaints at The Little Love Café. So, I have had to calm down and be an adult. Over the last few days, Noah is growing on me. I let him kiss me earlier. Big mistake.'

Esme squealed. 'Oh, my goodness – you two have kissed again after all this time.'

'Why was that a big mistake?' Phoebe filled up my wine glass.

'We kissed and then he got up and left. No explanation. He left. Walked away. I have gone back to hating him again.'

Phoebe studied my face. 'You still like him though – don't you?'

My reply was instant. 'No, I don't still like Noah Coombes after all these years...'

Both Phoebe and Esme stared at me until I took a swig of my wine and cracked. 'Oh God, I have never stopped liking him.' Tears rushed to my eyes. 'I have been thinking about him for twenty years.'

Phoebe took my hand. 'Talk to him, Alice.'

'I never stopped thinking about him. Frankie says that when Noah left, he built a little house in my head and has spent the last twenty years popping in and out of it.'

'He's come back into your life for a reason,' Esme said. 'There obviously was a reason. Maybe you both needed to grow as people first?'

'Rocco said he was jealous of Noah and me because we have been given a second chance.'

We drank some more wine, and I considered what Esme said. After Phoebe fell asleep on her rug, Esme and I decided to stagger home.

'Mummy.' Now Lucas was shaking my arm. He was sat up in his bed. 'I have a belly ache.' Hauling myself off the camp bed, I felt the room sway. With a thumping headache and breath like that of a wild dog, I reach for my fluffy pink dressing gown. Why did I drink so much wine?

Five seconds later Lucas vomited all over his bed and me.

CHAPTER TWENTY-THREE

@BabsTheScienceFictionFan: We met in the science fiction section of our local book shop years ago. His act of love is to buy me books I have been wanting to read for ages. Here's today's gift. Lovely coffee. #GiveLoveGetLove #LittleLoveCafé

@EmmaHappilyEverAfter: I was catching some rays on the beach, and he bought me an iced coffee. So happy and your flower wall is beautiful #LittleLoveCafé #GiveLoveGetLove

@DonnaThomas: Thanks to Alice at the #LittleLoveCafé we are getting married on Friday and she's made a miracle happen. Money has always been tight for us and my cancer hasn't helped. We thought getting married was going to cost more than what little money we have saved so we were on the verge of cancelling it - but Alice has saved the day. We can't thank her enough and watch this space for our reception pics on Friday at the #LittleLoveCafé

Noah is sat by the door to the café as I walk in on Tuesday. To say I feel exhausted is an understatement. Lucas was ill all day yesterday. Dad was working so I had to sort Lucas out and battle my hangover. Today Lucas is brighter and at home with Dad. I, however, still feel rough.

'Look, Alice, about the other day...' His face is pale, and his summer blue eyes are pinkish and housed inside two purple rings. 'I'm sorry about...'

My heart is beating so loud I am surprised he can't feel the vibration. I don't say anything and head towards the counter. He follows me. 'We need to talk.'

'You're right, Noah, we do. You can't kiss me like that and suddenly walk away.'

He opens his mouth, and our first customer of the day comes striding into the café. We both groan as the opportunity is lost.

On my break I head over to the gift shop to see how Esme is doing after our wine session on Sunday. As Lucas had been so poorly yesterday, I didn't have time to go see if she was okay. I have a little niggle that she won't stand up to Joy. Frankie and I spent years at school trying to make her do that, but it never worked.

As I cross over the promenade, I look up at the doorway of the gift shop and gasp. Esme is grinning at me and modelling a new sharp bob which grazes her jawline. It frames her face perfectly and accentuates her amazing cheekbones. 'I did it,' she cries out as I get closer. 'I cut my hair.'

Throwing my arms around her I blink back tears of joy. 'Esme, you look so beautiful.'

'It's made me feel different,' she gushes. 'Joy hates it.' We both laugh and hug again.

'I'm so proud of you, Esme.'

She ruffles her silky bobbed hair. 'Keith loves it.'

'Have you told Joy everything yet?'

Esme's smile fades. 'I haven't told her I am not going with her yet. That's going to take some doing.'

'Small steps,' I say, reassuringly.

She takes hold of my hand. 'I want to thank you for what you said the other day about following my heart and lending me that amazing book.'

'You don't have to thank me.'

'Well, I am going to keep following my heart and one day I will be the motorbike and not the sidecar. Wish me luck.'

'Stay strong. I believe in you.'

I walk back to the café in shock over Esme's hair transformation.

It's not until late afternoon that things get quieter in the café. Noah waves me over to the counter. There are two couples sitting in, and they are both near the window so out of earshot. My heart thuds. He holds my gaze and then bows his head. 'I got married five years ago.'

I gasp. 'You got married?' I can feel blood draining away from my face. Noah met someone who he loved enough to marry. My stomach nose dives towards the floor.

'What's the matter?' He's studying my face. 'You look like you've heard someone has just died.'

I shake my head. 'You got married – that's a shock.'

'Alice, you're now a parent – that was a shock for me too.' He flicks his eyes to his Timberland boots. We both go silent. I speak first. 'So, you kissed me, and you're married?'

He shakes his head. 'Becky and I are separated.'

My mind is trying to work out what Becky looks like. I bet she's tall, willowy, and blonde. Probably a model.

'Did you and Becky have kids?'

Noah shakes his head. 'No, I wanted them, but Becky didn't.' He takes a deep breath. He stops and lowers his head. 'Becky looks like you. In the early days she had red hair like yours. She's dyed it since then. When we first got together, I used to pretend she was you. It's not been easy for Becky. We've not had the best marriage and...' His words fade away. 'She is also the daughter of my dad's boss at work. Dad thought she was great.'

'Oh,' I say, ignoring the sinking feeling in my tummy. I used to pray that Dave Coombes would one day like me. It was hard having a boyfriend whose father didn't want you anywhere near his house.

Noah fiddles with a heart-shaped menu. 'Becky and I got married because...' He stops and drops the stone. 'Well, you know how persuasive fathers can be. Becky and I had some good times, but we argued a lot. We have spent half our married lives screaming at each other.'

'That was just like it was with Pete. We could have represented our country in the Olympics for shouting matches.'

Noah doesn't look up. 'I was the one who told Becky I wanted to leave her. Dad's taken it badly. We're not speaking.'

'Oh, Noah, I'm so sorry.' I place a hand on his shoulder. 'I know how close you were to your father.'

His eyes are studying my face. 'I've always wanted to come back here and see you again. This sounds weird but you never left my mind. I know it's been a long time and we're both adults now, but I never stopped thinking about you. I knew I had to find some answers to the questions which have been in my head for years.'

'What are those?'

His pink lips break into a smile. 'I have spent what feels like a lifetime wondering what happened to you, Alice.'

'Me too,' I whisper.

He envelops my hand with his. 'I wanted to tell you about Becky. I wasn't sure how you'd react.'

I smile. 'Thanks for being honest with me. How's Becky doing?'

'We've been living apart for a year. She's okay and has been seeing a man from the next village, but I sense she'd like us to get back together.' He rubs his forehead. 'I know that's what Dad wants.'

'I'm sorry, that sounds stressful.'

His hand touches mine. 'I need answers, Alice.'

'Answers?'

His tanned fingers entangle themselves in mine and he gently squeezes my hand. In a flash I am back to being a teenager again. We're holding hands and gazing into each other's eyes. Electricity is fizzing up and down my arm. 'What happened to us all those years ago? We both have different versions of how we ended. I want to find out the truth and get to know you again, Alice.'

CHAPTER TWENTY-FOUR

Noah is behind the counter making two Luscious Lattes for table four. We've been open an hour and, in that time, we have served two newlyweds, two recently engaged couples and a couple expecting their first child. They all looked loved-up and happy.

Yesterday we only had one couple who argued in The Little Love Café and that felt like an achievement. My social media campaign about giving acts of love has proved popular. We've had people sharing surprise plane tickets, plates of delicious food, perfume and aftershave purchases and surprise flower deliveries at work. Our favourites are the guy who treated his girlfriend's dog to a luxury grooming session and the woman who placed a love note inside her boyfriend's football boots. Throughout the day I regularly check our socials and share as many customer stories about love as I can.

I am leaning on the counter waiting for Noah to finish the drinks. 'I had to take up boxing to get over my anger of us splitting up all those years ago,' Noah says, casting me a cheeky grin.

'Boxing?' With a smile I say, 'You never had much upper body strength because I always beat you at arm wrestling.'

Noah laughs. 'I let you win because I wanted to kiss you, Alice.'

I let out a sigh. 'Well, once I had accepted we were over, and you were not going to write back, I found your favourite T-shirt stuffed down the side of my bed. I set fire to it in the garden to get over my anger at you.'

He grins. 'I also volunteered to do a sponsored kiss-a-thon at the sixth form and kissed away my anger at you.'

Noah and I were always competitive when we were younger. I could feel the old rivalry between us coming back. A memory popped up at the back of my mind. 'I also made a man doll which looked like you and inserted pins into it.'

His eyebrows rocket up his forehead. We both laugh. 'I can't believe you made a voodoo doll version of me,' says Noah, shaking his head in bewilderment. 'That beats my sixth form charity kiss-a-thon.'

He places the lattes on my tray, and I go deliver them. When I return, he asks, 'When did you and Pete get together?'

'It had been about six months. Pete had been walking me to and from school every day. He'd been my shoulder to cry on and he'd spent hours listening to me talk about you. On weekends he would take me out and get me smiling again.'

'You and Pete never struck me as having couple potential. The first time I ever met Pete, you and he were arguing over him fixing your bike.' He laughs. 'You told Pete a bike chain was not supposed to dangle on the ground after someone had allegedly fixed it. Poor Pete looked embarrassed.'

'Pete and I mostly argued all the time we were together. It was a long six years.'

'Did you see anyone after Pete?'

I think back to when Pete broke up with me the first time. We were both in our early twenties and we'd grown tired of the arguments. 'I moved out of Dad's and went to live in a flat with two girls I used to be lifeguards with. I dated a few people and had several drunken one-night stands with lads on holiday at the local caravan park but I think Pete had put me off long-term relationships.'

'Didn't you get back together after Lucas was born?'

I cast my mind back to Pete still living his bachelor life once Lucas was born. The hours I spent waiting for him to come home, the arguments over his penchant for casinos on a night out, the rows over money and the time when I broke my ankle, and he couldn't be bothered to come and give me a lift home from A&E. 'Yeah, we did. Pete had been my comfort blanket for years. The second time around wasn't great. I don't think he wanted to be a father. Lucas was a surprise for both of us.'

Not wanting to think too hard about that painful time, I turned the conversation back to Noah. 'Did you see anyone other than Becky?'

'I dated a few girls before Becky. No one special.'

The subject of Becky makes me feel uncomfortable. To my relief, a couple come into the café, and I seat them near the window and take their order.

As I walk back to the counter, I remember the time after Noah left and Pete had told me how Noah had gone silent on him as well. While Noah makes their drinks, I say, 'Can I ask you something?'

'Sure. Anything?'

'Why did you never contact Pete after we broke up?'

Noah's eyebrows arch with surprise. 'I did contact him.'

My heart grinds to a halt. 'Really?'

He nods. 'Pete and I exchanged emails for a while.'

'He told me you and he stopped speaking when you left.'

Noah shook his head. 'I asked about you once and Pete said you were enjoying your freedom. That made me sad, so I never asked again.'

An uncomfortable feeling passes over me. 'Why did Pete lie to me? I will be having a word with him when he drops Lucas off tomorrow evening.'

Dad is at work until 4pm so I've had to leave the café, collect Lucas from school and bring him back to the café. On the way to school this morning, Lucas and I talked a lot about how Mummy needs him to be a good boy. I reminded him of how brilliant he was the night he gave the lost wallet back to the couple on the beach. 'We give purses and wallets we find back to people, don't we, Lucas?' He nodded. 'We don't take them out of handbags either.' He gave me a thoughtful look while shoving his finger up his nostril. I can't believe I am saying this to my six-year-old. 'This is Frankie's café, so no running across seats and no drawing on teacakes.'

Settling Lucas down at the booth nearest the counter I get out his pens, scrap paper and his Batman figures. 'You are going to be a good boy for Mummy.'

Lucas nods and points to the heart-shaped menu. 'Can I have a milkshake?'

'I'm going to make Lucas a milkshake,' I tell Noah. He nods and heads off to take table three's order.

Lucas is quiet for about twenty minutes which is unusual. I've been able to clean down some of the tables, check social media and think about what I am going to say to Pete. But then I glance up at the pink booth Lucas was in. I gasp. It's empty. 'LUCAS.' My heart stops. Oh God, where is my son? Frantically I scan The Little Love Café for a little boy running around clutching a variety of handbags and wallets.

Voices at the far end of the café catch my attention. Noah is crouched down beside Lucas, and they are both inspecting a plastic Batman figure. Throwing down my dish cloth I race across the café. 'Lucas, I told you not to leave your seat.'

Noah rises to his feet. 'Batman has hurt his arm. I was seeing whether I could mend it for him.'

'Oh...'

Lucas holds aloft his plastic figure who now has what looks like a pink napkin sling. 'Noah made Batman better.'

'I made Batman a little sling.' Noah smiles and sends a train of tingles shooting across my chest.

To my horror I catch sight of something sticking out of Lucas's pocket. I can feel the blood drain from my face, It looks like a man's brown leather wallet. Oh God, while Noah has been doing something lovely, my son has stolen his wallet. For goodness' sake, I am raising a professional pick pocket. 'Lucas,' I hiss and gesture to the wallet.

Noah chuckles. 'He's keeping it safe for me. At one point he was more interested in my wallet than Batman.'

'Lucas, give Noah his wallet back please,' I say, before wiping a layer of sweat from my forehead and wishing Lucas liked other things, other than wallets and purses.

Noah and I lock up the café. Once we get outside, Lucas is tugging on my arm. 'Can we go play on the beach, Mummy?'

I turn to Noah. 'You're not working tomorrow so I'll see you Friday for the wedding party.'

'Can I come to the beach with you both?'

Lucas cheers and I hold out my hand to Noah. 'Come on then.'

We walk along the shore together and watch Lucas

paddling in the sea. I untie and remove my trainers. My bare toes wiggle with joy as I liberate them. Golden rays of sunlight dance on the water before us.

Noah drapes his arm over my shoulders. 'Do you remember the names we were going to call our kids?'

The memory of Noah and me cuddling on top of our rock after school discussing the names of our future children comes rushing back. As we both adored listening to his dad's vinyl Elvis albums, it was a given that our children would carry on our love of the King of Rock and Roll. 'Elvis and Priscilla.'

A wide smile spreads across Noah's tanned face. 'I didn't think you would remember.'

'Noah, I remember everything about us,' I say in a quiet voice.

We cast our gaze out across the dark blue sea. He bends down to pick up a smooth pebble. 'You are the only one I've met who appreciates Elvis and vinyl.'

I smile. 'Everyone at school used to think we were weird listening to Elvis on your dad's old record player.'

'This is nice,' he says, pulling me to a stop. We stand and face each other. He's grinning at me.

'What's so funny?'

'I was jealous the day you were in the Snug with Rocco.'

I cast him a mischievous grin. 'Were you?'

'The next day when we had that argument in the café, the one where I asked whether you fancied him, I realised how much I still fancy you.'

'Really?'

'You had this sexy wild look on your face, and I wanted to shut you up with a kiss.'

I smile and he plants a kiss on the top of my head. 'No one has ever come close to you, Alice.'

'Really? I don't believe you.'

'No one has ever kissed me the way you do,' he whispers, turning my face to his by placing a finger on my chin and placing his mouth over mine. This time he doesn't break away abruptly. When we pull away, he smiles, and we carry on walking.

CHAPTER TWENTY-FIVE

I've been home half an hour when Pete and Lucas arrive. Dad's gone to see an old friend, so I have the house to myself. The café had a steady flow of customers today, which was good. I was on my own as it was Noah's day off. Even though I tried to put aside what Noah had said about him and Pete staying in touch after he left, I kept chewing it over in my mind.

Pete picked Lucas up from school and took him for an ice cream. Now Lucas bursts through Dad's back door babbling away about his favourite flavour – mint choc chip. I watch his little mass of black curls race through the kitchen. The sight of him laughing and joking with Bean soothes my anxious state over what I am going to say to Pete.

Once Lucas is playing with his Batman figures in the living room and is out of earshot, I turn to Pete. He's stood by the back door looking out across Dad's vegetable patch. 'Why did you lie to me about Noah contacting you after he left for Ireland?'

Pete looks taken aback. He runs a hand through his black curly hair. 'What?'

'You heard what I said, Pete. Why did you lie to me?'

'That was years ago, Alice,' he mumbles, before bending down to pick up one of Lucas's tennis balls which is outside the doorstep. 'You need to let the past go.'

'No, Pete, I will not let this go.'

He lets out a heavy sigh. 'I loved you, Alice. I wanted to protect you from him.'

'I never needed your protection, Pete.'

He looks at me. 'The second he gets back, and you start working together, he starts filling your brain with stuff that happened twenty years ago.'

'It's important to me,' I exclaim. 'I have a feeling you're not telling me everything and now I want to know the truth.'

He lets out a sarcastic laugh. 'The truth? Well, the truth is that I loved you too much, Alice. From the moment we first met in nursery I've always loved you. I can still see you with your long red hair, blue eyes and cute smile asking me to play on the climbing frame with you. In primary school I used to fight any boy who wanted to sit next to you. When Noah told me he'd asked you to be his girlfriend, I hated him. My so-called best friend was going out with the girl I'd spent years loving.'

'Did Noah know you liked me?'

Pete shook his head. 'I only had to look at Noah with his angel-like blond hair and tanned face to know who you were going to choose. You were always going to choose him over me. I hated those years you and Noah were dating. Having to go to school every day and seeing you with him. Listening to Frankie day in, day out telling me how great you and Noah are. The day Noah left for Ireland, I knew he wasn't coming back. I'd spent years wanting you to be mine.' Pete studies the tennis ball. 'Noah broke you into a million tiny pieces, Alice, and I was the one who put you back together.'

My heart is pounding against my chest. 'But you lied to me?'

He lets the ball drop. 'Alice, it doesn't matter. The past is gone now. I lied to protect you from Noah.'

'If you'd have been truthful and told me you were still in contact with Noah, I could have...' I stop as Pete's glaring at me.

'What, Alice? You could have left me again for Noah?'

'Mummy,' Lucas rushes into the kitchen, 'can I have tea?'

Pete ruffles Lucas's hair. 'This is who we should be focusing on, Alice. Our son.'

A car door slams. Dad is returning. His eyes light up as soon as he sees Pete in the doorway.

'What a nice surprise,' gushes Dad, giving Pete a hug.

Pete grins. 'Guess who has been filling your daughter's head with nonsense, Brian?'

My neck and shoulders stiffen.

Dad's smile fades. He looks at me. 'Alice, I was worried this would happen.'

Pete lifts a squealing Lucas up. 'Brian, I told her to stop listening to Noah and start focusing on this little guy.'

Dad beams with pride at Pete and Lucas. 'Such a wonderful sight. You three make a wonderful family.' Emotion and anger are rising in me. I disappear upstairs as Dad says, 'Don't you agree, Alice?'

Anger at Pete for lying to me and at Dad for continuing to view Pete as some sort of hero bubbles away inside as I lie down on my camp bed. Closing my eyes I also feel a twang of sadness. Dad would never be like that with Noah. He would never rush to welcome Noah like he does Pete.

'Alice,' calls Dad. 'Come down here, I have news.'

Hauling myself up I walk downstairs to find Pete sat on the sofa grinning. Dad rushes over to me with his phone. 'Pete has been helping me persuade Scott to pay us back some of the money we lost with the wedding cancellation.'

'What?' I gasp, looking at Dad and Pete.

Dad goes to stand by the sofa and places his hand on Pete's shoulder. 'Pete has been crafting my emails to Scott. Well, Scott has just emailed to say he's transferred a sum of money to my bank account.'

'Scott told me he never had any money.'

Pete nods. 'He might not have any money, but the point is it wasn't fair for your father to pick up the costs when Scott was the one who caused the cancellation.'

Dad positions his glasses on his nose and stares at his phone. 'The money is in my account.'

'Does it help with the loan, Dad?'

He nods. 'It's a sizeable amount and yes it does help. His mother stepped in to help him out. I want to transfer some to you, Alice.'

'Why?'

'You lost money too, thanks to Scott. I am sending you some now.' He points to the pile of rental brochures on the coffee table. The properties are all within a stone's throw from Pete's house. 'It's enough for a rental deposit on a flat or a cottage.'

Pete rises and puts his arm around Dad. 'Brian, I am so pleased.'

Dad beams. 'I can't thank you enough, Pete.'

Once Pete goes home, I make tea for Lucas and Dad. As I put Dad's plate down in front of him, he looks up at me. 'Pete is a good man, Alice. He told me he wants you and Lucas to be a family again.'

Every muscle in my body tightens. 'Dad, I don't love Pete.'

My father shakes his head with disapproval. 'That upsets me, Alice.'

CHAPTER TWENTY-SIX

I t's the day of Donna and Jon's wedding reception. I have come to the café early to decorate. My head is crammed full of thoughts from last night, Pete's admission that he disliked Noah for taking me away from him; Pete helping Dad to get money from Scott; and Dad's face when I told him I didn't love Pete. After tea Lucas and I went upstairs as I didn't feel comfortable sat downstairs with Dad.

Ava knocks on the café door and I look up with surprise. 'Your shift doesn't start for another hour.'

She grins and comes in. 'I thought you'd need a hand, so I set my alarm for early.'

'Okay, well do you want to pump up the gold balloons?' Ava nods and heads toward the balloon pump.

'How are you, Ava?'

'Good, even though we were all out last night.' She giggles. 'It got a bit messy, and we all ended up on the beach after drinking too much cider.'

'I remember those days,' I say, with a knowing smile. 'Do you not have a hangover?'

Ava shook her head. 'I feel fine.'

I look at her face which is glowing, her two bright eyes and her hair which is neatly styled into two plaits. She's wearing a smart white shirt which has been ironed and a black skirt. I recall how rough I felt the day after drinks at Phoebe's. 'You wait till you're older. The other night I had some wine with friends. I felt so rough the next day and the day after. It wasn't helped by my little boy having a tummy bug at the same time.'

Ava's eyebrows shot up her forehead. 'I'm so glad I am seventeen and don't have kids.'

We both laugh. 'Listen, how are you and Will now?'

Ava grins. 'On Tuesday we came out of our respective friendship zones.'

'That's great – so are you together now?'

She playfully rolls her eyes. 'Alice, it's so uncool to say things like, "Are you together now?" No one likes a label. Will and I have gone back to our friendship zones for now. We might wander out of them again on Saturday.'

'That sounds stressful.'

Ava laughs. 'It's very chill. Becoming boyfriend and girlfriend is way more stressful.'

'Alice,' she says, after she's pumped up several balloons. 'You don't know anyone who is looking to rent a flat?'

'No – why?'

'My parents have a little flat above the ice-cream parlour on the seafront and they are struggling to find someone to rent it. Mum suggested I speak to you as you might know someone.'

'What's it like? The flat?'

Ava beamed. 'It's lovely. Two bedrooms. If you look out of the living room window you can see the beach and the sea.'

'Oh, wow, it sounds fabulous. I'll mention it to a few people.'

Noah has arrived. He looks so handsome in a blue fitted shirt and smart beige trousers. While Ava is busy sweeping outside the café, Noah and I are having a cuddle behind the counter. I am losing myself in his beautiful aftershave which is a delicious aroma of lemon and wood pines.

'Hello,' he whispers making a huge smile spread across my face. I close my eyes as he presses his lips against mine. We engage in a slow and lingering kiss. His lips are soft, warm, and inviting. 'You look gorgeous, Alice,' he says, admiring my pink dress. 'It's a shame we have to work today, and we can't go down to the beach.'

When Ava comes back inside, Noah and I break away. We all get to work on making The Little Love Café ready for its first wedding reception.

As I move tables and chairs so that I can mop the floor I think about the flat Ava mentioned. Somewhere like that would be perfect for Lucas and me, plus it would give Dad and me some much-needed space.

Pam hurries into the café carrying a huge cake box. 'Your cupcakes are here. Do you want a peek?'

We all gather around a table, and she opens the box. 'Alice, my baker followed your instructions.'

The two-tone pink and cream vanilla cupcakes in a rose design look fabulous. 'Pam, they look great.'

Ava lets out a little coo. 'They're so pretty and they are the same pink as The Little Love Café.'

I follow Pam out to the back of the café. Her beautiful silvery hair is busy trying to escape the clip which is holding it up. 'How are you, Pam?'

She rubs her forehead. 'Still stressed. Doctor says my blood pressure is sky high. It's all my ex-husband's fault.'

'Why is that?'

'I went into this cake wholesale business with him when we first met. Now we've split up and I must rely on him for the baking. Neither of us can stand each other.' She looks at me. 'You're Brian's daughter – aren't you?'

'You know my dad?'

She smiles. 'Sure do. I worked in his bakery. His cakes were always out of this world. Much better than my ex-husband's.' She giggles. 'I never said that.'

'Please take care, Pam.'

'I'll be fine.'

Once Pam has left, I walk over to where Ava is hanging up balloons. 'Ava, I would be interested in your parents' flat.'

'Great,' gushes Ava, taking out her phone. 'Let me message Mum. She will be pleased. Sunny, the guy who works at the ice-cream parlour, has been renting it but he's moving out today. He's got a job in Cornwall.' She taps something into her phone.

'Sunny is moving away?'

She nods. 'Lilly looked upset at the youth club last night.'

Her phone vibrates. 'Mum says are you free to look around it tomorrow? I can bring the key to work and show you during a break.'

'That sounds like a plan. I better try and see Lilly.'

The wedding reception has gone to plan. Noah, Ava, and I make a great team. I thought seeing Donna in my wedding dress would have brought back my old emotions but to my surprise I have felt nothing but pride and happiness at seeing it on her. Her children were angelic and made their parents proud. We did a round of photos in the café and then everyone trooped outside for beach pictures.

As happy guests leave, Donna throws her arms around me and squeals. 'Thank you, Alice.'

Her beaming smile fills me with a warm glow. 'You look

amazing in the dress too and I can't believe how well it has gone.'

She grins. 'I loved how our wedding reception food was rose cupcakes served with coffee, tea and hot chocolate.'

Jon, Donna's new husband, wanders over. 'My beautiful wife and I are so grateful for what you've done for us, Alice. We can't thank you enough.'

'It was a pleasure. You've brought so much love and laughter to this place today.'

Donna gives me a playful nudge. 'Every one of our guests has promised to deluge social media with Little Love Café selfies.'

'That was my fee,' I say, with an ear-to-smile.

@DonnaThomas: Today we got married and had a wonderful wedding reception in The Little Love Café. If you read my blog you will know about my fight against cancer and the financial hardship it has brought upon my family. We couldn't afford a big wedding, but we wanted something special. The Little Love Café answered all our prayers by letting us use their beautiful café for free.

The Little Love Café's social media lights up as Donna's followers like, love and share her post. Her guests also tag the café into their wedding reception selfies.

After dinner I work late to make sure all the selfies of the café are shared, and I reply to all comments. Using the café as a wedding reception venue worked as the shots of the happy couple standing in front of the golden beach and coastline are stunning.

I climb into my camp bed feeling proud of what The Little Love Café achieved today.

CHAPTER TWENTY-SEVEN

A va leads the way to the flat above the ice-cream parlour. We go up the stairs at the side of the old Victorian house and make our way to the top.

She opens the door to the flat and we walk through a little hallway to the living room that has been painted in a soft blue. Against one wall is a cream sofa and a set of coffee tables. Shelves line the opposite walls and below is polished wooden flooring. A giant window floods the room with light. The flat looks out onto the promenade, the beach, and the shimmery blue sea. There are two spacious double bedrooms both with sea views. The shower is encased in a cute sunflower yellow wooden beach hut and a little kitchen presides at the end of the living room. It has gleaming new white cupboards and a breakfast diner table.

A little burst of excitement rockets across my chest. 'Ava, this would be perfect for me and Lucas.'

'Well, Mum says it's yours if you want it.'

I stand at the living room window. The beach today is dotted with young families playing frisbee and football. If I peer to the right, I can see the winding coastline and the tall grey cliffs. If I peer to the left, I can see the pink café at the end of the beach.

'Oh, Ava, I love it. Tell your mum I need to talk to her about the contract and stuff.'

On the way out I catch sight of Lilly in the ice-cream parlour looking gloomy. 'Ava, I'll meet you back at the café. I need to see Lilly.'

'Hey, Lilly,' I say, as I walk into Blue Cove Bay's ice-cream parlour. Inside the walls are painted sunshine yellow and adorned with photos of delicious iced treats. It's one of Lucas's favourite places. He will be over the moon to find out we will be living above it.

In the summer it is always full of tourists and holidaymakers clutching beach towels, sun hats and small children in swimming costumes. They prop their inflatables up against the counter whilst they choose their perfect ice cream. I survey the contents of the freezer, the selection of ice creams in a multitude of flavours from salted caramel to hazelnut to blueberry muffin. When I was young, I used to spend ages deciding my flavour, which would always make Frankie impatient. He knew his scoop combination hours before we entered the parlour.

'Sunny's gone, Alice,' Lilly says, wiping a damp cheek. 'There was a reason why we didn't get together at the painting night. He was getting ready to leave Blue Cove Bay.'

I went over to where she was sat. 'What did he say?'

'He says he needs to go experience the world,' she sobs. 'He says we are young and have our lives ahead of us.'

'Did you tell him about how you feel?'

She nods. 'He doesn't feel the same way about me.'

Pulling Lilly into a hug I let her cry on my shoulder.

She says, 'I have loved him from afar for years, Alice. All through school and after we left. We worked in here together, scooping out ice cream, flirting over chocolate flakes, sharing secret jokes about our ice-cream customers and squirting each other with strawberry sauce. Now I feel like someone is scooping out my heart.' She grabs a handful of napkins and wipes her face. 'You got over heartbreak, Alice. What's your advice?'

Half of me wants to laugh and tell her that I would be lying if I said I got over heartbreak, but I sense she doesn't need to hear that. Before I can think of something sensible to say, Lilly grabs her phone. 'I'm going to message Elliot, Sunny's best mate. I can go out with him and—'

I see myself in her all those years ago, turning to Pete to make Noah jealous. The memory of forcing myself to fancy Pete comes rushing back to me. Hot on the heels of this one is how when he kissed me, I always imagined he was Noah. It wasn't a great idea of mine. Maybe unconsciously I knew Pete fancied me and I played on that. My mind goes back to when Lucas had just been born. He was wrapped in a towel and in my arms. I recalled looking down at him and thinking about Noah, not Pete. Guilt wraps itself around me. Instinctively I place my hand over Lilly's phone screen. 'This is my advice: don't contact Elliot.'

Lilly stares at me. 'What? You don't know Elliot.'

'I don't know Elliot, but I know about revenge. After Noah left for Ireland, I started dating his best friend. That was my revenge. At first it felt fine but over time all my anger and sadness about Noah came out. His best friend and I argued all the time. We never stopped fighting. Looking back now that was all my unresolved anger spilling out. Revenge feels like a good thing to do at the time, but you are setting you both up for pain and misery.'

Lilly shakes her head. 'Elliot has always had a thing for me...'

I snatch her phone away. 'You're not listening to me, Lilly. I ended up having a child with Noah's best friend. That was how far revenge took me. I love my little boy to bits but when he was born it was Noah I thought about and not his dad. I still feel guilty about that.'

She's staring at me.

Tears rush to my eyes, and I blink them away. I hand her phone back to her. 'Don't let revenge eat you up inside. Give yourself time to heal but then focus on your life.'

'What about Sunny?'

'Let him go for now,' I say, 'if it's meant to be he'll come back.'

She hangs her head. 'I can't carry on working here as it reminds me of Sunny.'

'Maybe you need a change?'

She runs her hands over the counter. 'The owner of this place has another ice-cream parlour in Brighton. It needs a manager, and the owner has suggested I do it.'

'Lilly, that's great. Go do it. Get out of Blue Cove Bay and make some new memories.'

She shrugs. 'I don't know. I'll think about it.'

The café is insanely busy for a Saturday when I return from consoling Lilly. I don't have time to tell Noah about the flat until we are half an hour away from closing. His face lights up. 'Alice, that's amazing. When are you going to tell your dad?'

'Sooner the better. He can't say anything as he's been leaving rental property adverts around for days. Dad's house is small, and I think he will like his peace and quiet back.'

'Have you thought anymore about Pete?' Earlier I'd told Noah about what had happened last night with Pete and how he'd admitted lying to me about staying in contact with Noah.

'I need to talk to him again.'

Noah nodded. 'I've been doing some thinking about what happened. I remember getting your email the day after I'd arrived in Ireland. I tried to call Pete as breaking up was the last thing I wanted, but his dad said he was out or something.'

'Pete must have called me the day after as I remember him confirming what you had said in your email. I got angry, shut down my email account and created a new one so you couldn't contact me. I remember phoning Pete back to give him my new email address. A bit dramatic, I know, but I was heartbroken and sixteen.'

I scratched my head. 'Pete came over to my house after you'd left on that Sunday as I remember as we listened to CDs in my room, and I was upset.'

Noah nibbled on his thumbnail. 'I could be wrong but hear me out. Would Pete have been able to access your email back then?'

I thought back to when I was a teenager and the old house layout. 'I used Dad's computer back then. It was always turned on in his study. Dad and I both had MSN email and it was always on...' I stare at Noah. 'Do you think Pete sent that email pretending to be me?'

'Look, we know from what he told you last night he was jealous of me and was prepared to lie to you about staying in contact with me.'

I clamp my hand over my forehead. 'I gave Pete my letters to post. Oh God, I need to speak to him.'

CHAPTER TWENTY-EIGHT

'You're moving out?' Dad seems shocked. He's put down his knife and fork to stare at me. It's Sunday and I've cooked his favourite roast chicken dinner with crunchy roast potatoes, veg and thick gravy. Lucas has gone to Phoebe's house to play with Flynn, which has given me some time to speak to Dad. Lucas assured me as we got out of the car that he would not go anywhere near Phoebe's purse or pick his nose.

'Yes, Lucas and I will be moving into our new flat on Friday.'

'Oh, I see,' mutters Dad. 'Can I ask where?'

'The flat above the ice-cream parlour.'

He rubs his forehead. 'Why have you not looked at those properties I showed you?'

'Dad, I can make my own decisions on where Lucas and I will live.'

An awkward silence descends upon the table. I push a piece of potato around my plate and wait for the inevitable Pete comment.

'Lucas would have loved to live near his father, Alice.'

Irritation bubbles inside of me. I drop my fork, sending it clattering across my plate and look across at Dad. 'How many times do I have to tell you, Dad? Pete and I are not getting back together.'

Dad looks taken aback. He takes out his handkerchief and dabs his sweaty brow. 'I'm sorry, Alice. I found what happened with your wedding quite shocking and I want you and Lucas to have some stability. To me, Pete is...'

'Dad, please stop bringing up Pete at every opportunity,' I snap. 'If you must know I feel guilty about not loving Pete. Every night when I say goodnight to Lucas I silently apologise to him for not loving his father. I don't love Pete and I never...' I pause. 'I never have loved him.'

Dad lets out a heavy sigh and pushes his plate away. 'Is this about Noah Coombes? Because if it is, I am going to be very cross.'

'Listen to yourself,' I say in a loud voice. 'I am thirty-six years old and you're still trying to tell me who I should and shouldn't love. Dad, I can make my own decisions.'

Dad lets out a wail of frustration. 'He is not welcome in this house, Alice.'

'Why do you dislike him so much? You never told me why you and Noah's father fell out.'

'That family have driven a wedge through us, Alice.' Dad rises from his chair. 'I've lost my appetite.'

I follow him into the living room. 'What did Dave Coombes do?'

'Leave me alone, Alice,' Dad says, before marching over to the mantelpiece. 'I don't want to talk about it.'

Returning to the table I clear away, wash up and put everything away. When I enter the living room Dad is watching an old *Antiques Roadshow*. He looks up at me. 'I think you moving out is a good idea, Alice.'

'Yes, I agree.'

He nods. 'We all need some space to think and collect our thoughts.'

I go upstairs and lie on the camp bed. Agitation at Dad is nibbling away at me. I stare up at the ceiling. This feels like I am fifteen again, lying on my bed after arguing with Dad over Noah. I don't want to move out and my relationship with Dad to deteriorate as Noah and I are getting close again.

Taking out my phone I decide to distract myself with Facebook by reading about other people having fun.

Rose has tagged me into a post on Facebook. The caption reads, 'Happy days.' It's a photo from years ago of Mum, Rose, Frankie, and me outside their house. Frankie's wonky fringe makes me smile. He'd asked me to cut it in the bathroom as he believed it was too long. To this day I still don't know why he asked nine-year-old me to grab the kitchen scissors and hack away. Rose screamed when she saw it. As it was the summer holidays and Frankie liked his lopsided fringe, she left it a few weeks before marching him down to the barbers.

My eyes linger on Mum and Rose. Their heads are pressed together, Rose is laughing into the camera, and both are clutching glasses of wine. They were the best of friends. An idea pops into my head. Rose is probably the only person in the world who knows what happened between Dad and Dave Coombes. If I am to sort this mess out with Noah and Dad, I need to know what happened.

I message Frankie to ask him how things are, how Rose is coping with her treatment and to say that I need to speak to Rose.

Later, I send another text to Pete asking him to call me. After what Noah told me in the café, I am now certain Pete is connected to that email Noah received and to my missing letters. Pete has been ignoring my texts and voicemails. Earlier I took Bean for an extra-long dog walk to Pete's house. His Golf wasn't parked in his drive and all his windows were shut.

He doesn't reply to my text.

CHAPTER TWENTY-NINE

It's Tuesday and I am back at work after my day off. Dad and I have barely spoken, and Pete still hasn't replied to my texts. A teenage girl with poker straight, chestnut brown hair and amazing winged eyeliner taps me on the arm as I hurry past clutching empty coffee cups. 'Do you have free wifi here?'

'Yes,' I say, pointing to the password printed on the back of the menu.

Grinning she taps it into her phone and then turns back to me. 'I am a YouTuber. Do you mind if I film in here?'

Her boyfriend grins. 'You're seriously going to vlog our date, then?'

She nods. 'I told my followers last night I was coming here, and I was inundated with people getting excited about us two having a coffee date in a romance-themed café.'

'Isn't that a bit odd?' her boyfriend asks. 'You're filming our date?'

'I think it's going to be fun. You must improve your topics of date conversation though, as last week's discussion on what you ate in your break at work will not go down well; nor will your other topic about which flavour Pot Noodle you prefer.'

'So, are you saying all of your twelve thousand followers will be watching our date?'

She nods and her boyfriend shakes his head.

I get excited about having YouTubers like this girl interested in The Little Love Café. This is exactly what we need. 'Can you use The Little Love Café hashtag?'

As I return to the counter, I spot Pete casually wandering into the café. Irritation bubbles inside my stomach and my shoulders and neck stiffen. He looks up and smiles. Taking him by the elbow I steer him towards one of the empty booths. Noah casts me a worried look as I glance back at him.

'Why haven't you text me back, Pete?' I hiss.

Yawning, he scratches his mass of black curls and smiles. 'I was on a stag do. What do you want?'

Blood is rushing past my ears and my mind wheels out the memory of Noah telling me about the email he received from me all those years ago. Through gritted teeth I hiss, 'Did you send an email to Noah pretending to be me when he left?'

Pete's smile evaporates. In a fraction of a second, I know he's guilty. I've looked into those blue eyes of his so many times. He used to try to lie about his secret casino trips and spending money we didn't have.

'I– umm... I–' he stammers.

'You lied, Pete. You sent that email pretending to me – didn't you?'

He stares at me. 'I didn't, Alice.'

Someone has turned up the heat on my cheeks. They are flame hot and my eyes are stinging. Emotion and anger are rising inside of me. 'You sent that email, and you didn't post my letters to Noah – did you?'

Pete squirms and fidgets in his seat. He remains silent and looks away.

My angry voice is loud and shrill. 'You lied, Pete. You told Noah I didn't want to go out with him.'

Pete's eyes darken. 'I have always loved you, Alice. When he came to live in Blue Cove Bay, he stole you from me.'

Out of the corner of my eye I can see the teenage YouTuber holding up her phone at Pete and me. 'Got to film this drama,' she says. 'This is much more interesting than our date.'

Pete sits up and runs a hand through his hair. 'The past has gone now, Alice. I can't believe you are publicly embarrassing me over something that happened twenty years ago.'

'Your lies ruined my life, Pete.'

He rises from the booth. 'I saved you from a lifetime of heartbreak.'

I stare at him face on. 'That's a joke, Pete. You gambled away all our money; you never helped me with our baby son; and then when I came to my senses, you stormed off to London for two years.'

His eyes flash with anger. 'You used me to get back at HIM.'

The Little Love Café has quietened. Everyone's gaze has followed Pete's finger, which points at Noah.

'You never sent my letters – did you?'

He laughs. 'I shoved them in the bin.'

Everyone gasps and rage like hot lava ripples through me. 'Get out of this café, Pete.'

To my horror Pete turns to Noah. 'Thanks for stealing the love of my life. I don't suppose you've told her about those rumours back then regarding your father and *her* mother.' He lets out a sarcastic laugh and turns to me. 'Goodbye, Alice. Say hello to Brian for me.'

Pete walks out as Noah rushes out from behind the counter. He guides me out the back of the café as everyone around us returns to their conversations. I am shell-shocked. In my head all I can hear is Pete saying *those rumours.*

Wrapping his arms around me, Noah pulls me to him. 'We're going to get to the bottom of this,' he whispers.

I pull away from him. 'Did you know about these rumours?'

He flicks his eyes to the floor. 'I did but I never believed them.'

'You never told me?' I take a step back in shock.

Noah runs his hand through his hair. 'I asked my father about them, and he said nothing happened between him and your mum.' He tries to stroke my cheek, but I bat his hand away. 'Noah, you never told me what people were saying about my mum.'

'Alice, it was harmful gossip.'

I take off my apron. 'I need some fresh air.'

I walk up to the promenade and sit on a bench. My head is a swirling mass of thoughts. Were these rumours why Dad took a dislike to Noah? Why had Noah not told me? I find a gang of white-tipped waves to focus on. They race towards the shore as cackling seagulls cheer them on.

Someone comes to sit beside me. I look up and see Esme. Without warning, hot, salty tears spill over my cheeks and she puts her arms around me. Once I have let all my frustration and anger spill out of me, I tell Esme everything. She listens and strokes my hand.

'You need to speak to your dad, Alice.' She sighs. 'I never heard any of these rumours if that makes any difference.'

'I'm angry at Noah for not telling me.'

'He made a mistake in not telling you, but he probably didn't want to believe the rumours either. I mean they were about his father. He also probably knew how much you loved your mum.'

I nod and wipe my wet cheeks.

'Your mum was an angel, Alice,' says Esme. 'She once shouted at Joy for being nasty to me.'

I look at her and she grins. 'Yes, that's true. Joy was forcing me to jump off the old pier into the sea and I didn't want to. Your mother came to my rescue.'

'I'm glad Mum helped you. Thanks, Esme.'

She places her hand over mine. 'Don't be mad at Noah.'

He's serving a couple on table three when I enter the café. When he's finished, he comes over with a sheepish look to his face. 'Alice, I'm sorry,' he says. 'I should have told you. The thing is, those rumours were about my own father too, and I chose to ignore them once he assured me nothing had happened between him and your mum. He did say that she had become a good friend to him, and they always shared a joke or two when they were on a long hike. I also used to sit by you on our rock and I could tell you felt close to your mum by the cliffs. You would talk so much about her and your father that I didn't want to hurt you with cruel small-town gossip.'

Leaning my head against his shoulder I allow his arm to circle my waist. 'It's okay, I understand.'

'You mean a lot to me, Alice. You always have.'

I look up at him and he leans over and kisses me.

We have a half an hour left until closing time. I'm in a booth on my own struggling to process the events of today. My head feels like a tornado has passed through it, leaving an array of havoc and chaos.

Reaching for my phone, I log on to The Little Love Café's Facebook account and groan. A few customers from today have already left comments with the words, *romantic drama in the #LittleLoveCafé*. One person has commented to say:

Shouldn't we be using the new Heartbreak Café name?

It has already got several likes.

A Rocco Reid fan, has posted:

Why are we shocked to hear this? You can only order a cup of misery and sadness at the #LittleLoveCafé. They are probably still busy sweeping up Lil Tia's broken heart.

This has garnered an eye-watering number of likes.

A new notification appears and my heart stops. A customer has added a link to a Matilda's Life YouTube video and today's post – *Heartbreak at The Little Love Café* – *check out my new post #LittleLoveCafé*. Matilda's video opens and I am stood screaming at Pete. All my hard work at turning public opinion around has been a waste of time. My chest aches as I imagine Frankie seeing this. I delete the comment and the link and pray Frankie has not seen it.

CHAPTER THIRTY

Frankie has his face in his hands and talks through the gaps between his fingers when the video call connects. 'Just tell me everything, Alice.'

I've stayed late in the café to speak to Frankie in private. Noah left half an hour ago.

'Oh God, I am so sorry. Please don't fire me.' My heart is hammering against my ribcage. This is the conversation I have been dreading. 'Pete made me so angry. Please, Frankie, I promise to–'

He lifts his reddened face at the camera. 'Let me stop you there. Can we talk about what has been going on because when I checked the other day, everything was great. You'd managed to silence the naysayers; the Rocco Reid drama had calmed down and the wedding reception looked stunning. Once again, I find myself reaching for those stomach settlers as some YouTuber has posted a shocking video of you and Pete yelling at each other.'

'Oh God,' I cry, placing my face in my hands. 'This is all my fault.'

'Alice,' snaps Frankie. 'When are you going to learn to control your emotions?'

I shake my head.

'Did you know she was filming in the café?'

I nod. 'She asked me if she could film.'

Frankie lets out what can only be described as a deafening howl. 'Alice, the next time a YouTuber comes into my café, take your arguments outside. Even Mum saw the clip and she said, "It's like watching a soap opera, Frankie." I had to remind her that I own that bloody café and I don't expect to see you and Pete auditioning for *Eastenders*.'

He takes a drink of water and I want the ground to open and swallow me whole.

'Tell me what's been going on,' Frankie says, after calming down.

Taking a deep breath, I tell him everything; how Noah and I have learnt to work together, how I ran my promotion, how I turned around the Donna and Jon situation and how Noah and I have grown close. I also tell him about Dad, Pete, and the rumours.

Frankie's silent for a few moments and then turns to whisper something to his mum in the background. Rose comes into view. Nausea swirls around in my belly as Frankie gets up to put his arm over her shoulders. He lets her have his chair. My guilt at causing him stress over The Little Love Café gets so tight I can hardly breathe.

Rose smiles. 'Hello, Alice.'

'Hey, Rose.' It's so nice to see her. 'How's life with Frankie nursing you?'

'He's brilliant, Alice. I am so glad he was able to come out here and support me. Your YouTube clip caused much debate here.' Her smile fades. 'I watched the clip and Pete said some hurtful things. I shouldn't be the one telling you about the rumours as your father should be doing this. It will upset you, Alice, and I'm sorry.'

Fighting the urge to shout about how everyone should stop treating me like a child I regain my composure.

'I'm sorry about keeping this from you.' She takes a deep breath. 'I want you to know that the reason I didn't say anything was that I never believed what your dad claimed. One of the reasons why I moved back to Sydney was because of your father.'

'What?' I notice Frankie is standing behind Rose.

She takes a sip of water. 'I didn't believe Brian. Julie was my best mate. I knew her years before she met Brian. I knew my best mate more than he did. She would *not* have had an affair with Dave Coombes.'

'An affair with Noah's Dad – what?' My shoulders and neck feel like someone has inserted a rod of iron inside them.

'Your father started to overthink the rumours after your mum died.' Rose takes a sip of water. 'People said it was grief playing with his mind. He found some photos of your mum and Dave Coombes sat together during a hike. They looked close and then at the wedding reception he got drunk and confronted him. To Dave's credit, he denied it. I moved to Sydney because I couldn't believe what Brian was saying. It hurt me that he believed all that gossip, so I decided to move away.'

'Really?'

Rose nods her head. 'Brian and I have been mates for years. He's a good man but I think he's wrong.'

My response shoots out without a second thought. 'Mum wouldn't have had an affair with Dave Coombes. She loved Dad; I know she did.' My childhood memories are of her cuddled up to Dad on the sofa, she and Dad watching her beloved *Star Trek* videos and coming into the kitchen to see her kissing Dad. My heart is hammering away inside my chest.

'Alice, look at me,' urges Rose. 'Your mum and Dave Coombes having an affair was a ridiculous rumour. She and

Dave were close, but your mum would never have cheated on your father. If she had, I would have had a stern word with her. Believe me. I know what it's like to be on the receiving end of that.'

'Why did Dad believe the rumour then?'

Rose sighs. 'Your mum loved hiking and she did loads of things with the hiking club. She was always out with them on a Saturday.'

'I remember watching her pull on her boots when I was younger,' I say. 'She used to make me laugh by saying they were stinky. Every Saturday Dad and I would wave her off.'

Rose smiles.

'Even as a child I could feel Mum's excitement on the morning of one of her walks. She'd be laughing as Dad poured her tea into a flask and would always moan about how she had packed her rucksack.'

Rose leans closer to the screen. 'Dave Coombes joined the hiking club, and they became friends. He was lonely and needed someone to listen to. Noah's mum left him for his best mate and it really cut him up. I think he'd had a battle with booze and hiking was his way of dealing with that.'

She pauses and takes a breath. 'Dave Coombes was an attractive man back then. He had a Harrison Ford look about him; tall, well built, square faced and wavy brown hair. Dave had quite a few admirers in Blue Cove Bay.'

I gesture for her to continue.

'What you need to understand, Alice, is that your father has never had much confidence. When we were all teenagers, he was the shy one. Your mum made the first move with their relationship and asked him out, which was a big thing back then. I don't think he'd had many girlfriends. After they got married Brian would always joke and say that your mum could have done better.'

She takes a sip of water and I recall the old photos of Mum and Dad in the family albums. Dad would always be at the back of any gathering and if there was one of him and Mum, he would always stand behind her. I never picked up on Dad not having much confidence.

Rose continues. 'Your father used to get upset at hearing she'd been walking with Dave. Your parents had a series of rows and there were a few occasions where your mum ended up sleeping in my spare room.'

'I never knew this.'

'They made friends the next day but talking about the hiking club became difficult for your mum.' Rose fidgets in her chair. 'It got to the point where she chose not to mention Dave being at hiking club and if Brian asked her whether Dave had been there, she lied and said he'd stopped going. She claimed it wasn't worth the hassle. Looking back, she should have talked to your father about his insecurities, I think your dad assumed Dave had left the hiking club. But Dave hadn't left.'

An uncomfortable feeling passes over me.

Rose takes another sip of water. 'Your dad also has a lot of guilt over not being with your mum when she died. He's very protective – which I am sure you know. Anyway, on the day she died, your dad didn't want her to go hiking. He claimed the conditions were bad. Your mum loved an adventure, and she loved difficult hikes. Brian told me she'd shrugged off his worries and walked off telling him she'd see him later.'

I sense Rose is building up to something as she keeps wetting her lips. 'Dave Coombes was with your mum when she died on the coastal path.'

Noah's dad was with Mum in her final moments. 'But I thought she was with her hiking club when she slipped?'

Rose nods. 'She was with her hiking club and there are few

in the town who were there. The trouble was that Dave was there too. Your mum died in Dave's arms.'

'Mum died in Noah's dad's arms?' Tears rush to my eyes, and I blink them away.

'Your father was told this and he took it badly,' sighs Rose. 'He thought Dave had left the hiking club. He claimed Julie had been lying to cover up their affair. I don't know whether it was shock or grief, but your dad became obsessed with the rumour that before she died, your mum and Dave were having an affair. He confronted Dave Coombes at a wedding reception, and you know how that ended. All this negativity and fear has turned Brian into a different person. I spent years trying to convince him Julie would not have been unfaithful. This is why Brian hated the Coombes family so much.'

'This is why he's getting stressed about Noah being back.'

Rose nods. 'He's scared, Alice. He's been afraid of you knowing the truth for years. Seeing you with Noah has reawakened all that bad stuff.'

'Thank you for telling me, Rose.'

She shakes her head. 'I shouldn't be the one telling you this. I'm sorry it got to this.'

'I appreciate you telling me.'

Frankie gets back in his chair. 'Look, Alice, you've been through a lot. I am not going to fire you. I have messaged this Matilda and asked her to take down the YouTube video. Even though you deleted it on Facebook, the link has appeared on Instagram and X.

'Thanks, Frankie.'

'You look like you need a glass of wine. Before I go, how is everyone in Blue Cove Bay? Any local drama I should be aware of?'

'Joy is selling the gift shop. Wants to move to North Devon.'

Frankie's eyes widen. 'How's Esme taken this?'

'She doesn't want to go and has started standing up to Joy.'

He scratches his stubble-coated chin. 'Esme has spent years telling us all she's not going to let Joy walk all over her. It never happens.'

'I think you might be surprised to hear she's changing. After all these years I finally think she's going to do the unthinkable and stand up to Joy. I lent her a book which she loved and she got her hair cut into a short bob a few days later. Can you believe that? Esme has cut her hair. It looks amazing. She has also revealed she and Keith from the bookshop have started dating.

Frankie's mouth has fallen open in surprise. 'Blimey, Alice, that's big news. What book did you lend her?'

'*The Approval List* by Celia Black – you know the one...'

He grins. 'The one you read and a week later you asked Pete to leave. A word of advice – do not leave that book around The Little Love Café or I'll come back to no business whatsoever.'

We both smile and it feels like old times again. After ending the call, I get up and spot Noah at the door. In his hand is a bottle of wine. I'm an emotional and snotty mess by the time I unlock the door and let him in. He pulls me into a hug and holds me tight. 'Tell me everything,' he instructs, gesturing me to one of the booths. After removing his jacket, he goes to fetch two Little Love Café mugs and pours us both some wine.

Everything comes out in a snotty, tear-fuelled torrent. After, Noah is silent. He traces the outer edge of his mug with his thumb. 'I didn't know she died in Dad's arms.'

'Nor did I.'

Noah looks shocked. He takes my hand. 'Alice, listen to me. I need to talk to my father about this. Hearing all this is making me uncomfortable. I also need to talk to Becky.'

'Becky?' I gasp.

'Alice, I want to be a part of your life.' He leans over and kisses me. 'I want us to be together, you, me, Lucas... and Batman.'

We both chuckle at his Batman comment.

'I need to go back to Ireland. I want to talk to Dad about what happened all those years ago and I want to tell Becky that I want a divorce.'

'You're leaving me *again*.'

Cupping my face in his hand he whispers, 'I'll be back to meet you down by our rock very soon.'

'How long will you be gone for?' Hot, stinging tears are filling up my eyes.

'You need to believe in me when I say that I *will* be back, Alice. I don't want to live a life full of regrets and what-ifs anymore. You are the one and only person I have ever truly loved.'

Half of me wants to believe him. He's saying things with sincerity, and I must believe in him. The other half of me is slipping into a pit of despair and frustration. What if Becky convinces him they need a second chance? Noah and I might never be together. Maybe we are destined to be apart?

CHAPTER THIRTY-ONE

It's Friday, the day Lucas and I move into our new home above the ice-cream parlour. Noah left for Ireland yesterday. It was an emotional goodbye and I tried not to listen to my brain telling me history was repeating itself. We all know what happened the last time Noah left for Ireland.

We asked Jake, Frankie's boyfriend, if he would help on a temporary basis. Jake agreed as his father was out of hospital and making good progress after his stroke. I have the afternoon off work as Jake is covering for me.

Dad seems to have forgotten about our heated discussion on Sunday and has been helping me take our belongings to the new flat. We have even shared a joke or two about how much stuff I have acquired over the years.

Once I've made up our beds, I pull Lucas into a hug. He giggles and laughs as I tickle him. 'Do you like our new home?'

He nods. 'Can I have an ice cream now?'

Dad chuckles and ruffles Lucas's mop of curls. 'You won't forget Grandpa and Bean, will you?'

Lucas throws himself at Dad. 'No, silly Grandpa.'

Dad goes to the living room window. 'What a fabulous view!'

'It's great, isn't it?' The sea is calm this evening. Waves are taking their time to reach the shore and when they do, they break with little fuss. A few chattering seagulls are circling above, and the orange sun is sitting above the horizon.

Dad nods. 'I bet you'll be glad to not sleep on that old camp bed tonight.'

I laugh. 'It has crossed my mind.'

He looks at me and I feel the urge to ask him about Mum and those rumours. The words are on the tip of my tongue. I want to ask him why he can't talk to me about what happened. I get that I was young when Mum died but there have been lots of occasions since then when we could have sat down and talked. But Noah has advised me not to say anything to Dad until he has talked to his father.

Once Dad has left, Lucas and I have a rummage through my boxes. Lucas squeals with delight after pulling out his favourite game, Hungry Hippos. To celebrate having our own place we have a game which ends with Lucas rolling about in hysterics. After a drink of warm milk, I tuck him up and read him one of his Batman stories. His eyes are closed before I've even finished.

My flat doorbell goes as soon as I sit down on my new sofa. It's Phoebe and Esme clutching several bottles of wine. 'We have to celebrate your new pad,' says Phoebe as she steps inside and plants a soppy kiss on my cheek. 'Congratulations, Alice.'

Esme hugs me. 'This is a new start for you, Alice.'

We troop upstairs and they admire my new living room. 'This is nice,' coos Phoebe. 'In the summer you can sit on your sofa and curtain twitch at all those hunky male surfers.'

Wine poured, Esme and I take the sofa and Phoebe sits on the floor with some of my cushions. 'Your new hair looks amazing,' she says, admiring Esme's chic bob. 'You have the cheekbones I always wanted when I was younger. The ones which give your face definition.'

Esme blushes. 'I never knew my cheekbones existed until I had my hair cut off.'

Phoebe pats me on the knee. 'How are you after your chat with Frankie's mum?'

I'd updated them both on our newly created WhatsApp group chat.

'It's been on my mind and earlier I did want to say something to Dad, but Noah is trying to get the truth out of his father, so I stayed quiet. I didn't know Dad was insecure about Mum and I had no idea they'd been arguing over Dave Coombes.'

Esme puts her arm over my shoulders. 'It must be hard finding out things about your parents' marriage.'

I nibble on my thumbnail. 'I want to believe Mum and Dave Coombes were friends.' We all take a drink and I wonder what Noah will uncover in Ireland. I need to change the subject as I'm feeling anxious. 'So, how's Liam?' I ask Phoebe.

A grin spreads across her face. 'We've stopped shouting at each other.'

'Oh, really?' I say, with a smirk.

She nods. 'The other evening Flynn lost Piggy.'

Esme and I both cast her puzzled expressions. She explains, 'Flynn still loves his comfort blankie, called Piggy. It's a grubby pink blankie, with a smiling pig's face on it and he still won't sleep without it. Even though Flynn assures me he doesn't take Piggy off his bed, Piggy goes missing. That blankie must have a mind of his own and goes missing daily, sometimes hourly. Anyway, the other evening I was taking Martha and Flynn to stay at their dad's, and I had to go into Liam's shop to complain about something before we left. While I am talking to Liam, Flynn drops Piggy on the floor. We leave and then an hour later my ex is having a meltdown on the phone about Piggy being missing.'

'So, what did you do?' I ask.

Phoebe flicks back her brown curly hair. 'I had to phone Liam, and he came to open his shop. He bought his kids too. Anyway, I think he's a decent guy. He showed genuine concern for Piggy and got on his hands and knees to search under his records. I was grateful when he pulled out Piggy from underneath the 'Country & Western' section. He offered me a cuppa once I had returned from taking Piggy over to my ex-partner's house.'

'Did you take up his offer?' I ask.

She grinned. 'He made me a cuppa and we and chatted while his kids played in the shop. He's asked for some advice on how to do newsletters and student promos.'

Esme giggles. 'This sounds promising.'

Phoebe shakes her head. 'Nope. Way out of my league. His late wife must have been a model.'

'But you like him though?' I ask.

She laughs. 'It's hard not to like him, he's so good looking and he's one for making cheeky comments.'

'That's always a sign,' I say, taking a sip of my wine.

Esme nods. 'That's how me and Keith started.'

Phoebe takes a swig of her wine before saying, 'I think romance nowadays is a bit overrated. Don't get me wrong, I love what Frankie has done with The Little Love Café, but men aren't interested in being romantic. They're nothing like the guys in romcom films. I think my ex-partner put me off romance.' She turns to Esme. 'Right, we need an update on Joy. Have you told her yet?'

Esme shakes her head. 'Not yet, but I'm building up to it.'

'We have faith in you,' I say, giving her knee a tap.

Phoebe points to Celia Black's book, *Always You,* the one I bought from her shop a few weeks ago, on my coffee table. 'Did you enjoy it?'

'Loved it,' I gush remembering the final part where the two exes realised they still had feelings for each other. 'Especially the end where he turned to her and said, "It was always you".'

We chat some more, drink our wine, and relax. 'How's the café?' Phoebe asks, refilling my glass.

'Frankie wants me to work hard at turning things around again while Noah is away,' I explain. 'Lucky that YouTuber agreed to take down her video. I feel so bad for Frankie as he doesn't need all my emotions ruining his business.'

Phoebe took out her phone. 'A friend of mine messaged me today. She works at the *Blue Cove Bay Chronicle*. She's seen your café and wanted me to ask whether you've heard about the National Award for the Most Innovative Café?'

'No, I haven't heard about that award. Why?'

'Well, if I send you the link she sent me. I think The Little Love Café could do well.'

A warm bundle of excited energy shoots up my spine. 'Do you really think so?'

'The closing date for submissions is next week and I think the winner is announced early May. If you win, you get national press coverage and I think the owner gets a cash prize.'

Phoebe flashes me her phone to show me the details. 'This competition could give Frankie's café the amazing lift it needs. He can also get some much-needed kudos for coming up with the idea of The Little Love Café. With Rose being so unwell, this is the type of boost he needs right now.'

Esme places her hand on my arm. 'Plus, it will stop you worrying about Noah.'

Phoebe looks at me. 'You're worried about him?'

'I feel like it's history repeating itself. Him going to Ireland and promising to come back.'

'You've got to believe in him, Alice,' says Esme. 'It sounds cheesy, but you are going to have to believe in love.'

Phoebe nods. 'Turning the café around is your version of hiking to Base Camp Everest. That's your mountain.'

CHAPTER THIRTY-TWO

Waking up in the new flat is a different experience. Drifting in through my bedroom window are the sounds of waves barrelling onto the shore, an overexcited dog barking like crazy on the beach, a gang of noisy seagulls, a small child having a tantrum about wanting an ice cream and an exasperated parent telling them the shop's not open yet.

There's no rush as Jake is covering this morning. He was so sweet as he said Lucas and I should have the opportunity to enjoy our new home. I look at my phone. There has been no word from Noah. An uncomfortable feeling takes hold of me. In my head I hear Esme's voice from last night, *You need to believe in love.* I need to believe that Noah will return, and we will finally be together after twenty years of disastrous relationships. It feels easier to say it than do it.

Thoughts about Dad and Mum creep into my mind. What happens if the rumours were true and Noah's dad tells him the unthinkable – that he and my mum did have an affair before she died. My stomach performs a nauseating spin.

'Mummy, can we build a den like we used to do...' Lucas is at the door in his pyjamas. He stops mid-sentence. I know what he wanted to say. Before Scott came along, Lucas and I were always building dens in my bed. We used to have such fun sitting underneath a duvet propped up by my old pogo stick looking at his picture books and giggling with each other. Scott stopped the den building. He said it made a mess of the bedroom and Lucas should make them in his own bed. I stupidly went along with what Scott said.

Scott's not here anymore, I remind myself. This new flat means Lucas and I can go back to our fantastic world of bed dens. 'Let's build a den, Lucas.'

He comes racing in and before long, he and I are building a den, comprising of my duvet cover, all our pillows and a clothes airer to give it height. Once it is finished, he goes to fetch a Batman book and we sit inside and read it together.

After we have showered and changed Lucas helps me unpack more stuff from the many boxes I'd stored at Dad's house. A few were from my time living with Scott. My mind drifts back to when I'd first met Scott on a dating app.

Lucas was still little and we were living in a flat above one of the clothes shops in town. Pete and I had broken up for good and I found myself looking for love again. A girl I used to work with in Mick's old beach café recommended a dating app she'd met her fiancé on.

Scott was handsome with sun-kissed blonde hair, a golden tan and an eye-watering athletic figure. Looking back, he reminded me of Noah. Initially I liked the idea of a long-distance romance. After a whirlwind romance, where one of us would go see the other at weekends, I was whisked away for a romantic weekend, and Scott asked if Lucas and I would go live with him in Surrey. Days later, Lucas and I moved into Scott's fancy three-bedroomed house on the posh housing estate. He proposed two months later.

In one of the boxes is Lucas's old school uniform from the

primary school he went to when we lived with Scott. Lucas and Scott never bonded. I used to put that down to Lucas being ill so much. From the day we moved into Scott's house; Lucas caught every bug imaginable. He was always ill and missed a lot of school. Every germ made a beeline for him: chicken pox, chest infections, a rampaging stomach bug, a persistent cough, and several heavy colds.

Holding up the school jumper, I look over at Lucas who is climbing over our new sofa. Since returning to Blue Cove Bay, he has had one tummy bug and that only lasted two days. The version of Lucas back then was very different to the one now hanging off the sofa and sticking his tongue out at me. The Lucas who lived with Scott and I was pale, sickly, and tired. I wonder whether that was because Lucas wasn't happy back then. 'Lucas, did you like Scott?'

The reply is instant. 'No, Mummy.'

'Do you like living here?'

He stands on the sofa and cheers. 'Yes, can we go have an ice cream for breakfast?'

After a celebratory ice-cream breakfast, Lucas and I go for a walk along the beach. As he races to pick up shells from the sand and I watch the waves rush in and out, my relationship with Scott is still on my mind. On the surface everything seemed okay, but he wasn't right for Lucas and me. I was always trying to fit in with a group of posh school mums who had produced an array of angelic children. They were never unwell and they never got caught rummaging through the purses and wallets of strangers.

Scott also used to make it difficult for me to come home and see Frankie and Dad. There would always be a problem with the car or a reason why I couldn't visit. Perhaps Scott's affair did Lucas and me a favour? We were not able to be ourselves with Scott.

Maybe what happened with Scott was a blessing? Maybe heartbreak is not meant to just hurt you, maybe it's meant to show you that the person you think you love is not right for you. This is what it was doing with Scott. He wasn't right for me, or Lucas and I know that now. Pete wasn't right either although that took several years to fall apart. I take a deep breath of salty sea air and feel a little lighter inside.

The Little Love Café is busy when I join Jake later. Dad has taken Lucas to the cinema, so I don't have to worry about childcare.

While Jake makes the drinks for table two, he listens as I tell him about the award. 'If the submission is successful, we will be visited by a set of judges and then we would hear officially at the start of May.'

'This sounds great, Alice,' says Jake. 'I just wish we could stop couples coming here to have a row. This morning, I had two arguing couples. One woman told her partner he could stick his engagement ring where the sun doesn't shine. She then put it on social media and tagged us in.'

I can feel my shoulders drooping and a worried frown spreads across my face. Celia Black's book appears in my mind, quickly followed by Phoebe's words: *turning the café around is like your mountain.* Standing up straighter I decide it's time to put my trust in Noah and in love and sort out the café. Like me, Noah has spent twenty years wondering what happened between us. He was one the one who came back to Blue Cove Bay to find answers. My failed wedding meant that I was back here to fall in love with him again. Noah will come back. As Rocco Reid said, Noah and I have been given a second chance. Standing straighter, I grin at Jake. 'We're going to turn things around, Jake,' I say confidently. 'Somehow, we are going to make Heartbreak Café a distant memory.'

Later as we lock up the café, my phone bleeps. It's a message from Noah.

> Becky has agreed to a divorce. Now I need to go talk to Dad. I can't wait to see you again x.

Jake grins as I squeal with celebration and give him a hug. 'You started to believe, Alice.'

Once Lucas is asleep, I take out my laptop and pull together The Little Love Café's submission for the Innovative Café Award. I use a mixture of Noah's photos from social media, a few wedding reception shots, a lot of examples of our customer's stories on Instagram and a lengthy piece on the café, its location, its owner Frankie, and the events coming up like *Treat Your Grandparent*.

At two in the morning, I press send on the submission.

CHAPTER THIRTY-THREE

It is Tuesday and I'm on my way to the café. Jake is coming in later. As I leave the promenade to cross the beach I am greeted by a shimmering blue sea. I watch a couple of men wrestle with a sail on their boat and then make my way towards the little pink café. On the steps, a young man with jet black hair is sat looking forlorn. He lifts his head as I approach.

'Are you okay?' I ask, rummaging in my handbag for The Little Love Café door keys.

Wiping his eyes, he lets out a sigh. 'She had something to tell me.'

'Sorry – who?' My café keys have disappeared to the bottom of my bag.

The man sniffs. 'My girlfriend... well, my now ex-girlfriend. She brought me here to confess to having an affair with a guy from work. This place is being renamed Heartbreak Café – right?' The young man's pale and tear-stained face triggers an ache inside my chest.

I stifle a groan as all my optimism from the weekend oozes out of me. The café has reached a new low if customers are not even waiting for me to open to announce a break-up.

They're doing the dumping on the steps. This is not great timing in view of my submission for the award. Finding my keys, I take a deep breath and ignore the cloud of doom and gloom. I must believe in the café. With a kind smile I shake my head. 'No, this is The Little Love Café. Do you want a free coffee?'

The young man climbs onto a pink stool. 'Latte, please.'

I get to work on waking up our coffee machine.

'My name is Richard,' he announces. 'My ex is called Belinda. We'd been seeing each other for a few months. I met her at music college.'

Passing him a pink bowl of sugar, I can see so much sadness in his face. 'Sorry, Richard. I recently had my heart badly broken, so I know what it feels like.'

He sweeps a strand of greasy black hair away from his face. 'I don't know why she had to dump me on the steps of your café. I thought we were going for a romantic beach walk.' He sighs. 'I knew it wasn't going to work. Belinda hated my harp music.'

My ears prick up. 'Harp music did you say?'

He nods. 'I'm a professional harpist although at the moment I'm unemployed.'

'Do you own a harp?'

Richard is now giving me an odd stare. 'Yes, I do. Several in fact.'

Fidgeting with a tea cloth I wonder whether this is a good time to ask him whether he wants to help me. Having a harp playing in the background would be a great touch for this café and soothing harp music might go some way to soothing our troubled customers. Belinda, whoever she is, might have done me the biggest favour ever.

'Look, Richard, I can't pay you much, but how about you fetch your harp and become The Little Love Café's harpist?'

Richard scratches his head. 'What?'

'I want to give my customers a unique romantic experience. Harp music to me screams romance.'

'It's not a small instrument and Belinda was the one who had the car. Mine broke down a few months ago. It is still not fixed as I got carried away with Belinda and forgot to take the car to the garage.'

'I can sort out getting the harp here.' I'm wondering whether Jake still has his van.

'If you need me, I can start next week,' announces Richard with a heavy sigh. 'Right now, I feel terrible. I think I need to go home and lie on my sofa.'

Shaking my head, I place my hand on Richard's arm. 'Trust me, Richard, rest is not what you need. Lying on my dad's sofa led me to basically stew in my own negative thoughts when I was sad. It's better to be up and about keeping yourself busy.'

'But I've just had my heart broken...'

Taking his hand, I give it a reassuring rub. 'Start that new project today, Richard. Don't go home and stew in negative thoughts.'

He rolls his amber coloured eyes. 'I get the feeling I don't have much choice.'

A smile takes over my face. Jumping off my stool, I pull him into a giant hug. 'Richard, Belinda did you a favour by hooking up–' I stop myself. 'In time you will look back and thank her.'

He breaks free. 'Do you think so?'

To my relief Jake still has his van and assists Richard with bringing his golden harp into The Little Love Café. We move some chairs and tables and slot his harp into the corner of the café. Richard is now playing and is filling The Little Love Café with beautiful harp music. Judging by the dreamy smiles from our customers his music is creating a romantic atmosphere.

We are half an hour away from closing. Jake is pointing to

someone behind me. I spin around to see Pete. 'Alice, can we talk?'

Every part of me tenses.

'We need to talk,' he says.

I can hear Frankie's voice in my head: *Control your emotions.* If Pete and I stay in the café and talk, it will end in a screaming match and that won't be good for business. I need to go outside and talk to Pete.

Jake gives me the nod to say he will cover for me. Pete and I step out of the café. A silvery mist has crept in from the horizon. It looks like someone has laid a giant blanket over the inky blue sea.

We stand by the railings at the edge of the promenade. Hot, bubbling anger is shooting up inside me by the time we get there. 'Do you know how much pain and embarrassment you caused me?'

He flinches and raise his hands. 'Okay, I'm sorry. I get it. I'm not proud of what I did.' He looks out towards the misty horizon.

'A YouTuber filmed us arguing. They put the link on social media and Frankie saw it. I am trying my hardest to make a success of Frankie's business. I didn't need that.'

Pete closes his eyes and pinches the skin above his nose. 'Everything got to me the other day. I couldn't breathe and I exploded, said some things which were not very nice.' He chuckles. 'Communication between us was never great – was it?'

'You can say that again,' I snap. 'Why did you throw away my letters and send that email to Noah pretending to be me?'

Pete leans on his elbows and folds his hands together. 'I loved you, Alice. Noah had gone and everyone kept telling me it was unlikely he'd be back. I took my chances. Do you know how hard it is to keep on loving someone when you know they don't love you back? I slipped up. It was a terrible mistake.'

'You have been lying to me for years.'

'All right, I do know all this, Alice.'

'What about all that you said about Mum too? I had to call Frankie's mum. I wanted her version of what happened with Mum and Dave Coombes.'

Pete hangs his head. 'I wanted to hurt you and Noah. It's been on my mind ever since. If you must know I've not slept properly.' He looks back at the café over his shoulder. 'Where is Noah?'

'He's gone back to Ireland.'

Pete stares at me. 'What?'

'Noah came back for answers about us. If Noah and I are going to have a future together we need to address this issue between our fathers.'

Pete scratches his hair. 'Look, your dad knew about your letters and how I was throwing them away. In fact, he encouraged me.'

Blood is rushing past my ears and my heart is pounding against my chest. 'What?'

'Your dad wanted Noah out of your life. After I'd thrown away the first few, I got guilty. I finished school early and went to talk to your dad.'

'Why did you talk to *him*?' I exclaim, running my hands through my hair. 'For goodness' sake, Pete. Why didn't you talk to me?'

He shakes his head. 'I wanted you all to myself and to do that I needed your dad on side. Yes, before you say anything – I was a manipulating little so-and-so.'

'What did Dad say?'

Pete blows the hair out of his cheeks. 'He congratulated me. Your dad hated the Coombes family.'

'Bloody hell, you and my father were thick as thieves. Why didn't you tell me about those rumours to do with Mum? I mean we've had some screaming matches over the years, and you've never said anything.'

'Yes, Brian and I were close,' explains Pete. 'He made me promise to not talk about the rumours to you. The other day was the first time I'd seen you both together. All my anger and frustration came up and I found myself thinking of something to say which would really hurt you.'

Pete shoves his hands in the pockets of his jacket. 'If I could change the past, I would. It hasn't got me anywhere – has it? I was kidding myself back then. I thought in time you'd love me. In the back of my mind, I knew you still loved Noah.'

Lucas's face appears in my mind. 'If you were able to go back in time we wouldn't have Lucas, would we?'

Pete's face softens. 'You're right. You and I did do something right.'

We smile at each other. I haven't fully forgiven him, and he knows this, but it's a start.

CHAPTER THIRTY-FOUR

I t's the day of our *'Treat Your Grandparent'* promotion. Ava has done an amazing job at promoting the event on her social media and through her youth club links. After an hour of being open, the café is a sea of teenagers and grandparents. To make extra space I gave Richard the new harpist the day off.

For once the café is full of laughter and chatter. As I deliver drinks I can hear all sorts of conversations; some teenagers are assuring their grandparent that they are studying hard, some students are admitting that they haven't been studying hard but are doing their best to turn the situation around and others are being open and saying their social life is more important than college work. The phrase, 'treat your grandparent' has been used liberally – as from what I have seen most grandparents are paying the bill.

Even though I am pleased to see the café come alive, I can't stop thinking about Pete throwing away my letters and what he told me about Dad knowing. I'm still in shock at how much manipulating they were doing all those years ago.

Last night, I struggled to get to sleep. Every time I closed my eyes, I was whisked back twenty years and replayed the memory of me asking Pete to post my weekly letter to Noah. Why didn't I post the letters myself? Anger and frustration at the sixteen-year-old version of me kept me awake for hours.

I'm taking an order from a young man and his grandmother. He points to his grandmother. 'This is Nana Elsie and she taught all of us grandkids poker when the adults weren't looking. We'd be summoned over to her house for lessons.'

I smile at his grandmother who winks at me. The young man carries on. 'We used to have a card school during every family get-together. I made the mistake of thinking Nana would either let me win, or the skills she had taught me would turn me into a gambling whiz kid.'

'Why on earth did you think that?' his grandmother asks, making me giggle.

The young man shrugs. 'I've always believed I am your favourite – I am the only grandchild to go to university; I got all A-grades in my A-levels, and I mowed your lawn for years.'

His grandmother smiles at him. 'You know I don't have favourites and you also know that I am very competitive.'

He turns to me. 'She would win every time, collect all her winnings – which included a lot of my hard-earned money from mowing her lawn – and ask me to top up her sherry glass.'

'I was teaching you a valuable life lesson. Don't gamble and don't trust sweet old ladies.'

We all laugh, and the young man playfully rolls his eyes. 'You are such a legend, Nana.'

I really enjoy listening to customer stories now, which is a surprise.

After delivering drinks to tables one and two, Ava catches my attention. 'This is my best mate, Georgia.' Ava introduces me to a tall girl with pink hair, who is furiously chewing gum and sporting shimmery purple eye shadow. 'Georgia has brought her great grandpa. He's called Harold.'

I smile at Georgia and glance at Harold with his tufty white hair, his twinkly blue eyes, and his wide smile. 'I know Harold. He used to fix Dad's car. When I was little. I used to love going with Dad to pick up his car as Harold would always give me a little packet of sweets.'

Georgia leans in and whispers, 'Great Grandpa Harold is trying to get Pearl to go on a date with him. Pearl over there. She is Will's great nana.'

'I know Pearl too,' I say, looking over at Pearl sat opposite her great grandson, Will, at a table alongside Harold and Georgia. Pearl, whose hair is cut into an elegant silver bob, has dressed up for the occasion and is in a pink jacket and skirt. She's deep in conversation with Harold. Will has clearly got bored as he's stuck his earphones in and is staring at his phone. A quick glance around proves he's not the only teenager doing this, a few have their earphones in, however some are still talking to their grandparent.

'Has your great grandpa been successful in his dating quest?'

Georgia lets out a heavy sigh. 'Grandpa has been asking Pearl out on a date every Monday at the Senior Tea & Chat morning for the past five years. Pearl always turns him down.'

'Blimey, I never knew this. Your great grandpa doesn't give up – does he?'

Ava giggles and Georgia rolls her eyes. 'I've told him he needs to play it cool with Pearl, but he still asks her out every Monday.'

After serving a few tables, taking a lot of photos of smiling teenagers with their arms wrapped around their proud grandparent and overhearing one girl asking her grandmother whether she fancies accompanying her to a beach party later, I walk past Harold's table. 'Alice,' he calls out, gesturing for me to sit by him as Georgia has gone to sit with Ava and her nana.

With a smile I sit down opposite him. Pearl is talking to a lady two tables along. Harold beams at me. 'This is great,' he says, 'I've really enjoyed today.'

'Thanks, Harold, that's good to hear.'

'How's your father? I see him at the supermarket most days.' Harold gestures to Pearl. 'I'm always running errands for Pearl.'

'Dad's good,' I say.

Harold leans over the table. 'Pearl has just agreed to go on a date with me after five long years.'

I gasp. 'Really? Harold, that's great news.'

To my amazement he grimaces. 'There is a catch.'

I giggle. 'What sort of catch?'

He coughs and looks around him to check no one is listening. 'I've been wanting to tell someone. Will you promise me you won't say anything?'

'Harold, I promise.'

'To go on a date with Pearl I have to help her carry out a secret mission.'

I chuckle at him. 'A secret mission? Are you two now working for MI5?'

He erupts into a coughing fit. Once it has eased and I have made him drink some water, he sighs. 'Pearl knows how much I love her and that I will do anything for her. She's a crafty one, my Pearl. Do you know we were once childhood sweethearts?'

I nod and glance at Jake who looks like he needs a hand back at the counter.

Harold carries on. 'In 1951, Pearl's family moved into the council house next door. Pearl had beautiful shiny dark hair that made me think of raven feathers and she had slender deer-like legs which carried her swiftly up and down our street. I'd never seen a girl like Pearl before. Pearl was the girl who broke all the rules.' He smiles. 'When her mother told her not to get her Sunday best dress dirty, Pearl would go climbing the tall trees in it at the end of the street. She wasn't like the other girls who played hopscotch and skipping with old washing line ropes. Pearl wanted excitement, danger, and everything her parents didn't want. When we were older Pearl, and I went to a few dances. Sadly, though, our love was short-lived as my mother wanted me to marry Edith Barnes; and Pearl married Bert. So, now Pearl and I find ourselves widows and neighbours. Every day we talk to each other over the fence, walk into town and every Monday I take her to the Senior Monday Tea & Chat. Neither of us are getting any younger and I love her with all my heart.'

'Harold, I need to go rescue Jake,' I say, pointing to the queue of people.

He grabs my hand. 'Do you want to know the secret mission?'

I spot Ava. To my relief she starts helping the customers. Hiring Ava is one of the best decisions I have made. I turn back to Harold. 'Tell me the mission?'

He grins. 'Pearl believes there are two lonely souls in Blue Cove Bay who need a helping hand.'

I wonder who these two lonely souls are. They must attend the Senior Monday Tea & Chat session. I am curious though. 'A helping hand? Do they have mobility issues, Harold?'

In my head I am imagining an elderly lady who is unable to get to the community centre due to health reasons but is desperate to see the love of her life. He also struggles to get to the community centre. Maybe Harold and Pearl are hiring a taxi for one; or bringing the Monday session to them.

Confusion flashes across Harold's face. He ignores my question. 'Pearl says if I help her carry out this plan, I can take her out on a date.'

'Yes, but what exactly do you have to do?'

Sitting back, he scratches his head. 'Deliver some letters.'

'Letters? Is that your secret mission?'

Harold nods. 'Pearl wants me to do the delivering.'

'That sounds lovely.' My fictitious elderly lady has received a love letter from the love of her life, hand delivered by Harold.

'Oh well, good luck, Harold.' Rising, I give him a wink. 'If you need a hand, let me know.'

His face lights up. 'Really? That's very kind of you.'

Pearl appears by Harold's side. She gives me a mischievous wink. 'Are you chatting up my man, Alice?'

'Is it obvious?' I say, making Harold laugh.

I walk back to Jake who is grinning at me. 'I saw you having a heart-to-heart with Harold over there.'

'He's embarking on a secret mission, so he had to fill me in on all the details.'

Jake places a Luscious Latte on a tray together with a Flirty Flat White. 'That sounds intriguing.'

'The community centre runs a Senior Monday Tea & Chat group. From what Harold was saying, it sounds like a hotbed for romance. I need to do some café promo over there.'

Jake grins. 'You've changed, Alice. A few months ago, you'd run in the opposite direction at the first sign of romance. Now, you're hunting it out.'

CHAPTER THIRTY-FIVE

As I leave the school gates after dropping Lucas off, I hear a shout and see Phoebe hurrying after me. Her face is pink and the curls at the front of her face are stuck to her forehead. 'He's invited me and kids to his house for tea and a playdate.'

'Who are we talking about?'

Her eyes are shining. I know who she is referring to.

'Liam. Didn't you see him stood by me in the playground?'

I shake my head. 'Lucas was having a meltdown because I wouldn't let him look inside my purse. That's great though. You've gone from hating him to going on playdates.'

She casts me an anxious look. 'Liam's little boy is an angel compared to Flynn. I'm already worried about Flynn's obsession with opening drawers and cupboards in other people's houses. He loves a good rummage through someone's sock drawer. Do you think I should forewarn Liam?'

I shrug. 'I always forewarn people about Lucas's penchant for purses and wallets. If left unsupervised Lucas will come home with a wad of cash and a collection of cards.'

Phoebe and I both start to giggle. She links her arm through mine. 'Some parents are raising future geniuses, sporting prodigies and celebrities whilst we're raising future...'

'Criminals?' I say, and we both erupt into laughter.

I stare at the email from the Innovative Café Award co-ordinator and my heart skips a beat. My submission has secured us a judge's visit to the café in two weeks. 'Jake,' I call out, 'come here, quick.'

'Congratulations,' he says, returning from taking table four's order. He comes to read the email over my shoulder. 'Your submission must have been really good.'

'It was a team effort, I just pulled everything together.'

He makes up an order for table four. 'So, we have two weeks to make The Little Love Café great.'

'Yes, hopefully we can put all our issues in the past and shake off the Heartbreak Café reputation.'

Once he's made two Flirty Flat Whites, I deliver the order. The couple on table four are celebrating their recent engagement. 'Here's your coffee,' I say with a smile, placing pink cups in front of them.

The woman has black hair which hugs her shoulders, piecing green eyes and enviable dewy skin. 'This is not what I was expecting.'

'In a good way?' I ask, surveying the other tables to make sure no other customers are waiting to be served or need drinks.

'Rachel, leave it,' hisses her fiancé, casting me an awkward look.

The woman ignores her fiancé. 'I must do this. My friend had an awful time in here a few weeks ago. She was really upset. I reckon you must have got rid of the miserable woman who ruined my friend's engagement.'

My heart grinds to a halt. Was I that miserable woman?

The woman continues. 'It was bad. Her fiancé did a live proposal, and this woman was supposed to record it. Anyway, she didn't because she had issues and my friend's been so upset.'

She's talking about Michelle and Jason. *That was me.* In a few seconds I am wrapped in a cloak of guilt and shame. I was the one who ruined Michelle and Jason's proposal.

The woman smiles and surveys the café. 'I'll tell my friend the miserable woman has gone.' She turns to me. 'Do you know what happened to her?'

I want the ground to open and swallow me whole. My stomach performs a nauseating spin cycle. Half of me wants to lie and say we got rid of the miserable woman. It would be easy – however what happens if Michelle comes back to the café and sees me? The other half of me wants me to be brave and take responsibility for my behaviour.

'It was me,' I say, as the woman's mouth falls open in surprise. 'You're right. I did ruin your friend's proposal and I feel bad about it.'

An awkward silence descends upon me, the woman, and her fiancé.

'What are you going to do to put it right?' The woman asks, as her fiancé hisses, 'Rachel, stop this.'

'Put it right?' My voice crackles. 'Well, would Jason and Michelle like to come in here for free coffees?'

To my horror the woman takes out her phone and taps out a message. Her fiancé is mouthing the word *sorry* at me and shaking his head.

'Michelle says she would like to accept your offer of free drinks. She and Jason will come in soon. I think it's right that you get a chance to apologise to them.'

'Yes of course,' I say, forcing out a smile, before hurrying back to the counter.

'Are you okay?' Jake asks, glancing at me.

I gesture towards table four and explain what happened with Michelle and Jason and what the woman said to me. Jake casts me an uncomfortable look. 'You're brave, Alice. I would have lied and gone for the easier option.'

On my break I head for the gift shop to see how Esme is doing. When I arrive, Joy is leaving the shop, arm in arm with Eric from the guesthouse. Joy casts me a huge smile. 'Alice, how lovely to see you. Have you heard the news? We have sold the gift shop business.'

'What? You've sold it?'

Joy nods. 'Esme and I are leaving Blue Cove Bay to start a whole new life in North Devon.' She playfully tugs on Eric's arm. 'I can't wait. Can you, Eric?'

He laughs and shakes his head. Then they saunter off down the promenade. Esme is tear-stained and emotional behind the gift shop counter. She looks up as I rush over to her. 'My nightmare has come true, Alice.'

'Have you not told Joy you don't want to go?'

Esme shakes her head. 'I tried to last night, but I wasn't strong enough. Joy started shouting about what Mum would say if she was still alive, how as twins we are meant to stay together in life and how she needs me for our new business.' She wipes her wet cheek with the back of her hand.

'Oh, Esme, I'm so sorry,' I say, pulling her into a hug.

'I don't want to go,' Esme sobs. 'I'm a grown woman who can't say no to her twin sister. It's pathetic.'

'Okay, what's the worst Joy can do if you refuse to go?'

Esme looks at me. 'What do you mean?'

'What's the worst that will happen? Joy goes off to North Devon with Eric and you stay here. Is that so bad?'

'Joy will never speak to me again and I will feel guilty for the rest of my life.'

I rub Esme's shoulder. 'Joy has been horrible to you for thirty-seven years. She's controlled every aspect of your life, and she's also made you run this place by yourself. We both know you manage this place whilst she gallivants around Blue Cove Bay.'

'Yes. True.'

'I don't understand how Joy not speaking to you and leaving you here is any worse than what you are going through now.'

Esme stares at me. 'You have a point.'

'Who is this buyer? This has all happened quickly.'

'Joy put it up for sale last week without telling me. An anonymous buyer has made her an offer.'

I place my hand over Esme's. 'Be brave. Come on, Phoebe and I will be here for you.'

CHAPTER THIRTY-SIX

When I return Jake is wearing a mischievous smile. Something is going on and that smile is a giveaway. He hands me a tiny slip of paper. 'This is for you.'

I take it and uncurl it. Gasping I see that it reads:

Meet me down by our rock in Blue Cove Bay right now, Noah x.

Jake's face has gone blurry. I ask, 'Is this a joke?'

He shakes his head. 'I'll cover for you. Go now.'

I hand him my apron and race out of The Little Love Café. Once I am on the beach, I yank off my shoes and sprint towards the distant figure by the rock. My legs burn as I pick up speed, but I don't care. All I can think about is Noah's come back to me. He gets closer and soon he's jogging across the sand towards me. We meet and he lifts me high into the air.

'You came back.' I wrap my arms around his neck. 'You're back.' His lips find mine and we engage in a long and sensuous kiss. He breaks away first. 'I promised you I would.'

Hot tears spill down my cheeks. He laughs and wipes them away with his thumbs. 'Come up here.' Without hesitation I slip my hand into his. Holding Noah's hand again has a warm, reassuring feel to it. My hand feels like it's come home. He lets me go first as we climb up our old rock.

I can't believe what's up there; a pink and white gingham picnic blanket containing two Little Love Café coffees and a plate of Cuddle Muffins. Once he's clambered up, he grins. 'Thought we could celebrate.'

I fall into his arms. 'I've missed you so much, Noah.'

'I'm back for good, Alice.' He kisses my hand. 'I never stopped thinking about you when I was over there.' His summer blue eyes study my face. 'Will you be my girlfriend again?

'I want to wake up with you; I want to cook your dinner; I want to play Batman with Lucas and I want to walk on this beach with you.' Noah's eyes are dancing with excitement. 'I want to drink wine with you; take you out, watch films with you and I want to wake up with you by my side.' He presses his lips against mine. 'Well?' He murmurs.

'Yes, Noah, I will be your girlfriend again.' After we have kissed and hugged, I rest my head on his shoulder. 'What happened in Ireland?'

Noah fiddles with the top of his plastic coffee cup. 'Becky was better than I expected. She'd also met someone while I have been away. He's a local farmer and they've been spending a lot of time on his farm.'

I take a sip on my coffee. 'How do you feel about that?'

Noah turns to me and smiles. 'I told her I was happy for them both which is true. She deserves some happiness.' He squeezes my hand. 'She was happy for me too.'

My heart has swelled so much I think it's close to pushing out my ribs. 'This is like a dream come true.'

Noah kisses my forehead. 'I know what you mean. Listen, I also talked to my father.'

My shoulders sink as he reaches over to his rucksack. He takes out his phone and places it beside us. 'I went back to Ireland to talk to Becky and to my father. With my father, I wanted to tell him my news, that I was moving to be with you, and to find out what went on with him and your dad all those years ago.'

My heart is thudding. I have this awful sinking feeling Noah is going to tell me something which is going to hurt. Taking a deep breath, I regain composure. I must stay strong and believe in Mum's love for Dad.

'As you can imagine things got intense with Dad. This is not one of his favourite subjects. We came close to having a fight and if it wasn't for Becky's farmer friend I think Dad would have floored me.' Noah runs his hand through his blond hair. He takes a deep breath. 'Before your mum died, my dad got close to her.'

This is excruciating. My hands are gripping the blanket so tightly my knuckles have gone white.

'Apparently on one walk your mum gave him a hug as he was upset. He got carried away and he kissed her.'

'He kissed her?' My heart grinds to a halt.

Noah lets out a heavy sigh. 'Dad said it was his fault. He was emotional and he misread your mum's signals. A few of the hiking club saw and that's how the gossip began.' He pauses and stares at my face. 'Dad assured me it was just a kiss. Nothing more. And your mum didn't speak to him for a few weeks after it happened.'

Closing my eyes, I take a deep breath. 'I cannot tell Dad this.'

Noah continues. 'Dad was with her when she died, and he

told me that she told him to tell your dad and you that she loved you. Those were her last words.'

I blink away tears and find myself looking up at the cliffs towards the coastal path. Noah gives me a moment to gather my thoughts.

'What happened at that wedding reception?'

Noah fidgets and squirms. 'Dad was really cut up when she died, and he admits things got out of hand at that wedding. There had been a lot of gossip in the town about him and your mum. Your dad was also grieving and he lamped my dad before he could explain what happened. His pride took over and here we are.'

'But why did it drag on for years?'

Shrugging, Noah nibbles at a muffin. 'My dad was a proud man back then and didn't like the fact your dad had nearly knocked him out.'

Noah pulls me to him, and I rest my head against his broad chest. 'We have to talk to your dad, Alice.'

CHAPTER THIRTY-SEVEN

'I'll go see Dad tonight,' I say to Noah, as we walk hand in hand, back across the beach after work. Earlier we'd talked about us both walking over to Dad's to have a clear-the-air discussion. The more I thought about it, the more I felt uncomfortable, and it didn't feel fair on Dad. He is going to have a big enough shock when I announce Noah and me are together. 'Let me do this on my own.'

'Are you sure?' He gives my hand a gentle squeeze.

'Yes, I want to try and get him to talk about Mum. I think it will be easier if I do it.' The idea of taking Noah scares me as Dad is probably going to get very angry.

'Will Lucas be with you?'

I shake my head. 'Pete's picking him up from school and taking him back to stay over.'

Noah pulls me to a stop. His arms circle my waist, and he pulls me closer. 'Are you going to show me your new flat first then?'

I arch my eyebrows suggestively. 'You could stay over tonight. Lucas is away.'

'Where would I sleep?' He smiles and plants a series of tiny kisses on my neck. 'Your sofa?'

With a giggle I say, 'You can... but it's a small sofa.'

'Okay,' he says, with a playful wink, 'the sofa it is.' His boyish smile makes me light-headed.

'Why don't I message you when I am back from Dad's, and you can come over and I'll show you around, plus... sort out that sofa for you.'

'It's a deal.'

It feels like a long walk to Dad's house. My palms are already sweaty, and my heart is beating like a drum against my ribcage.

He opens the door and welcomes me in. 'This is a nice surprise, Alice. Come in.'

Bean is excited to see me and starts barking. I give him a good scratch behind his ears. 'How are you, Dad?'

We walk into the kitchen. Dad's kitchen always feels warm and inviting. It's like stepping back in time as he's had the same cupboards and units for years. 'I have some news,' says Dad, making me flinch. 'I've been laid off from the supermarket.'

'What? Oh, Dad, I'm so sorry.'

He shrugs and pours water into his kettle. 'I'm all right. Do you fancy a cuppa?'

Once he has made us two mugs of tea we sit opposite each other at the dinner table.

'I'll have to look for another little job,' he says, with a sigh. 'I don't know whether anyone will employ me at my age.'

I cover his hand with mine. 'Of course they will, Dad. You're amazing.'

He shrugs. 'I never really enjoyed the supermarket, if I am honest. Lately I've been thinking about baking, but I don't want to go back to running my own bakery.' He stares at his hands. 'I like making things. Shelf stacking and sitting on the supermarket till never gave me an opportunity to make something.'

I smile at him. 'Lucas and I are always willing to be your cake testers.'

We both laugh. He looks at me. 'So, what's going on with you? How's the new place and more importantly – how many ice creams has my grandson consumed?'

'The flat is lovely,' I say. 'Lucas and I like watching TV together on an evening and the yellow beach hut shower unit has proved a big hit with Lucas. He has two showers a day now. You remember how hard it was to get him to have one a few months ago?'

Dad chuckles. 'I love him so much. He did cause havoc here when you both lived with me but since you've gone, the house has felt empty. I miss hearing Lucas singing and shouting.' He takes a sip of his tea. 'I'm sensing you have come to tell me something, Alice.'

I take a big breath. 'Noah and I are back together.'

Dad looks like he's been frozen in time. His sea-grey eyes have darkened, and his mouth is open.

'Say something, Dad,' I croak.

The atmosphere has changed. His eyes narrow and anger flashes across his face. 'You know how I feel about Noah Coombes. He will not be welcome inside this house.'

'Dad, I never stopped loving Noah.'

He shakes his head with disapproval, and my anger rises. 'You've never given Noah a chance, Dad.'

Dad slams his hand on the table making me flinch. 'I don't want anything to do with Noah Coombes or his family.' The air between us has become thick and charged.

'Will you tell me why you and Dave Coombes fell out all those years ago?'

Dad rises from the table and pours his tea away. 'I don't want to dredge all that up again.'

'Well, I want to know.'

'Alice, please leave,' says Dad. 'I don't want to talk about this anymore. You've upset me enough by telling me you are getting together with that man.' He turns to face the window with his back to me.

I get up from the table as all the things that Pete told me flood my mind. 'When were you going to tell me about you and Pete colluding and throwing away my letters to Noah?'

Dad turns around with a look of shock. 'How do you know that?'

'Pete told me. He said you'd congratulated him when he admitted to you what he'd done with the first couple of letters.'

'Alice, I was worried about you.'

Tears are filling up my eyes. 'Dad, I was mortified that Noah never replied. That decision you and Pete made has impacted my life.' My voice crackles with emotion. 'Do you know how upsetting it is to hear your father was happy that your so-called friend was chucking away your letters to the love of your life.'

Dad is staring at the floor. 'I was protecting you, Alice.'

'From whom? You never took the time to get to know Noah. I can't remember when you and he were in the same room together.'

He looks up and stares at me. 'I knew his family, Alice. That was enough.'

I baulk at his comment. 'Dad, you fell out with Noah's father, not his family.'

'I had good reason to protect you from the Coombes family.'

A tear rolls down my cheek. I wipe it away. 'Tell me the reason.'

He shakes his head. 'Alice, please leave.'

~

I'm tear-stained and snotty when I fall into Noah's arms as we meet outside the ice-cream parlour. He helps me find my keys and we go upstairs to the flat. On the sofa he holds me close as I tell him everything that was said between Dad and me.

Noah wipes my tears away with his thumbs. Once I have finished, he whispers, 'It will all work out, Alice, I promise.' He kisses my forehead. 'I know your dad is holding on to a lot of stuff from the past but he won't want to lose you.'

'Do you think so?'

Noah nods. 'We are going to get through this together. Maybe we should give your dad some space and put all our efforts into getting the café ready for the judge's visit.'

'Maybe,' I murmur, as I turn to face him. His mouth finds mine. His kiss is long and lingering. Lifting me into his arms he carries me to my bedroom. Laying me down gently on the bed he smiles. 'Do you want me to go sleep on the sofa?'

I pull him down and his warm soft lips find mine. 'You have that wild look on your face again,' he murmurs.

'I've waited twenty years for this.'

He laughs and kisses me. 'When we were teenagers the only place, we could go was our rock and it wasn't the comfiest of places. The beach was better although sand was an issue...'

'Noah, stop talking,' I say, with a grin. 'I've been waiting a *long* time.'

CHAPTER THIRTY-EIGHT

We are a week away from the judge's visit next Wednesday. Noah has replaced Jake and working at The Little Love Café has never felt so good. Noah has stayed over my flat twice since he returned. Each time it's been amazing to wake up beside him in bed. I have had to pinch myself to ensure this is not a dream. We've also had an evening in with Lucas. Noah sat through an entire Batman movie with an excited Lucas telling him what was going to happen in the next scene.

Dad and I have not spoken which has been upsetting. I thought he would have come to speak to me. Noah has been supportive and keeps reassuring me that Dad and I will be okay.

I'm on my way back to the counter with an order for table six when Georgia, Ava's best friend, taps me on the arm. 'Alice,' she says, 'Great Grandpa Harold is in hospital.'

Her news makes me come to an abrupt halt. 'Is he going to be okay?'

A worried look takes hold of her face. 'A nasty chest infection. We are all hoping so. I went to visit him in hospital, and he gave me these envelopes. He said you know about his secret mission.'

She hands me a plastic bag. Inside are two cream envelopes containing letters to be delivered.

'But he never gave me any instructions about his secret mission,' I say.

Georgia fiddles with her pink hair which today has been plaited down one side. 'Grandpa said that if these two letters are not delivered, Pearl won't go on a date with him.'

Noah comes over and peers over my shoulder. 'What's up?'

'Georgia's great grandfather is Harold Brown. He's been asking Pearl out every Monday at the Senior Tea & Chat session at the community centre for five years and she finally said yes. However, there was one condition: he had to complete a secret mission for her. Now he's in hospital and wants me to do it for him. All I know is that he had to deliver some letters.' I open the bag. A huge waft of lavender perfume comes out, making us all step back with surprise.

Georgia giggles. 'Will's nana loves a scented letter. She's been dousing Will's birthday and Christmas cards in perfumes for years. I bet she's sprayed the envelopes.'

I take out the envelopes. On the front of one is the letter P and on the other envelope is the letter L. 'Help me, Georgia. Who are these for?'

Georgia studies the envelopes. 'They're both sealed so we can't be nosey.'

Noah chuckles. 'Good luck, Alice.'

I look at the envelopes and try to think of two elderly Blue Cove Bay residents who have the same initials. I'm about to give up when it hits me. 'Phoebe who owns the bookshop and Liam who owns the record shop.'

Georgia casts me a puzzled look. 'Why are my grandpa and Pearl sending those two a scented letter?'

'Oh, my goodness,' I gasp. 'Phoebe and Liam are the two lonely souls your grandpa was talking about. Also, Phoebe told me she'd spotted Harold and Pearl giggling in her bookshop when she was arguing with Liam. That's it. Your grandpa and Pearl have been doing a spot of secret matchmaking. They must be trying to get Phoebe and Liam together.'

Georgia makes a face. 'This is super cringe.'

I turn to Noah. 'Are you okay to cover me? I am going to have to deliver these. Phoebe will laugh when I hand over her envelope.'

He nods and I take the envelopes. Georgia taps me on the arm. 'Great Grandpa kept telling me that this is a secret mission. Even though I don't think it is very cool, we can't let Great Grandpa down.'

'Don't worry. I know Phoebe.'

She shakes her head. 'You can't just give them to Phoebe and Liam. That will blow the mission. I think you're going to have to sneakily drop them at the bookshop and the record shop.'

'Really?'

Georgia nods. 'If Grandpa passes over this will have been his final wish.'

I stare at her. 'Harold can't pass over yet as he's not had his date with Pearl. I will sort this.'

I walk into town with the two envelopes in my bag. How am I going to deliver them without Phoebe or Liam spotting me?

As I enter the bookshop, Keith spots me and comes over. 'Phoebe has a secret admirer,' he whispers. 'She's on her tea break out the back pretending to sort out new orders but I know she is trying to work out who it is.'

'Really?' I try to sound surprised.

He nods. 'They've been leaving her cryptic messages in envelopes on bookshelves. It's been so exciting in here lately. I was worried about handing in my resignation the other day, but this development has helped me.'

'Resignation? Keith, you can't leave this bookshop. Who will I turn to when I need a cracking gothic thriller recommendation?'

He grins. 'I have always liked you, Alice. Yes, I am off to pastures new.'

I think about Esme, and I wonder whether she knows. To hear Keith is leaving will be upsetting for her. The way she talks about him, and the way her face lights up at the mention of his text messages is lovely to see, especially as I never heard her talk like that about Steve.

'Where are you going? Not another bookshop I hope?'

'I have a few irons in the fire,' he chuckles. 'I have told Phoebe I don't want my successor in here to be better than me.'

'It's going to be tough for Phoebe to replace you, Keith.'

He casts me a mischievous grin. 'I sense things will be changing around here.'

'What do you mean?'

Keith straightens his red bow tie. 'I have to say that these messages have been an unexpected plot twist for Phoebe.'

I smile at Keith, who always gives every situation a book angle. 'What do you mean?'

He chuckles. 'The messages arrive in heavy lavender-scented envelopes. Her secret admirer loves a lavender spray. So far, the messages have been about how pretty her eyes are, how her smile makes their day and yesterday's message was about how they might be soulmates.'

'Wow.'

Keith nods. 'The plot twist is that she and Liam have been getting close over the last few days. I knew she fancied him the second he strode into this shop to introduce himself to her when he first moved here. The way she gazed at him when he

229

removed those dark shades said it all. Then we had all the arguing with each other outside which, I might add, has followed a "typical enemies to lovers romance" plot. I have read too many of these romances to know that underneath all these dramatic rows are two beating hearts that long to be entwined. I have seen the way Phoebe and Liam struggle to stop gawping at each other. When Liam helped her find Piggy and invited her over for a playdate, I knew we were onto something.' He leans closer and whispers, 'I think she wishes it was Liam writing the messages, but he doesn't strike us a lavender letter type of guy.'

A customer goes to the till clutching two books. Keith looks up and grins. 'I better go and do my day job, as opposed to gossiping to you.'

After he hurries away, I head for the romance section, with its tea-for-two display. While Keith is busy telling his customer that the books they have chosen are his all-time favourites, I carefully take out the envelope marked P and slide it next to the teapot.

To avoid detection, I wander into the crime section and then casually stroll out giving Keith a wave.

On the right of Phoebe's bookshop is the record shop – *Vinyl Dreams*. Painted a pale peach colour, its front window is adorned with an array of colourful albums and single sleeves, posters advertising local gigs and a selection of funky Vinyl Dream T-shirts for sale. When I enter, I assume the tall guy with the swept back brown hair, the strong jawline coated in stubble and piercing blue eyes is Liam. He is talking to a group of students about an album. I can see why Phoebe was struggling to argue with him, he's very handsome.

I don't know where to put the final envelope. To my relief two record enthusiasts enter his shop and stand by the heavy metal record storage crates. I loiter behind them and discover the jazz section. Carefully I slip out the envelope and rest it on top of the vinyls. After faking an interest in classical music vinyls, I leave the shop.

Noah grins at me as I come back into the café. 'How did it go?'

'Successfully delivered. Keith in the bookshop told me that Phoebe and Liam are getting closer which is good. Let's hope Harold and Pearl's matchmaking works. Have I missed anything?'

Noah shakes his head. 'Pam came and was stressed as usual. She's received your order for the judge's visit next week.'

'Great,' I say. 'It's all coming together.'

Grabbing hold of my waist Noah pulls me into a hug. 'We have one problem though.'

'Oh, no – what?'

'I don't think I have had enough kisses today, Alice.'

CHAPTER THIRTY-NINE

'Can I go to Grandpa's house?' Lucas asks, as I make him his breakfast and at the same time reply to Phoebe's latest WhatsApp message to Esme and me – titled, *'Would either of you date a man who likes to send lavender scented love letters?'*

Hearing Lucas say this makes my heart ache. There has been no word from Dad since we argued over a week ago. Lucas has asked me every day if we can go see him. With some unexpected help from Pete, I have juggled the childcare and the school runs this past week. Dad normally helps with Lucas, but he hasn't contacted me to arrange any days.

'We will see Grandpa soon,' I say, putting his cereal in front of him.

'I miss Grandpa and Bean,' groans Lucas.

Leaning against the work surface I close my eyes and rub my temples. The ongoing situation with Dad and the visit from the award judges on Wednesday is getting to me. It's Sunday and the café is closed today which is a blessing as I am tired, and I don't know what to do about Dad. Noah is coming over later and we're going to play football on the beach with Lucas as the weather is going to be warm and sunny. Jake is meeting us too, which will be nice.

After I have replied to Phoebe's message with a *'Definitely, everyone loves a scented love letter,'* and smile at her shocked face emoji response, I find Dad's mobile number. My finger hovers over the text message button. I want to tell him that this has gone on for long enough and it's making Lucas upset. I stop and scroll up at the *'talk to me, Dad'* text messages I have been sending him since we fell out. He's read each one but has not replied. I stop myself from sending him another which he will ignore.

Once he's finished Lucas runs off to get ready for his first shower of the day. I wash up his cereal bowl with a smile and go to help him.

Noah turns up later. He's wearing a white T-shirt, navy blue knee-length shorts and trainers. His blond hair is messy and windswept. He looks so handsome I can't help but kiss him before we have said hello.

'This is a nice welcome,' he says, with a grin. 'How are you?'

I force out a smile, but Noah reads my mind. 'You're worried about your dad?'

'Lucas keeps asking about going to see him.'

Noah lets out a heavy sigh. 'I never thought us getting back together after all these years would make your father behave like this. Alice, I'm so sorry. Look, tell him I will never step inside his house or go anywhere near him.'

'That's not practical, Noah. We can't spend the rest of our lives making sure Dad never encounters you.'

Lucas rushes into the living room and grins at Noah. 'Do you like football?'

Noah nods. 'I'm brilliant at football.'

Lucas giggles. 'Not as good as me.'

Noah rises from the sofa. 'Let's go and see how good you are, Lucas.'

Lucas leaps into the air and cheers.

We're on the beach. Jake has arrived and volunteered to go in the makeshift goal. Noah and Lucas are taking it in turns to score goals. I love the way Noah is helping set up goals for Lucas and giving him advice on how to kick the ball.

Phoebe's messages throughout the day have been making me smile. Her latest question to Esme and me is:

> Would you date a man with over-the-top flowery handwriting and who writes cryptic messages about you being his anchor? I don't want to be anyone's anchor.

Someone comes to sit next to me on the towel. I look up to see Lilly from the ice-cream parlour smiling at me. She gives me a nudge. 'I wanted to say thank you for the advice about not dating Elliot, Sunny's friend,' she says, tucking her long brown legs under her. 'It was good advice.'

'I'm glad. How are you?' I ask, noticing a new sparkle to her eyes.

She grins. 'Well, I got the manager's job of the ice-cream parlour in Brighton. It feels the right thing to do.'

I throw my arms around her. 'Lilly, this is great news.'

She rises to her feet, 'I better get back. Can I ask you something?'

'Sure.'

'If Noah and you had kept in touch and he had returned from Ireland years ago, do you think you'd still be together now?'

I watch Noah lift a giggling Lucas into the air to stop him scoring a goal. The sight of them floods my body with happiness. 'I don't know, Lilly. We were both so young. What I will say is that our time apart has made what we have rekindled so special.'

She smiles. 'Thanks, Alice. Maybe Sunny and I will meet again in the future?'

'You never know, Lilly. Now, go to Brighton and enjoy yourself.'

As Lilly walks away my phone vibrates. It is Pam, the cake supplier. Why is she phoning me on a Sunday? 'Hello, Pam.'

'Alice,' she gasps, 'my ex-husband has broken both his arms. He played five-a-side football for the first time in years yesterday and the silly old fool clattered into another player. He's now in hospital.'

'Oh, Pam, I'm sorry to hear that.'

'Alice, I can't supply your cakes.'

My heart grinds to a halt and the blood drains away from my face. 'Oh... I see.'

'My ex-husband is the baker, Alice. The wholesale business doesn't run without him.'

I gulp as my brain goes into a tailspin. We can't run out of cakes and pastries the week the judge comes.

'Don't you have someone in reserve?'

'No, we don't because my ex-husband is too pig-headed. Our business is screwed with this accident, Alice. I was stressed before this; now I'm on the edge of a nervous breakdown.' Her voice is wavering and crackling. She's emotional.

'Okay, Pam, calm down and take a breath. Let me go and think about this.'

'Alice, I know this is an important week for you. I am so sorry.'

'I'll get back in touch later. Take it easy, Pam.'

She lets out a nervous laugh. 'With all our bills to pay and all our customers expecting cakes, I can't take it easy.'

Noah comes over as I end the call. He sits down beside me, and I tell him what's happened.

'I will have to find a new wholesale supplier,' I say, hugging my knees. 'We will cope somehow. What a week for this to happen. I feel sorry for Pam. This accident will put her business back weeks.'

Noah shakes his head. 'There's one person who can help us and Pam.'

'Who?'

'Your dad.'

I stare at him. 'Dad?'

He nods. 'We need to go see your father and sort out this mess once and for all.' He helps me to my feet. 'Jake, any chance you could have Lucas for an hour or so?'

Jake gives us a thumbs-up. 'Alice, give me your key and I'll go watch Batman with him.'

After saying goodbye to Lucas, Noah and I head for Dad's house.

As we walk, Noah takes out his phone.

'Who are you texting?'

He looks at me. 'My father.'

I gasp. Noah nods. 'It's time they talked to each other.'

Once we arrive at Dad's house I knock on the door. I am trembling and all the saliva in my mouth has drained away. Noah is standing beside me on Dad's doorstep.

CHAPTER FORTY

The second Dad opens the door and spots Noah beside me his face turns thunderous. 'You are not welcome here. Please leave.'

I shake my head. 'This situation has gone on for too long, Dad. It ends today.'

'Please don't do this, Alice. I'm angry enough.'

I reach out and touch his hand. 'Dad, please do something for me. I'm not asking for much. Just listen to what we have to say. If not for me, do it for Lucas.'

Something flickers across Dad's face, and it softens slightly.

'Let's not carry this argument on, because Lucas is getting upset about not being able to see you. That's not fair,' I say, blinking back tears. 'He's only six and he doesn't understand why he can't see his grandpa.'

Dad leaves the front door open and walks into the kitchen. I take Noah's hand and lead the way.

In the kitchen Dad is sat with his head in his hands. I go to him and put my arms around him. At first, he's resistant but I don't let go. Eventually he turns and we hug each other. Tears stream down both of our faces.

'What happened to us?' Dad says, as he pulls back from my hug. His cheeks are damp and his eyes pink and watery.

I smile at him and wipe away one of his tears with my thumb. 'We love each other far too much, that's the problem.'

Noah holds his phone up. 'Brian, there's someone who wants to talk to you.'

Dad looks over and lets out a heavy sigh. Dave Coombes is on the screen via FaceTime. 'Brian, it's been a while.' Dave scratches his now bald head. 'If I don't do this, I'm going to lose my son. I love him and I want him to be happy.' Dave pauses to take a sip of water. 'Nothing happened between Julie and me. She loved you, Brian. There was not a hope in hell for me. It's time to bury the hatchet. Grief does strange things to us. I should have told you that her last words were that she would always love you and Alice.'

Dad's sobs fill the air. I let him bury his face in my shoulder. 'Dad, it is over. Nothing happened. There was no affair.'

'Brian, I hope this will help you to build a bridge with my son whose only crime was to love your Alice with all his heart. Take care.'

Dad turns to Noah and with a trembling arm offers him his hand. They shake and smile at each other. 'You did this for Alice – didn't you?'

Noah nods. 'I just want to make her happy, Brian.'

Dad sits up straight. He turns to me and kisses me on the head. 'Please forgive me, Alice, I think I have been a bit silly. This past week since we argued has been awful. It has, however, allowed me to do a lot of thinking. I'm sorry for meddling in your relationship all those years ago.'

Standing up I grab the photo at the back of the shelf. 'She always loved you, Dad.'

Tears stream down our cheeks as we gaze at Mum's radiant smile.

I make us all a cup of tea and even find a box of biscuits in one of Dad's cupboards.

'Have you met my grandson, Lucas?' Dad asks Noah.

He nods. 'Lucas is a great kid, Brian. We have been playing football on the beach and Lucas has been showing me his moves.'

We all smile and drink our tea.

'Dad, we need your help,' I say, once we have all drained our cups. 'My submission for the most Innovative Café Award has secured us a visit from the judges on Wednesday.'

'Congratulations,' says Dad.

'We have a problem though. You know our cake supplier, Pam? Her ex-husband is her baker, and he's broken both his arms. So she can't supply our cakes.'

Dad looks at me. 'Pam Reynolds – the one who used to work in my bakery?'

I nod. 'Pam is in a mess and–'

He smiles. 'You want me to help Pam?'

'Would you?'

Dad pulls me into a hug. 'I have a lot of making up to do to you, Alice. Do you have Pam's number?'

CHAPTER FORTY-ONE

I t's here, the day the judges visit. For the past three days Noah and I have been working hard to make sure the café looks its best and we have been trawling social media to find positive love stories from our customers to share.

Noah has been repainting some of the pinks walls where there are noticeable marks. They now look great. Dad has been a legend and stepped in to help Pam. They've agreed he will help on a temporary basis until her ex-husband can return to work.

I haven't seen Esme or Phoebe although we have kept in touch on WhatsApp. Phoebe has updated us on her mystery letter sender and apparently, she must meet them today at a secret location which will be revealed later. She and Keith have been spending their time in the bookshop searching through their book customer database to try and work out the identity of Mr Lavender. Phoebe thinks her mystery love letter sender is an older man who recently bought a book titled – *The Joy of Growing Lavender*. This has caused some debate in the bookshop as Keith believes the man is married and has just celebrated his wedding anniversary.

Esme has been a little quiet which has been worrying. Once the judges have visited, I am going to go see her.

We are an hour away from the visit. Richard is playing his harp and table four have just ordered two Flirty Flat Whites and two of Dad's special chocolate brownies which have become quite a hit.

A couple enter the café and the man says, 'Oh, Belinda, I think I love you.'

The name 'Belinda' makes me look at Richard. He's scowling at the couple kissing each other while waiting for a free table. That's his ex-girlfriend, the one who cheated on him. I walk over to Richard. My heart thuds. This could cause us a problem. 'Everything okay?'

He grimaces and nods. 'Belinda is here with her love interest.'

'I know but I need you to stay strong as it is a big day for us.'

With a heavy sigh he nods. 'I'll try my best.'

'I won't sit them near you.'

I show them to a table at the opposite end to Richard.

On my way back to the counter with their order I look up to see Jason and Michelle before me. I knew they would come back to The Little Love Café, but I didn't realise it would be today. We stare at each other for a few awkward seconds. I take a deep breath as it's time to put things right. I outstretch my hand. 'Please accept my sincere apologies, both.'

Jason shakes my hand and then Michelle does the same.

'All drinks are on the house plus you can have two free brownies,' I say, guiding them to a table.

'That's very kind of you,' says Michelle.

'Have a look and I will pop back to get your order.'

Noah smiles at me. 'Is that the couple who were annoyed when you stopped filming their proposal?'

I nod. 'I feel good for apologising and their drinks and cakes are free.'

Noah points towards Richard and his harp. 'Is he crying whilst playing his harp?'

I gasp and look across at an emotional Richard. 'Oh God, visible heartbreak is the last thing we need.'

I hurry over to Richard. 'Let's go get some fresh air.'

He looks up and nods.

After guiding him outside I listen to him tell me about how Belinda hurt him and how painful it is to see her with her new love interest. 'Richard, I know how you feel. A few weeks ago, I was like you. Do you know what I learnt?'

He shrugs.

'Heartbreak does hurt us, but it also can redirect us in life. Maybe heartbreak is telling you Belinda wasn't right for you.'

'She didn't like my harp music.'

'That's a huge part of you, Richard. Don't you want to be with someone who likes every part of you?'

He nods and a faint smile appears on his face.

'Richard, I need you today. This café needs you.'

We walk back into the café. Noah looks up and gestures to me that new customers have entered. I turn around to see Joy and Eric. She beams at me. 'We're here to celebrate our two-month anniversary.'

I smile and show them to a spare table. Joy looks up at me once they are both seated. 'This is also a farewell celebration as we're leaving Blue Cove Bay.' She grins at Eric. 'Me and Eric are running away to start a new life together.'

Eric nods. 'With your sister too.'

Joy frowns. 'Yes, and Esme.' The way she says it is like Esme is an afterthought. Anger at Joy bubbles inside me. The urge to spill a drink over Joy is strong. I find myself willing her to have a milkshake so I can tip it over her. They order two cappuccinos and as I walk back cursing her, I hear Frankie's words in my head. 'Control your emotions, Alice.' He's right. Getting angry at Joy today will not help my award submission.

We are half an hour away from the judge's visit. I am nervous and Noah is too. A few couples from yesterday have shared happy selfies and I have added them to our social media stories.

I'm loading up a tray when I hear a familiar laugh behind me. I turn around to see Phoebe and Liam. She grins. 'Guess who turned up at my secret location – outside The Little Love Café.' She points to Liam. 'He was also receiving lavender-scented love letters.'

'So, Phoebe, this is Mr Lavender? Nice to meet you Liam.'

'I guess so,' he says, with a smile. 'I've been hoping, well praying, Phoebe was my secret admirer.'

Phoebe turns to him with a look of surprise. 'Really?'

Liam nods. 'Yep, although we were going to have to talk about your love of scented letters.'

They both giggle. I notice how he's giving her an adoring gaze. They will make a beautiful couple. I like the way her curly fringe is gently tousled and parted in the middle of her forehead and her curls are bouncing off her shoulders. She is stunning, and he is tall and striking.

'Let's get you both to a table.'

Phoebe is surveying the café. 'It's quite nice in here. I love the harp.'

I give Richard, who looks happier, a wave. 'Yes, he was a great find. Have a seat, both of you, and I will be back to take your order.'

As I am clearing away table two's cups and plates, someone hurries past my shoulder. I look up and I spot Esme marching over to Joy's table. An uncomfortable feeling takes hold of me as I spot Esme's stern expression. 'Joy, I have something to say,' Esme announces in a loud voice. Joy turns around to smile at her sister.

'Oh God,' I mutter. The judges will be here any minute. I hurry over to Joy's table.

'I'm not coming to Devon with you.'

Joy's smile evaporates and conversation in the café quietens. All eyes are on Joy and Esme.

Joy replies, 'I'm sorry, Esme, what did you say?'

Esme clears her throat. 'I'm staying in Blue Cove Bay. You can go to Devon on your own. This is my life and I am going to live it the way I want to live it.'

A look of thunder passes over Joy's face as Noah comes up behind me. 'The judges are outside.'

I need to defuse the situation. Taking Esme's elbow, I lead her away. 'Come with me. This is not the time or the place.'

'But...' she says, as Joy rises from her seat.

I guide Esme past the counter and to the back of the café where the paint tins are. 'Stay here,' I bark.

I meet Joy head on as she marches towards me. 'Where's my sister?'

'Not now, Joy. Please sit down.'

She tries to barge past me, and I block her with my foot. Leaning in close to her, I hiss, 'Leave your sister alone. You've done enough damage to her over the years. Go sit back down with Eric.'

Joy stops and stares at me.

I give her my hardest stare. 'Joy, I said go sit back down.'

To my amazement she turns and makes her way back to her seat.

Noah and I greet the man and the woman judge on the steps. 'Hi and welcome to The Little Love Café.'

We lead them into the café as Richard plays his best piece of harp music. I guide them to a special table in the corner and offer them both a heart-shaped menu.

Noah and I nervously survey the café while they look at their menus. I spot the couple at table six in the far corner casting each other cold stares. Nudging Noah, I point them out. 'Offer them free brownies,' I whisper. To my relief Dad's brownies seem to stall their agitation with each other.

The judges enjoy their drinks, and they love Dad's brownies. Once they've finished, they ask me a series of questions about the café and Frankie. After the last question has been answered they thank me for my time and tell me they will be in touch. The woman turns to me as I lead the way out. 'Have you seen your social media today?'

I gulp. Has something happened that I don't know about? Has someone complained? My heart beats like a drum. Has Heartbreak Café been trending again?

Noah appears behind me. 'Yes, we have and we're over the moon.'

I turn to Noah, and he gives my shoulder a reassuring rub.

Once the judges have left, Noah takes out his phone and shows me Rocco Reid's Instagram post. It's a photo of him with his arm around a young woman with a little girl on her hip. The caption reads:

A few weeks ago I got into difficulty. I was rescued by Alice Hiddleston from The Little Love Café. Not only this but she made me realise that a celebrity life is not for me and that I should be with this one @FreyaHicks – the only girl I have ever loved. Freya has agreed to be my girlfriend. My next film – *Always You* – will be my last as I want to be with Freya. I know you will all support me and give Alice and all her team at The Little Love Café some love. Rocco x

'Our little café is trending for all the right reasons,' says Noah, as he pulls me into his arms. 'I love you, Alice Hiddleston.'

CHAPTER FORTY-TWO

Esme, Phoebe, and I are all sat on a bench on the promenade watching tourists bob about on giant inflatables in the sea. After the judges left, I rescued Esme from the back of the café, and we came here. Phoebe has just joined us.

'I'm sorry I nearly ruined your big day,' says Esme. 'The courage to go tell Joy hit me and before I knew it, I was marching over to the café.'

I take her hand and give it a gentle squeeze. 'You didn't ruin it. Everything worked out in the end.'

Esme nudges Phoebe. 'How's Liam?'

'Gorgeous,' giggles Phoebe. 'When I saw him waiting outside the café holding his scented envelopes, it felt like I had won the lottery.' She lets out a comedy sigh. 'He can play his music as loud as he wants.'

We all erupt into giggles. 'What I don't understand,' she says, 'is that if I never sent Liam those letters and he never sent me letters – who has been playing matchmaker?'

Esme and I both casually shrug and look away.

Phoebe takes Esme's other hand. 'Any news on the buyer of the gift shop?'

Esme shakes her head. 'No, I guess this part of my life is coming to an end.'

I turn to Esme. 'What made you tell Joy today? Did something trigger you?'

Esme nods. 'Joy was lecturing me on what I was going to be expected to do in the new business.'

'I take it she wants you to do everything?' Phoebe asked, before rolling her eyes.

Esme grins and turns to Phoebe. 'How did you guess?'

We all smile and go back to watching the people in the sea.

'I decided after she left that I'd had enough,' explained Esme.

Phoebe nudges Esme. We all turn to see Joy and Eric walking towards our bench.

'Oh, no,' groans Esme. 'I'm going to have to be brave again.'

I squeeze Esme's hand. 'Your future happiness depends on it. You can do this.'

Joy's face is shadowy and taut. 'Esme, I'd like a word please, in private.'

Esme casts me and Phoebe a worried look. As she rises from the bench I grab her hand. 'Stay strong.' I watch her walk behind Joy who is stomping towards the gift shop. Without hesitation or thought, I am on my feet and chasing after Esme. She turns to see me behind her. 'Esme, you need a friend.' I look at Joy who is stood by the door of gift shop and glaring at me. 'Joy – you can say whatever it is you need to say to Esme to me as well.'

'Alice, this is a private family matter,' hisses Joy.

Esme shakes her head. 'I want Alice to hear what you're going to say.' She laces her fingers through mine, and I give them an encouraging rub.

'And me too,' says Phoebe coming to stand by Esme's other side. 'We'd all like to listen to how you are going to try and manipulate Esme into going to North Devon with you and running your new business while you do posh lunches with Eric.'

Joy looks at us one by one. 'Esme, please stop this. We're family...'

Esme shakes her head. 'Alice and Phoebe are my new family now, thanks, Joy. As I said in the café, I am not coming with you to North Devon.'

'You can't do this to me,' cries Joy. 'I need you. Esme, you're my twin sister.'

Esme stands a little taller and looks directly at Joy. 'I am your twin sister but that doesn't mean we have to live the same lives, wear our hair the same, live in the same town and run a business together. I am finally becoming the person I have always wanted to be. Last night I applied to foster cats for a local charity, and it made me feel so happy. I have a male friend who takes me out on day trips and makes me laugh. I also live in my hometown, Blue Cove Bay, and I am happy about that.'

I am blinking away tears of pride for my friend Esme. To hear her say all this is lighting me up inside.

'You'll regret this,' snaps Joy. 'When I get in Eric's car tomorrow with all my stuff you will come rushing out and beg me to take you with me.'

'I don't think she will,' says Phoebe. 'I think Esme will be happier than ever once you leave Blue Cove Bay.'

Joy mutters something under her breath.

'Is that all, Joy?' Esme asks.

'I'll come over tonight to say goodbye,' sneers Joy, 'when you are on your own and I can talk some sense into you.'

Esme gasps and before she can say anything I look at Joy.

'Esme is staying with me tonight, Joy, so why don't you say your goodbyes now.' Esme rests her head on my shoulder.

Joy lets out a heavy sigh and goes into the gift shop, slamming the door behind her.

'Did you mean that about tonight?' Esme asks.

'Definitely,' I say, pulling her into a group hug with me and Phoebe. 'You might have to sit through a Batman film, though.'

'Don't you want to spend the evening with Noah?'

I smile at The Little Love Café. 'Noah and I have the rest of our lives to spend an evening together.'

CHAPTER FORTY-THREE

It's the second week of May and the day of the announcement for the National Award for the Most Innovative Café.

Noah and I have dropped Lucas at school and are walking hand in hand along the beach to the café. Our jeans are rolled up to our knees and in our hands are our trainers – there's nothing sweeter than an early morning paddle. We stand for a few moments, savouring the azure blue sky, sun rays skittering over the water, and the gentle lapping of the waves. Noah gazes out towards the horizon and I stare down and see something glinting in the wet sand. Bending down I see that it's a tiny gold bracelet which has been brought back by the tide. Gently I wipe away all the bits of wet sand and seaweed. 'I'll stick this on our social media to see if anyone has lost it.'

Noah circles my waist with his hand and pulls me close. 'I'm glad I never lost you, Alice.'

'I am glad you came back, Noah.'

The Little Love Café is packed with happy couples. The winner of the award will be invited to a fancy dinner in London where they will be formally presented with their award. I'm sat at a table constantly refreshing The Little Love Café email account. Noah is sat by me; Richard is playing his harp and Ava is serving.

Ava added a photo of the lost bracelet to our social media pages and on the town's Facebook page. We're hoping the owner comes forward soon.

Noah places a hand on my shoulder. 'I believe in us.'

I lean my head on his shoulder. 'We make a great team, Noah.'

He chuckles. 'Once we stopped arguing. I am so glad we got a second chance.' Noah plants a kiss on my cheek. Underneath the pink table I cross all my fingers and toes.

I look across the café. Harold and Pearl are in the corner gazing into each other's eyes. The completion of his mission earned him a proper date with Pearl. Since then, they have been seen walking arm in arm around Blue Cove Bay and exchanging a kiss or two at the community centre. They did reveal to Phoebe and Liam that they were responsible for the lavender scented love letters and the matchmaking.

Dad has arrived with Pam from her bakery. Since he's been working alongside Pam, we have all noticed a change in them both. Dad seems happier than he was in the supermarket and Pam now wears her beautiful silvery hair down a lot more and she doesn't look so harassed. In fact, today I can see a brush of sparkly eyeshadow over her eyelids and her lips are pink and glossy. They're heading for the table. 'Any news?'

We all shake our heads. Phoebe and Liam have come over to the table, hand in hand. 'This is so exciting, guys,' gushes Phoebe. She puts her arms around my neck and pulls me into a hug. 'I am so proud of you, Alice.'

At the door I can hear Esme laughing. We all look up to see her and Keith walking in, arm in arm. It turned out Keith was the anonymous buyer of the gift shop. He bought it to free

Esme from Joy's clutches. She now manages it and he is her assistant. They are also dating which has made us all happy. Joy went to Devon with Eric and the last we heard she was struggling to run her new business by herself. After years of watching her make Esme do everything, hearing this is very satisfying.

'Have you heard anything?' Esme asks.

I shake my head. Keith holds up his crossed fingers. 'We're all praying, Alice.'

Ava comes over to the table holding her phone. 'The bracelet owner has been found, Alice'.

'Really?'

She nods. 'It belongs to one of our customers. She and her partner came here a few weeks ago, had an argument and she stormed out onto the beach.'

An uncomfortable feeling passes over me.

'They had a yelling match on the beach, and she lost her bracelet. Anyway they are fine, but she thought the bracelet he once bought her was lost forever. Isn't that great you found it?'

I smile at Ava. 'Perfect.'

Noah holds up the iPad. 'Frankie and Rose are on a video call. He said he wants to watch the result come in live.'

Frankie and Rose's happy faces come through on the screen as The Little Love Café email pings to signal the arrival of an email. Everyone gasps as I say, 'It's here. The email from the award committee.'

I go to open the email and Dad stops me. He turns to everyone who is gathered around and to the iPad screen. 'Before we find out, can I say how proud I am of my daughter, Alice, for all her hard work and Frankie for creating this wonderful place. I would also like to welcome Noah to our family and apologise to Rose. Julie is one very proud mum in heaven today.'

'Can I also say,' says Frankie from the iPad screen, 'that I am also proud of Alice. I knew she could turn this place around with Noah's help.'

Clearing my throat I rise from my seat. 'Before I open the email, I also want to say a few words.' Noah and Keith give me a little round of applause. 'I have worked so hard to turn this place around and give my wonderful, best mate in Australia something to smile about.' I turn to Frankie on the laptop screen. 'Frankie, I admit now giving me the job in my broken-hearted state was probably not a good decision.' Everyone around me laughs and Frankie grins. 'You can say that again, Alice,' he chuckles, which sends a ripple of laughter around the café.

I continue. 'I am not going to take credit for the idea of this café. This is Frankie's café, and I simply made a few tweaks and finishing touches... once I controlled my emotions. Turning this café around has been a team effort and I would like to thank Noah, Jake, Pam, Dad, Ava, Richard and of course Frankie. I also want to thank my two friends, Phoebe and Esme who drank far too much wine with me when I needed to vent and moan.' Both Phoebe and Esme cheer and clap.

With Noah holding my hand I open the email.

The National Award for the Most Innovative Café goes to... The Little Love Café in Blue Cove Bay.

After a lot of hugging, kissing, and crying down the laptop at an emotional Frankie and Rose, Noah and I head out onto the beach. Ava is managing the café whilst we get some much-needed time to process the café's victory.

'We did it,' says Noah, lifting me up and twirling around. He puts me down and we engage in a beautiful kiss. Once we come up for air we walk towards our rock. 'I can't wait to marry you a second time by this rock,' Noah says, with a grin.

'Really?' I gush.

He nods. 'Lucas can hold our rings.'

'Lucas has a thing for shiny things so we might have to talk to him about how he must hand over the rings and not put them in his pocket.'

We both giggle. While Noah climbs up our rock, I look at out at the sparkling sea. Just as the sea returns treasures like the lost bracelet hidden beneath the surface, love offered Noah and me the chance to rediscover our connection which we thought had been swept away years ago.

'Alice, come on,' shouts Noah, 'I want to kiss you up here like I did when we were teenagers.'

THE END

ALSO BY LUCY MITCHELL

I'll Miss You This Christmas

~

Instructions for Falling in Love Again

~

The Car Share

ACKNOWLEDGEMENTS

Thank you for taking the time to read my book.

Thank you to Betsy, Clare, Lexi and Tara from Bloodhound Books for bringing this book to life.

Thank you to Huw, Seren and Flick for your love and support.

A huge thank you to my two fabulous friends, Catherine and Sue who support me with each book and no matter what life is throwing at them, they still urge me to send a draft novel through so they can read it and give me their thoughts.

Thank you to my fellow romance author friend, Bettina Hunt, who makes me laugh every day and always encourages me to keep going when writing is hard.

Thank you to Rachel for your funny voice notes and friendship.

Thank you to Helen, Sacha and Susie who were in Croatia with me in 2019 when the idea for this book came to me. Helen – you and I were on our apartment balcony, getting some sun and scoffing Croatian chocolate biscuits when I had a brainwave about what next to write.

Thank you to Mum and Vez. I purposefully added a lot of coffee and cake into this book in memory of Dad who always loved a coffee and a slice of cake.

A NOTE FROM THE PUBLISHER

Thank you for reading this book. If you enjoyed it please do consider leaving a review on Amazon to help others find it too.

We hate typos. All of our books have been rigorously edited and proofread, but sometimes mistakes do slip through. If you have spotted a typo, please do let us know and we can get it amended within hours.

info@bloodhoundbooks.com

Milton Keynes UK
Ingram Content Group UK Ltd.
UKHW042152010824
446366UK00004B/68

9 781917 214179